THE CASE FILES
~OF~
JEWELER RICHARD

NOVEL

8

T0270047

WRITTEN BY
Nanako
Tsujimura

ILLUSTRATED BY
Utako
Yukihiro

Airship

Seven Seas Entertainment

HOSEKISHO RICHARD-SHI NO NAZOKANTEI
© 2018 by Nanako Tsujimura
Illustration by Utako Yukihiro
All rights reserved.
First published in Japan in 2018 by SHUEISHA Inc., Tokyo.
English translation rights arranged by SHUEISHA Inc.
through TOHAN CORPORATION, Tokyo.

Seven Seas press and purchase enquiries can be sent to
Marketing Manager Lauren Hill at press@gomanga.com.
Information regarding the distribution and purchase of
digital editions is available from Digital Manager CK Russell
at digital@gomanga.com.

Follow Seven Seas Entertainment online at
sevenseasentertainment.com.

TRANSLATION: T. Emerson
LOGO DESIGN: H. Qi
COVER DESIGN: M.A. Lewife
INTERIOR LAYOUT & DESIGN: Clay Gardner
COPY EDITOR: Meg van Huygen
PROOFREADER: Jade Gardner
SENIOR EDITOR: Nibedita Sen
PREPRESS TECHNICIAN: Melanie Ujimori, Jules Valera
MANAGING EDITOR: Alyssa Scavetta
EDITOR-IN-CHIEF: Julie Davis
PUBLISHER: Lianne Sentar
VICE PRESIDENT: Adam Arnold
PRESIDENT: Jason DeAngelis

ISBN: 979-8-88843-667-7
Printed in Canada
First Printing: July 2024
10 9 8 7 6 5 4 3 2 1

CONTENTS

CAST

Seigi Nakata

A Tokyo native who started apprenticing as a jeweler after graduating college, thanks to connections he developed at his part-time job. Just as his name—Seigi, meaning "justice"—implies, he's an earnest young man always looking to help others, even if he may be a bit lacking in tact at times.

Richard Ranasinghe de Vulpian

An English jeweler with a better command of Japanese than your average Japanese person. His incredible beauty would strike anyone, regardless of gender, utterly speechless. He has a weakness for all things sweet.

WHY ARE beautiful things sad?

I recall once asking that.

It wasn't the day my grandmother told me that beauty and sadness go hand in hand. She said those profound words as if she were stating the obvious, but it took a lot of courage for me, a young child, to ask her why.

My grandmother wrote someone a letter that day. She was always writing letters to someone, but whenever I asked who it was, she just said they were "a friend." I suppose she could say that with confidence, even though everyone on the estate knew she wasn't particularly close to anyone, because she didn't want the cloying oppression of friendships. I even believed, naively, that she might have many secret friends.

She slowly stood from her writing desk and turned to me, flustered by the gesture, and tilted her head eerily to the side.

"If everything in the world were beautiful, what would 'beauty' be?"

That question was much too difficult for me at the time. If the world was full of beautiful things, with not a single unsavory sight to be seen, wouldn't it be nice to experience nothing but beauty all the time? If the servants who thought I was creepy for not acting enough like a child, or if my father, who barely ever saw me and treated me like a piece of luggage when he did, weren't around... If the whole world were a pleasant place, wouldn't that be nice?

I said as much. My grandmother chuckled like a crow and set her hand on my head.

"Pleasant and beautiful are not the same thing at all. Beautiful things can be terrifying, and carry with them great pain. But the most important thing to remember..."

Was that beauty wasn't something you possessed.

Because beauty only existed when someone else observed it and declared it "beautiful."

I asked her if it was like how, if no one were there to call the beautiful fallen leaves beautiful, they may as well not exist. "Yes, exactly," she said.

I offered her the golden leaf I'd collected from the garden as a present, and she narrowed her eyes at me.

"What a beautiful leaf you've found. Do you like leaves more than flowers?"

I don't remember what I said at the time. I liked both, but flowers wilted and fell apart so quickly. In that sense, I preferred leaves.

I caught sight of the letter on top of her desk. Something that looked like a bracelet sat next to it, and I think I asked her,

"What is that?" Or maybe, "Who gave that to you?" Something to that effect. It was a string of ordinary natural stones that almost looked like a toy, though it did seem a little old for that.

She didn't respond and just twirled the leaf around her fingers. It was either an elm or an oak leaf, with a symmetrical, spindle-like shape and not a single insect bite taken out of it. I'd thought that my grandmother, who loved gemstones so much, might like it. It was a product of nature that was perfect in every way.

But that intent didn't quite make it across.

My grandmother, whose eyes sparkled like gems, looked down at the child looking up at her in silence and gave an exasperated laugh.

"You should be more assertive when you speak, Richard. You were born under a beautiful star, so you ought to make an effort to communicate more about yourself. I'm not saying you need to learn Sinhala—just use your own language. That's what I want for you."

I learned Sinhala. I learned French, Spanish, Italian, and other European languages even faster. I threw myself into studying Asian languages even as I was teased for it, with people telling me studying too much would damage my brain. It was like I was a fish and studying languages was the water of life. But the more languages I learned, the more my loneliness intensified. No matter which language's waters I swam in, I couldn't *live* in any of them. All I wanted was water, but I was beginning to feel like one of Princess Kaguya's suitors, tasked with searching for the impossible.

One of my cousins told me I was being conceited but still watched over me in my pursuits. My other cousin praised my talents, all the while pretending not to see me at all. It didn't really matter to me. It was all the same, either way. I was the only person living in my world.

I was still trapped in that world, whiling away my days, when I met her.

Prologue

THE CASE FILES
OF
JEWELER
RICHARD

AUGUST 9TH

Hello, it's Iggy from Sri Lanka again. I may not be the most consistent, but I have more or less managed to keep up this blog that I started to improve my writing skills. I greatly appreciate everyone who's taken the time to read it.

I'm going to be writing about pricing negotiations in Ratnapura this time.

This should be pretty obvious if you go through my posts, but I've been in a little mountain city called Ratnapura since the end of July. I've been working on stocking gems—so shopping, basically. Ratnapura is an old mining town that still produces sapphires and tourmaline. Its name means "capital of gems" in Sinhala, and there are records of Europeans coming here to trade for gems as early as the Age of Discovery.

My boss says it's one of the most interesting places in the world. Whenever I go there, it feels like every single person I meet is involved with the gem industry. Just about everyone has a parcel of gemstones (a parcel is like an envelope) in their pocket.

It's the kind of place where negotiations begin the moment you make eye contact.

And everyone is looking to trade.

This was my first time being trained in making a bulk purchase.

I'm sure the word *training* evokes images of a systematic process with reports, communication, and feedback. This was anything but. My training was just a steady process of meeting and negotiating with as many gem dealers as time would permit, with the goal of obtaining large quantities of products that seem like they'll sell and avoiding those that seem like they won't.

The thing is, whatever image the words *gem dealer* might evoke, most of the sellers here are men wearing sarongs and footwear that remind me of beach sandals. Nothing about it really screams "business." The town is typical of Sri Lanka in most other respects, too—there are hardly any paved roads, and if anything, it feels like the people here are just temporarily renting the space from Mother Nature. Just like Colombo and Kandy, it can only be accessed via a one-lane mountain road that takes four to five hours to traverse, and even with your seat belt fastened as tightly as possible, you're guaranteed to be totally worn out by the trip.

Still, every single building on the bustling city streets looked expensive. I'm struggling to find a good way to describe it, but as someone used to the shopping districts in Kandy and Colombo, the difference in budget was immediately apparent. The first time I came here, I let it slip to my boss that I thought so, and he praised me for being so perceptive. Most of the buildings here are owned by people who mined valuable gems and decided to invest some of the crazy money they made into starting their own shops. It's kind of cute.

There's a chamber of commerce-type institute in the middle of town for people who want to do business, but I'm working in a little hut on a hill some distance away, intently examining gemstones. It's a tiny building—barely six square meters—with nothing but a desk, chair, and light, located among a line of similar little shacks where I spend hours upon hours.

Whenever they get the call that someone from my boss's shop is here, a group of sellers whom he buys from fairly regularly— people you might call trustworthy, in a sense—come to the hut and show me the items they want to sell. It's always a sight to behold. Obviously, there are things like ruby, sapphire, cat's eye, alexandrite, and tourmaline, but also moonstone, spinel, kunzite, tsavorite, sphene, tanzanite, and even jade. There are always enough gems being brought in to open a jewelry shop. Big ones and small ones. Stones with stars and stones without. Stones mined in the area, stones that came in from who knows where. Heated and unheated. Stones dressed up in the names of more expensive stones, stones mistaken for inexpensive ones. Real and fake. Everything you could imagine. I can't help but wonder if the Chinese idiom "a jumble of gems and stones" was inspired by such a sight.

As for the price ranges, I'd prefer to leave it to your imagination, but I'll just say they were nigh boundless—from mineral show souvenir prices to high-end jewelry store window display prices. I'm very grateful my boss let me focus on just looking at real stones at first, rather than throwing me right into the deep end.

The vendors—or, rather, the sellers employed by the gems' owners—rarely complete a sale at the first price given. Fixed prices really aren't a thing in this world. What actually happens is you negotiate with the seller until you come to an agreement on a price, then buy what you want for that amount. But if the other party rejects your offers, negotiations are over, and they'll move on to try to sell to another person.

This might seem obvious, but there's no one here to tell me if the things people are trying to sell me are real or fake. Just like there's nobody to intervene if someone's selling stones that are obvious fakes on the side of the road to unsuspecting customers.

You need some heavy-duty machinery to definitively identify a given gemstone. Acquiring that level of proof isn't feasible when working in the middle of nowhere like this. Instead, it all comes down to whether or not you are willing to buy something, and all you have to rely on are your eyes, your experience, and your intuition.

As you might expect, the only people who come to sell stones to my boss are battle-worn veterans. It's not hard to imagine how they might see a brand-new jeweler's apprentice, who's getting his feet wet for the first time, as easy prey. Which is why I always have a more experienced coworker standing behind me when I'm training in Ratnapura.

His nickname is "Hawk Eye"—because of his sharp eyes and unique facial features. He doesn't have a mean look to him or anything, but as I was exchanging light banter with another jeweler, I knew what he meant when he said that his gaze could paralyze you with fear. Hawk Eye stands behind me while I'm encamped at the desk in the little shack, negotiating with gem dealer after gem dealer. Whenever he thinks my judgment is clearly off, he'll say, "Pardon," and give me some advice. He's basically a safety net, but it makes me want to die of nerves whenever I hear that "pardon" after a negotiation is complete.

Over the course of half a day—with breaks in between—I met at least 150 people. My final score was 14 "pardons." It was still impossible to say if that was the result of a streak of beginner's luck or quite the opposite. It would all depend on how things sold later.

In Ratnapura, people don't look at gems once the sun starts to set. They all know that gems are at their most beautiful—exactly as they're meant to be—in morning light. It's just a fact that gems look their best in natural light. This town isn't exactly kind to buyers, but it *does* let you switch out of business mode in the afternoon and enjoy some elegant tea and cake at an English-style café that inexplicably exists here. Which is pretty nice, if you ask me.

One of the unfortunate side effects of this schedule is that buying starts very early in the morning. I have to be ready and waiting by 5 a.m. This is a particular struggle for Hawk Eye...but I'll save that story for another time.

I think I just barely managed to stick to the three principles of buying: 1. Don't let it show on your face, 2. Don't let yourself be bound by obligation, and 3. Never tell anyone what item(s) you're interested in. As a result, my face was always aching by evening, which worried my coworker. As scary and strict as he might be when it comes to work, he does let me take it easy in my off time, and I'm always glad to have him around.

Even with a chaperone, the experience of using the company budget (and a lot of it!) to buy a huge quantity of gemstones was so intense that I had trouble sleeping afterward. It wasn't the thrill of the experience that kept me up at night but instead thinking about whether I made the right call by buying a stone at a certain price, or if I should have bought something I'd ended up passing on.

My colleague would scold me, reminding me that it was a waste of energy to worry about things I'd never know the answer to, and that I should spend only exactly as much time as is required to reflect on things and then use the rest of my time developing an optimistic attitude. I think that helped me strike a healthier balance. I guess I'm just going to have to get used to it all.

I know that was a bit long, but I'll end my notes about purchasing stones in Ratnapura here for now.

I hope I do even better next time. I'm determined to.

[EDIT]

I forgot to mention this, but at least with respect to the people I encountered during my training here in this city, 100 percent of the gem dealers were men. I'm pretty sure if a woman so much as walked down the pedestrian-packed Jeweler's Street (as I've decided to call it), she would have stuck out like a sore thumb. And I didn't see any women among the mine shafts in the fields, either. Maybe I shouldn't be surprised, considering it was dangerous manual labor, but it still took me aback to see just how male-dominated the space was.

I guess it's just that way more women than men wear jewelry, and yet when it comes to the trade side of things, it's almost all men. Maybe it's less that it's strange and more vaguely ironic.

AUGUST 10TH

Today I'm going to talk about transportation. I'm finally getting used to driving the three-wheeler I acquired the other day. I'm going to post a picture of it.

Ta-da! It's one of those three-wheeled scooters you see all around Sri Lanka.

The body is red and the seat and canopy are black.

As you can see, it has a lot of ventilation. There's seating for two people behind the driver, but since it doesn't have any doors, whoever's sitting in back has to be careful. If I just stuck some incense and stickers of Buddha and Hindu gods on the windshield, it'd look just like any of the taxis you see around here.

I didn't buy it new. I got it used for cheap off of someone in the neighborhood. If you've ever been to India or Thailand, you can easily picture how these scooters are typically used as taxis, rather than exclusively personal vehicles. While they're way cheaper than cars, they're still a big investment, so a lot of people who work as drivers actually rent them from someone who owns a big fleet. There's actually someone who operates a business leasing these three-wheelers near where I live. He offered to sell me some extra stock for cheap when they heard I was getting fed up trying to drive the car along those narrow roads.

I'm trying to keep it as nice as possible because I figure I'll end up selling it to someone myself in a few years.

That said, I was really surprised by how inexpensive it is to get your driver's license in Sri Lanka. I have an international driver's license, but I was curious, so I asked the owner of that lunch place I frequent, and he said that it costs about 30,000 Sri Lankan rupees! As a point of comparison, in my home country it would cost several hundred *thousand* Sri Lankan rupees to get your license. When I explained that, all the Sri Lankans there at the time burst out laughing. "If it cost that much, no one would get their license!" they all exclaimed. They had a point. Considering the average salary in this country, several hundred thousand rupees would be practically impossible. After all, it's not just the cost of a driver's license but the cost of living in general that's relative to the country you're living in.

I've never lived abroad before, so I find myself impressed by every little thing.

I wonder what I should do for dinner tonight? If I get too swept up in chores, it eats into my studies, but I do appreciate the change of pace. And now that I have the scooter, it takes me no time to get ingredients. Maybe I'll post photos later. Would that count as language practice? Well, whatever!

The other day, I was having some soup made from fish stock when this cute little stray mutt wandered into the house. I gave it some leftover fish and we had dinner together. There are tons of stray dogs in this area. Sometimes people feed them, and sometimes they don't. It's a pretty relaxed dynamic. It makes me wonder if the people here are less accustomed to the idea of keeping pets than the people back home. I guess I do see people raising chickens to eat whenever I go out into the countryside.

It was a very cute dog. I hope it comes back.

The stars were really pretty tonight, too.

AUGUST 11TH

I've been really busy lately.

You're probably thinking, "preparing for the festival in August?" Unfortunately, it's not that. I feel like I can hear someone saying that it's a shame to not go to the festival when I'm living in Kandy, but I have plans for an extended business trip. I'll post all about it when I get back, as usual.

I wonder how it's going to go. I'm kind of nervous—but I do get to see a friend of mine for the first time in a while, and fretting about it won't get me anywhere.

I just have to stay motivated and get ready for the trip.

AUGUST 12TH

I'm struggling to figure out what a good souvenir to bring back from Sri Lanka might be. Elephant-themed merch, maybe? But the person I'm looking to get something for doesn't seem like the type to enjoy trinkets. Hm... Alcohol maybe? Although Sri Lankans don't really drink much. The main thing I've been drinking here is a sweet ginger ale they call ginger beer.

You know, I guess there is that big Buddhist temple here in Kandy. Maybe something from there would be a safe option.

That reminds me, since I got some questions about this topic—right now, the only people reading this blog are people who found it on their own. I haven't shared it with my friends and family. I did start it to practice English at my boss's suggestion, but he's not a snoop. I told him I was doing it but also that I didn't have any questions for him and didn't need his advice, and that was the end of it. But it is a public blog on the web, so I suppose he *could* be reading it and just not saying anything to me.

Hmm. If anyone who knows me IRL is reading this, that would be kind of embarrassing. Would you tell me if you are? Just text me or give me a call. Please.

AUGUST 13TH

I appreciate everyone's concern about goods from the Buddhist temple not being the safest bet because religious items might be a touchy subject. The thing is, my friend and I do know each other reasonably well, and I'm pretty sure Buddhist items won't be an issue, but I do appreciate the concern.

This made me realize that I've never really had to think about religious souvenirs back home before. I guess that's probably because I didn't have all that many friends from different countries, or who openly practiced other religions, but now I feel like it's kind of weird that I never had to think about it.

Also, regarding my request last time, no one's contacted me yet. I still have my doubts, but I have no way to confirm my suspicions, so I guess I just have to assume that this is still my sanctuary for the time being.

I'm finished packing. I should get going. It is a work trip, but while I can't say exactly where I'm going, the food should be incredible. I can't wait! So please keep your spirits up as you wait for me! And pray that I'll come back safe.

Well, I'm off!

Le Premier Jour:
Day 1

THE CASE FILES
~ OF ~
JEWELER
RICHARD

T HE INTERNATIONAL AIRPORTS of the world were all so similar they could almost be siblings.

I'd only used the airports in Japan, England, Sri Lanka, Dubai, and Fort Lauderdale—which was less than ten in total—but they were all structured pretty similarly. They all had a massive entry hall plastered with airline logos, bag check counters, self-service check-in machines, security, duty-free shops, and numbered departure gates. I guess it made sense, since you were always doing basically the same things in airports, and they always had staff who spoke fluent English, not to mention passengers from all over the world.

And now, I could add France's Charles-de-Gaulle airport to the lineup. I gave a little nod to the immigration agent as a greeting. People with various skin colors were manning the line of booths as they stamped passports from all sorts of countries. I collected my big backpack from the luggage belt, continued along the moving walkway, and finally made it to the outside world again.

Just another twenty kilometers by taxi, and I'd be in the city of love. Paris.

France was the biggest country by area in the EU, the country that received the most tourists in the world, and a major agricultural power ranking fourth in the world's food security index. All the trivia I learned while studying for the civil service exam came in handy at times like this. Having just come from Sri Lanka, the difference in humidity made my skin ache. France's Mediterranean air was dry. Feeling the sun stinging my skin, I understood why so many people on the street had sunglasses on.

This would be my second time in Europe after my trip to England in college. The trip was expected to be about a week long—"about" because it might prove to be shorter, or it might end up being extended. Thankfully, it was summertime, so I made sure to pack a change of clothes that would dry quickly after being washed. I sure made the right call there.

I quickly hailed a taxi, climbed into the back seat, and gave the driver the address of my destination. He looked a little puzzled and asked if that was a hotel. I explained that no, it wasn't a hotel, it was just where I was meeting a friend, and handed him the map I'd printed out just to be safe. He laughed, looking a little bewildered, then asked if I was sure I didn't want to leave my bag somewhere first. I replied that I had nowhere to leave it, and anyway, it would be fine. It was light enough to carry.

"Are you here to have some fun?" His English was slightly accented and very fast. The middle-aged driver, who was balding, with half a head of sparse brown hair, gave me a kind look.

"I guess it could be fun or it could be work. I think it just depends on your frame of mind."

"Well, that sure sounds annoying. Where from?"

"Sri Lanka."

"Oh, you're Sri Lankan?"

"No, I'm Japanese," I replied, and he chuckled, amused for some reason.

"A Japanese man coming to France from Sri Lanka."

"Exactly."

"Okay, *on y va*," he said and started driving with the taxi windows still wide open. *On y va* was French for "let's go," if I recalled correctly. The wind felt nice as it blew through the cabin.

The driver went on to ask me some of the usual questions— how old I was, where I was born, et cetera—then started to talk about himself. His wife was Algerian, and they had a six-year-old who was very good at counting and loved Japanese food. Rent was so high that they were thinking about moving from the Paris suburbs to somewhere more rural. After we'd been driving on the highway for about ten minutes, he got a call in his earpiece and started to have a cheerful conversation with someone I assumed was family. He had a big smile on his face as he spoke.

Now that I was no longer in conversation, I installed the SIM card I'd bought at the airport into my phone and contacted the person I'd be meeting. In Japanese, not English.

"I landed on time. I'm heading to the spot by taxi."

A reply came almost immediately.

"Take your time."

"I'll be waiting."

I was glad to hear that.

As I listened to the sound of happy family conversation, occasionally interrupted by the sound of barking dogs, I closed my eyes in an attempt to relieve my jet lag. I felt like I was dreaming about having tea with a certain someone in the garden back in Sri Lanka, but I couldn't remember it when I woke up.

I deposited my bag at reception and entered the museum. When I got out of the taxi, the driver checked with me repeatedly to make sure this really was the place. I pointed at the sign and reassured him that it matched what I'd been given and that I'd be fine. I couldn't blame him for worrying—this really wasn't the sort of place you'd expect someone to head directly to from the airport by taxi, after all.

Le Musée de la Chasse et de la Nature.

This aristocratic mansion located in the northern part of the Marais is a museum. It's not a station or a hotel. Even if you were going to come here as a tourist, you'd definitely stop somewhere to put up your bag first. It felt a little out of place—this marble building with a garden, surrounded by bustling restaurants and hotels almost like central Tokyo. I was astonished by the grace with which it seemed to eschew expectations, and glad I'd changed clothes in the plane before I'd arrived. Though the scale was naturally completely different, the vibe of the place was exactly the same as the Claremont estate situated in the outskirts of London.

That Claremont estate was the family home of none other than a certain brilliant polyglot—a man whose beauty was so exquisite I felt foolish even trying to describe it in words, a proper member of British nobility, and my one and only boss, Richard. His background was reminiscent of a plate of caviar, truffles, and foie gras mixed with sea urchin, salmon roe, and abalone.

A lot had happened to both of us on that estate. Afterward, I learned that it was normal for British aristocrats to own multiple estates. Townhouses in London, vacation villas in the countryside, and big manor houses on land, if they owned any. Owning property came with its costs, too. I asked how they paid for the administrative upkeep, but Richard just gave me a vague answer about how they had it covered. That was the end of that conversation. I guess when you have that much money, you can just "cover" things like that.

Even if it was a Parisian museum, this place was cool and quiet. The Louvre, a museum in the very same city, was surely as loud and crowded as the shops lining the entrance to the shrine in Asakusa, but this place was completely silent. Had the whole place been booked out for us? There were no signs to indicate that it had been, but the fact that it was a possibility was terrifying.

I glanced over at the garden, pruned into perfect geometric shapes, paid the eight-euro entry fee, and ascended the massive marble staircase. I wondered if I was really going to see him. He was supposed to be waiting for me.

And when I got up the stairs, there he was, stepping out from behind a wall.

The man had golden-brown hair, pale, sparkling blue eyes, and almost sickly pale skin. He was wearing a beige jacket and pants with a similarly toned pale brown tie and a white shirt. It was a style I was familiar with—"colonial chic." Inspired by the sort of thing British people wore when the country was colonizing Sri Lanka and India and stuff.

He waved to me when he saw me.

"Haven't seen you in ages, Jeffrey."

"Hi. You know you can just call me Jeff," he said with a smile.

He was wearing rimless glasses today. I'd never seen him in glasses before. He explained with a chuckle that he usually wore contacts.

Jeffrey Claremont was Richard's cousin but also something of an older brother to him. His father was the current ninth Earl of Claremont, but his older brother, Henry, was set to inherit the title. The younger children of nobles in England were customarily given the title "the honorable," so in a formal setting, I'd be expected to refer to him as "the Honorable Jeffrey Claremont" and conduct myself in a suitably humble manner. Jeffrey, however, was a very candid guy who spoke Japanese just about as well as Richard did. He preferred sports jackets over suits, and brown shoes with laces over black ones. He was a cheerful guy who always lit up the room...normally, anyway.

After a mild exchange of greetings, he invited me further into the museum. His black shoes clicked along the floor. It wasn't just his clothes but his whole attitude that felt off.

"You didn't have any trouble finding the place, did you?"

"Nope, I took a taxi. The driver looked at me like I was crazy when I gave him the address. He was all like, 'Who goes anywhere but a hotel from the airport?'"

"Oh, right. Crap. I guess you didn't have anywhere to put your luggage. Are you taking the train later? I can have someone come to take your things for you. Gare de Lyon station, right?"

"Don't worry, I'm all right. I can carry my own bag just fine."

"...You really haven't changed one bit, have you?"

My frame of reference was probably all messed up by being used to Richard's impossible beauty, but Jeffrey was decently good-looking, too. Those round frames gave him the air of a gentle bookworm. It tugged at my heart to see him smile at me with that troubled look on his face—but maybe I was just seeing Richard in him.

"You know...this place is pretty incredible."

"It's a fairly new museum. I figured it'd be the perfect place for us to meet since it's quiet and not very popular with Japanese tourists."

A wild boar. A leopard. Deer. Deer. Deer. A polar bear in an imposing pose. A flock of owls hanging from the ceiling over visitors. A row of lions sitting like well-mannered house cats. And more guns than I could count. There were beautifully decorated gunpowder flasks and hunting-themed paintings as well.

I'd seen plenty of taxidermy in the National Museum of Nature and Science in Ueno, but this exhibit had an entirely different purpose. These rhinoceros, water buffalo, and deer heads mounted on the walls were hunting trophies. Before the Washington

Convention, folks of high status who enjoyed hunting as a hobby would preserve their most prized prey like this to show off their high scores, as it were, kind of like taking a fish print of a marlin. I supposed there was some historical significance to records of a sport influential people participated in in the past, but I found it hard to just enjoy the exhibit when I was so keenly aware of the pleasure they'd taken in this particular pastime. I guess to them, living in a world with no TV and no internet, these exotic animals were just products to be consumed.

It didn't look like there were any other visitors present, but Jeffrey kept conversation to a minimum as we progressed deeper into the museum. Finally, we arrived in a blue parlor with gold-framed paintings decorating one wall. The walls were a sapphire blue, a sparkling chandelier hung from the ceiling, and there were seats upholstered in flower-patterned fabric. There were no "no touching" signs on the furnishings in this museum. There were plenty of items on display that you could touch.

I looked down at where he'd gestured for me to have a seat and discovered that it was already occupied—by a taxidermied red fox, curled up on the chair. I jumped back with a shout and heard a hearty burst of laughter from behind me.

"Aha ha ha ha! I totally got you!"

"Please don't do that. What if I'd just sat down without look-ing? I'd never be able to pay for the damages."

"You'd never be able to pay for the damages, huh? Am I really hearing you say that?"

Jeffrey looked at me and flashed a smile that made my heart ache. It felt like ages since I'd seen him make that face. He was probably trying to use his villain smile, but it didn't really have the same effect now that I knew him better and he'd done so much to help me. He must've known that, too.

"There's only one reason I called you here today. It's about the incident in Fort Lauderdale."

"You've already apologized like a million times."

"Not that."

Jeffrey sat down on the open couch and invited me to take a seat next to him, as if he were entertaining a guest at his estate. He opened the leather document case he'd been carrying the whole time, pulled out a folder, and handed it to me. It looked like a personal dossier. A single bundle of A4 size pages. I counted ten pages as I ran my thumb along the edge. The first page had a photo of a person's face on it. An Asian man. One I happened to know.

"I believe you're already familiar with Vincent Lai."

"...I am."

The man had almond-shaped eyes and brown hair cropped into a model-like undercut. He'd been instrumental in resolving the mess Richard and I had been embroiled in on that cruise, while also ultimately turning out to be the source of the problem despite pretending otherwise. He'd been Richard's assistant when he worked in Hong Kong. He'd even called Saul "old man," and described himself as a Hong Konger living in the US.

Vincent...also known as "Vince."

The photo in Jeffrey's file was a portrait shot of him in a dress shirt with a sour look on his face. It looked kind of like a passport photo. He was a little plumper in the photo than when I'd met him. It was nothing compared to the old photo of him that Richard had shown me, but it made me think that this might be a slightly older picture.

But why was Jeffrey showing this to me?

When I looked up at Jeffrey before going on to flip through the rest of the pages, he still had that fake smile on his face. It made my chest prickle.

"Let me sum it up for you. He worked in Hong Kong as Richard's assistant from the age of 21 to 22. He was a bit sweeter and squishier back then, but still hiding something. He was my spy."

"Your spy?"

"Yes. I wanted information about Richard, so I paid him off and he passed it along to me. Not from the very start of his work as Richard's assistant—only starting about halfway through his first year. I was in just the right place at just the right time, because he had a sick family member and was in sudden, urgent need of money."

The lack of any hesitation in his voice made *me* flinch. Why was he telling me this now?

Jeffrey crossed his legs and shrugged, almost like he'd read my mind.

"Considering the circumstances, hiding it from you now is only going to make things pointlessly difficult. Let's not waste time, we've got secrets to reveal."

"...So does that mean that secretary of yours who stole my passport number was—"

"In charge of managing the information my spies collected, yes. My 'shadow handler' if you will. Once I thought the situation had been resolved, my mind was focused entirely on financial settlements, but things were much worse than I could have imagined. A rather foolish misstep on my part, if I do say so myself. Entirely missed my chance to play a more dashing villain..."

I hastily flipped through the documents. A page with what looked like his former address and a letter he'd sent Jeffrey. A copy of wire transfer statements. There were numerous payments with an impressive number of zeroes on each line. No personal information on any of Richard's clients but a great deal of detail about Richard himself: his daily routines, shops he frequented, even things he had said to Vince. It pained me to have to look through these while sitting next to Jeffrey.

The first seven pages were all related to Vince. The last three were about someone else entirely. There was a photo of a sweet little girl with blonde hair and amber eyes.

"I guess I shouldn't be surprised that someone who wants to be a government bureaucrat is this fast at scanning documents. This adorable little girl is Octavia. I believe you know her, too. You saw the video message she sent Richard, didn't you?"

I nodded. Octavia was the girl who'd sent us video after the incident on that luxury cruise, taking credit for the whole thing. She claimed to have sent Vince in to set me up and, apparently still unsatisfied with the maelstrom of stress she'd put Richard through, declared that he and his cousins, Henry and Jeffrey, should "not consider what [she's] about to do unfair treatment." She was a picture-perfect little terrorist.

She wasn't smiling in her photo, just staring off into space. The background was a uniform grey. The photo looked like it had been taken in a booth for an ID or something. It was hard to imagine a cameraman taking a photo of a little girl and not asking her to smile.

"Octavia Manorland. She's incredibly wealthy and currently resides in St. Moritz, Switzerland. She's seventeen years old and a citizen of the U.K. Richard was her tutor when she was still living there. Her parents have both passed away, and she doesn't let many people get close to her. You could say she's a very motivated—to borrow a Japanese term—*hikikomori*. As bright as she is, she doesn't seem to enjoy school very much. Naturally, as she is still a minor, she can't move funds without the approval of her guardian, but she will immediately fire any guardian that displeases her. She only lets people who do exactly as she says near her. So—how should I put this..."

"She gets to do whatever she wants?"

"Basically. She is a sweet girl, though."

Sweet? Jeffrey must know a side of her that I didn't.

He continued, "If I had to guess, she's probably using Vince to get at me, not Richard. She sent different versions of her revenge declaration video to me, Richard, and Henry. I'm the only one who's seen them all, and thankfully, the one addressed to me was the longest. I was so grateful I nearly cried. What a relief to find out she was the one behind that incident."

"Yeah, but why is she doing this?"

"You mean her motive? It's simple. She wanted Richard and Deborah to get married. And in the kerfuffle over the inheritance, I had to break them up."

The chaos surrounding Richard's marriage prospects had long since been resolved. And while my attempt to destroy a priceless heirloom had been wholly unacceptable, everything turned out okay in the end. It had even recast the history of the Claremont family in a more positive light.

That said...even if it had all worked out, you couldn't undo what had already been done. Richard's cousins couldn't change the fact that they'd pressured his fiancée to leave him. Or that Richard had cut ties with them and spent the next few years running to Sri Lanka, Hong Kong, and eventually Japan. Or that despite everything being settled, Richard would never have the same relationship with his former lover, Deborah, that he had before.

"The two of them met and grew close while working as Octavia's tutors. She was their biggest supporter. Her first and dearest goal in life was to attend their wedding. What a mess!"

Jeffrey sighed like a petulant child, jerking his legs restlessly as he sat. Richard must have been in college or graduate school when he was working as a private tutor in England. Vince met Richard five years ago, so this must have happened even before that which probably would have made Octavia around ten years old?

I tried to put myself back in my ten-year-old shoes. I would have been in fifth grade. It was easier to remember than I'd expected—both the good and the bad.

Obviously, no matter how young you might be when they happened, some wrongs are nightmarish enough to stick with you for the rest of your life. But the past is the past, and we don't have time machines. I think that as you get older, you gradually learn to accept that there are things you can't change. Whether you actually come to believe this or just get better at telling yourself "That's just how it is"...that's a whole other story. Still, you do get better at that sort of thing as you get older.

I lifted my eyes from the page and looked at Jeffrey. He was dressed more for a small party than a museum visit. He was a young, wealthy man and also an executive at an investment firm who worked primarily in the US. The glamour suited him. Still, I couldn't imagine he was enthused about having had to choose this outfit today.

He sighed. The look on his face was that of either a dashing villain or a hero who'd tried to play the villain and failed.

"I wonder if I could get her to take all her anger out on me. That would be a welcome compromise. But I doubt I can reason with her at this point..."

"I'm pretty sure Henry would tan your hide if he knew you were saying things like that."

"Ah ha ha! I didn't think you'd bring Henry up. You know, he's doing so much better now. He can drive like he used to, he's been working with other musicians online, and he'll even go out shopping to crowded stores occasionally. He could just have the people who work for us do those things for him, of course, but he said he wants to do it himself. That fact alone is the most impressive improvement to me."

"It really is impressive."

"Thanks. I know you mean it when you say that. But that's why I can't let anyone drag him back into that mire again, be they angel or devil, or acting in the name of justice or revenge. I just can't. I'm the one who started this fight, after all. Even if I say I was doing it for someone else, I'm the one who crossed a line to try and escape from a situation I was powerless to change."

The drama about the inheritance had done a mental and physical number on Jeffrey's older brother, Henry, a pianist and the heir to the title. His fear of what would happen to him should Richard inherit the family fortune was entirely prompted by social standing, vanity, pride, and jealousy—nothing particularly flattering. To Henry's credit, he at least turned it all inward. But no matter how strong someone might be, there's a limit to what they can keep bottled up. As the internal pressure threatened to explode Henry from within, Jeffrey tried to save him by doing something that would put him eternally at odds with Richard, a man who was like a little brother to him. As a result, Richard vanished from their lives.

No one would say Jeffrey had made 100 percent the right call there, but I can't imagine anyone saying he was 100 percent *wrong*, either, assuming they knew the circumstances. Not even a child. I felt like she might understand, even just a little, if we could only talk. Or maybe that was just what I wanted to believe.

If the thing Olivia couldn't forgive them for was their personal failings, maybe the issue was just a lack of understanding. None of this would have happened in the first place if something as simple as talking it out could have fixed things, but I *did* get the sense that communication breakdowns had contributed to the mess. Maybe talking to her wasn't really an option, though. I mean, she was a minor. I didn't know exactly how she got him to do it, but she was having Vince, an adult, commit near-criminal acts on her behalf. Even if she could brush that off for now, wouldn't it catch up with her in the future? I couldn't imagine Richard and Jeffrey hadn't thought about that.

I stared at Jeffrey's face, trying to figure him out. He flashed me a more reserved and mature smile.

"Let me guess, you're going to suggest that we take legal action to clear up her 'misunderstanding' before I take any other action?"

"Yeah. Um, how is it that you and Richard always know what I'm thinking..."

"Oh, please. I suppose if I had to guess, I might say it's just in our blood. Our grandma was an incredible woman—a master of seeing right through to the darkness in people's hearts. I think Richard inherited the majority of that talent, but I'm sure you already know that."

"Your grandmother?"

Before I could ask if she was the same woman who'd had the complicated love story with the previous Earl—back when he was the heir to the title—Jeffrey continued talking.

"We're trying. Even if she's a shut-in, she has to exist in this world. She can't remain *completely* cut off from everything. But Henry, Richard, and I all agreed that forcing her to do something against her wishes was out of the question."

"When did the three of you have time to get together?"

"You can thank the internet for that."

The singsong way he said that put me at ease, somehow. So they'd had a virtual meeting. He seemed to be trying to dodge any questions with that sparkling smile of his, but ultimately it meant that we—or at least Richard—would be continuing to tolerate her unreasonable behavior for the time being.

My eyes must've narrowed, because Jeffrey continued, speaking softly. "Well, there is one other thing about this situation. Should Octavia's plot inevitably drag outsiders—especially you, Mr. Seigi Nakata—into it, we will use whatever means necessary to resolve this, as the adults in the situation. The three of us are all in agreement on this point as well."

"You don't need to worry about me. But I guess you guys didn't conclude that an immediate intervention would be in *her* best interest?"

"For now—just for now. I'm sorry for being so behind everything, but there's still so much information we're missing. If she *is* just after petty revenge, however, I don't think you need worry."

A far-off look briefly crossed Jeffrey's face. I couldn't deny that the situation warranted more investigation, but Richard, Jeffrey, and Henry seemed to have some cards up their collective sleeves that they had yet to show me. Besides, there had to be a reason they couldn't just meet Octavia and had decided to not intervene yet.

I was pretty sure Jeffrey would tell me in his own time if I didn't pester him to spill the beans immediately. At least, I thought he would. He had to have a reason for not telling me everything just yet. I'd absolutely despised him the first time I met him, but now, I didn't think I could bring myself to hate him even if I tried.

Should we just wait a little longer? What was the right call? Which route did *I* want to take?

Jeffrey flashed me a flimsy smile. It was almost like he was telling me I could hit him if I wanted to.

I responded to his smile by looking him in the eye and nodding.

"All right, I understand. But please tell me once you know more."

"Of course. Thank you, my friend. I would love to tell you not to worry too much, but I imagine that's a big ask after that data breach. I'm not going to cause you any more trouble—I will promise that much. If I cause any more trouble for the person who's done so much for our family, I'm pretty sure Richard will make me his punching bag before I even have the opportunity to distract myself with whatever Octavia's up to. Besides, I do need to show you my good side sometimes, don't I? Richard's not the only one who gets to play the hero." He smiled. "The same goes for Henry."

I nodded appreciatively, then cut in with an, "Actually..." trying my best to sound nonchalant. "Does Richard know about Vince working as your spy?"

"...Yes. He picked up on it while it was going on. If he hadn't, he might not have gone to Ginza."

"And what about Vince?"

"Is he aware that Richard knows he was spying on him? Beats me. I have no way of knowing. I have no contact with him anymore."

I constructed an image of a shop much like Étranger in my mind. There were two people it that shop—not me and Richard, but *Vince* and Richard. I couldn't even begin to imagine what kind of relationship they developed or how they interacted with one another.

I was more or less satisfied with the answers Jeffrey had given me. When he opened his arms wide and asked if I had any other questions, one thought suddenly came to the forefront.

"I like your outfit."

"Really? You don't think it's a little too much? Thanks, though. I appreciate it. The theme I was going for was, 'a villainous young man from the 19th century, with a heart black as coal and wit sharp as a knife, even if he doesn't look it at first glance.'"

"I'm getting more, 'a 19th century friendly older brother figure who's a bit of a bookworm and is trying a little too hard with a fashionable suit.'"

"Are you sure Richard's not rubbing off on you a bit too much? I almost thought it was him sitting next to me for a moment. You really threw me for a loop last time you spoke to me on the phone in English, too. For a second, I wasn't sure who I was talking to. You should just be yourself, you know. Don't force it."

"You're not going to fool me with that silver tongue of yours. I'm serious, please don't do anything stupid. I'm begging you. For Richard and Henry's sakes, too."

"I know, I know."

I sure hoped he actually meant that.

Thanks to the nightmarish inheritance requirements set by the seventh Earl of Claremont, Henry endured a serious bout of depression and Richard lost the woman he loved. They'd both been mired in their own pain, but the person sunk deepest in that mire right now might just be the fellow in front of me, with his ever-present smile. The man who got his hands the dirtiest. The first person to volunteer when unsavory deeds needed to be done. I think I had some similar tendencies, but Jeffrey was much more capable and much better at hiding it. He deserved concern, too. Perhaps to a worrying degree.

I must have looked dejected, because Jeffrey ran his hand through my hair, as if petting a dog.

"Wah! Hey! You know I'm almost thirty if you round up."

"What a bizarre thing for a twenty-three year old to say. Your age has nothing to do with it. Sorry if I made you feel like I was belittling you. I was just trying to cheer you up. I guess we had better be on our way before the curator comes in here yelling at us for being a nuisance."

The Musée de la Chasse et de la Nature was an opulent little building. As soon as I picked up my bag and stepped outside, I was surrounded by the city. Paris. I didn't really have much of a mental image of the city—the Eiffel Tower, the French revolution, and crepes were about the extent of it. Was this really that same place? If you told me this was a new development in Marunouchi, I'd have believed you.

Jeffrey was messing with his phone as I looked for a taxi stand. He should be heading to the airport from here—when he heard I was going to be in France, he'd worked a quick half-day trip into his schedule. Mind you, I wasn't here to sightsee either. My real destination was a bit further south, and Jeffrey knew that, too.

I was about to say goodbye to him, bag in hand, when I noticed Jeffrey fidgeting restlessly. He kept looking at me like he had just noticed something. What was it? I just went ahead and asked.

"Oh, it's just...you have a good head on your shoulders, but you can be a little careless sometimes, so I was worried that you might have forgotten something. Maybe I just got my hopes up, but...you wouldn't happen to have a souvenir for me, would you?"

The raised inflection at the end of the sentence was both deliberate and very cute.

An awkward silence hung between us. A souvenir. I recalled how I'd written vaguely about that before I left. Not in an email or text to anyone, but on my blog

But I hadn't told Jeffrey about my blog. I hadn't even told Richard. I'd heard it was easy for misunderstandings to occur when you connected with people you know offline on the internet, so I decided not to mention the blog to anyone for the time being. It was the same reason I'd decided to use the pen name Iggy, even though it is a little embarrassing.

But...

"...You read it, didn't you?"

"Read what?"

"You did, didn't you?"

"I wish you'd be more specific. You know I'm not as good at Japanese as Richard is. But if you don't have any other business with me, that's fine. Ah ha ha. I wasn't actually expecting anything, I promise."

"Right. Well, I know it's not much, but this is for you."

I pulled a piece of candy from my pocket and offered it to Jeffrey. It was a piece of soothingly royal-milk-tea-flavored Japanese candy that my colleague would bring me from time to time. Jeffrey thanked me with a sparkling smile, and I asked again just to be absolutely sure.

"You really haven't read it?"

"Like I said, I haven't the faintest idea what you're talking about. Come on, I really don't know anything, okay? All right. So you're headed to Gare de Lyon station? I assume you're taking the TGV. We could share a taxi to the station. I can head to the airport from there."

"No thanks."

I explained that I was meeting someone else here and Jeffrey's expression faltered before he smiled again.

"Oh. Well, it's nice that you have lots of friends. I hope you have fun."

"You must have a lot of friends, too, Jeffrey."

"Do I, though? All I do is work all the time, so while I'm always gaining new acquaintances, my friends seem to be shrinking in number. I guess you don't have that problem. Maybe it's a me issue."

"...Do you count me among those 'acquaintances'?"

I was trying to be cheeky, but I regretted it the moment I actually said it out loud. But Jeffrey just laughed cheerfully and carelessly, like an aristocrat from ages past.

"I don't think you're either, and you don't have to be. You're someone both Henry and I care about. Take care of yourself. And don't neglect your mental health, either. I'll be seeing you."

I had just managed to nab a taxi, so I offered him a warm thank you and bade him goodbye as I left the museum. Jeffrey waved to me from where he stood. He matched the building so well it almost seemed in poor taste. I sincerely wished he wouldn't have to go through any more hardship.

The driver asking me, "Where to?" snapped me back to reality and I gave a clear answer in response:

"Tour Eiffel!"

The Eiffel Tower. The perfect spot to meet someone.

I softly stroked the unnatural bulge in my backpack. Hang on a little longer, Buddha.

This trip had started with an email from Richard. He explained the details to me at the end of July, the day after my first trip buying gems for the company in Ratnapura. I got the initial message in the car on my way back from Ratnapura, but he didn't give me the details until I made it to the house in Kandy.

If it had been another email with no sender name and the subject line, "Help Richard," it would have been an exact repeat of last time—but instead, this one came from Richard's mother, Catherine. The subject was "Vacances!" (French for "vacation"— a loan word that had become common in Japan in recent years.)

Richard looked at me like he was in the midst of a forty-hour long migraine when the subject was finally broached at the company residence in Sri Lanka.

"She...appears...to want to meet you...over summer vacation."

"Me?" I said, pointing to myself. Richard meekly nodded a few times.

Richard's mother, Catherine de Vulpian, was a French woman of noble descent. She and Richard's father had married for love but divorced after their only child was born. She was currently enjoying the single life, though I'd heard she was struggling a bit financially, due to having quite a few relatives in need of money. She had a queenly disposition, and her son looked just like she used to when she was younger. Theirs was a bloodline of incomparable beauty. I didn't really know anything else about her beyond that.

How did Catherine know who I was? Richard had essentially cut off all contact until a few years ago, but he didn't really seem the type to keep in close contact with his family under normal circumstances. I knew their relationship was kind of rocky, too, which made it even harder to imagine Richard talking to Catherine about how he had a Japanese apprentice who was being trained in Sri Lanka right now.

I asked Richard where she got that information. His face shifted from "horrible migraine" to "a jeweler ready to do battle."

"That concerns me as well. The body of the message itself is typical of her writing—not particularly coherent, concerned entirely with herself, excessively cheerful, and missing key details."

"So she's usually like this?"

"I misspoke. I don't really interact with her often enough to say if this is 'typical' for her, so I should have said it *was* typical of how she *used to* write. However...I cannot account for the source of the information in question."

Recklessly accepting a suspicious invitation, walking headfirst into a trap and causing Richard untold amounts of trouble. Now why did that sound so familiar? *Sorry, but I'm not going through that again.* But who knew—maybe it was just a coincidence, and Richard was struggling precisely *because* there hadn't been anything particularly unsettling about the email's contents. He wouldn't look so exhausted, otherwise.

"I mean, why not?"

"...Why not what?"

"Why don't I just meet her? Catherine that is."

Richard replied with a "what?" after a lengthy silence. Was my response really that surprising?

"I mean, I know you're going either way."

The beautiful man had no response to that. But his silence was an answer in its own right. Thinking back, I'm pretty sure he was wearing a white shirt and pale grey pants at the time. Not only had he just accompanied me to Ratnapura for my training, he'd even driven for four hours along the long, winding, impossibly bumpy road there. I'd driven on the four-hour return trip. He must have been exhausted, but I guess I shouldn't have been surprised that an aura of radiant sunshine seemed to surround him even at the worst of times.

"What makes you think that?"

"Do I really need to explain?"

I tried to see it from Richard's perspective. You know there's someone trying to entrap you, and that it's possible they not only contacted your mother but are using her to get to you. Either way, you'd be worried about her. You'd absolutely want to at least check in on her and probably wouldn't be able to rest easy until you did.

I explained my reasoning, and Richard let out an exasperated sigh.

"Sometimes I think it would be nice if everyone were as kind as you. Then again, it might be uncomfortably cloying if that were the case."

"I feel exactly the same way about you. Wait, does that mean I was right?"

"I can't deny that."

Surprisingly, there wasn't a hint of irony in his voice. He didn't seem particularly happy about the prospect of seeing his mother, but he also didn't seem like he was being forced to go visit someone who was in trouble. I was pretty sure I'd be making a similar face if I were put in a position where I had to go see my mother Hiromi like that. We didn't exactly have the kind of relationship where we might go see a movie or get dinner together, like friends. If anything, our relationship was awkward and uncomfortable. But she was my mother, so we found a way to get along.

It finally hit me why Richard had had such good intuition about that in the past. I guess it was something we had in common.

Richard was lying on his side on a tiled chaise lounge in the tropical garden, surrounded by banana and mango trees. I went back into the house to prepare some refreshments, and when I came back, he was still in the same position. I set a wooden tray down on the table we used to have tea outside. Banana chips, candied coconut, and the star of the show—pudding and chilled royal milk tea. A special spread. The exhausted man lifted his head and smiled faintly.

"...Thank you."

"You should eat something. Sweets are just the thing when you're exhausted."

"Indeed they are. But I'm more concerned about your answer earlier. Her demands aside, what reason do *you* have for coming along?"

Richard reached out a hand from the lounge, and I pulled the tray away.

I moved the tray of sweets about ten centimeters away from the mildly shocked man.

"......"

"Care to say that again?"

"...Why do you need to come along with me?"

Richard reached his hand out as he spoke. A feint, huh? Cheap tricks wouldn't work on me. I had a lot of confidence in my reaction time, thanks to all the years I spent getting beat up by my karate instructor from Ryukyu. I swiftly lifted the tray up and over my head like a woman carrying water from a river, and Richard looked at me, his lips pulled taut. He looked like an angry elementary school student on the verge of throwing a tantrum after taking a bite of a sour fruit.

I played dumb. "Care to say that again?"

"I see your stubborn streak has only gotten worse."

"You only have yourself to thank. I won't be a burden. I've even been studying French. I swear I won't repeat my disgraceful behavior from last time."

"You never learn. How many times do I have to tell you that the only promises I want from you have nothing to do with how you come across or how much you can do for me, but keeping yourself safe?"

"Well, that's just implied."

I didn't think I could take it. I'd never be able to forget what happened to him on that boat for the rest of my life. After I made it back to Sri Lanka, I'd spent some time ruminating on what happened. Even if Richard's comment about how that sort of thing had happened to him before was a slip of the tongue, as far as I was concerned, it just proved he needed someone to pull him out of situations like that and get him somewhere safe. And if he didn't have anyone like that despite needing them, well, my salary was going to magically transform into airline tickets to France. And I'd do everything in my power to find him. He might get mad at me for following him, but I'd apologize and he'd ultimately forgive me. Because he was just such a nice person.

In which case, taking me along from the start was clearly going to make things easier for both of us.

"Don't you agree?" I asked, holding the tray close to my chest. I wasn't about to budge. Today's Nakata pudding was a bit on the softer side and paired perfectly with the coconut shortbread biscuits Richard had been fond of eating lately. A scoop of vanilla ice cream from the freezer would only elevate it further. I made sure to mention that to Richard, and his expression soured even further. I guess he needed just one more push.

"...So you've been studying French?"

"Oui! Bonjour! Merci! Mademoiselle."

"Thank you for the rather...creative announcement of your decision. But you have two weeks."

Richard held out two fingers, his cheek still firmly planted on the backrest of the chaise lounge. With the background of all that verdant greenery, it almost looked like a shot from a movie.

"The vacation she invited us on is in August. That gives you two weeks to learn the language. During that period, I'll only be with you for two to three days, and only while you're in the field in Ratnapura or Colombo. You may call me, but not every day. France is an even more French-speaking country than you likely realize. Are you going to show me how motivated you are, *Monsieur Seigi Nakata*? I'd like you to show me what a young man who's surpassed the rather high hurdle of the first round of the Japanese civil service examination can really do when he sets his mind to something."

Catherine had to have spoken English when she was living at the Claremont estate...but I guess it would be better if I understood French, huh? Professor Richard's answer to that was a harsh glare and nothing more.

Besides, it wasn't like Richard and Catherine were the only people I'd be talking to while in France. Most of all, though, I was excited to hear him ask me to show what I could do. Learning to appraise gems and negotiate prices here in Sri Lanka was full of variables that were out of my control, but studying a foreign language, just like studying in school, was more like a speed-eating contest to take in all the nutrition—vocabulary, grammar, and the rest—that you could. And it was something I was good at. If he wanted me to show him what I could really do, I'd be more than happy to show him all I've got.

That said...

"I would appreciate it if you could give me some coursework..."

In response, Professor Richard made me give him my cell phone. After he finished inputting whatever it was he was typing, he took the tray from me and began eating his treats. I was relieved to see that, like a wilted plant given water, his pained expression began to vanish and he seemed to come back to life. He really did need to be given sweet things to eat when he was tired.

Since we only saw each other a few days a month, I ended up eating most of the pudding I made. This meant, however, that the stockpile of pudding in the fridge was growing. It was probably happy to have the opportunity to be eaten by him.

And so, I spent the next two weeks before the trip diligently studying French with the books and videos Richard had put on my phone.

"Hey, how long have you been in France? Do you live here?"

I struck a triumphant pose in my mind as I sat in the taxi on the way to the Eiffel Tower. After leaving the Musée de la Chasse et de la Nature, I shifted gears in my head and switched to French. I still hadn't learned stuff like the subjunctive mood and whatever, so I could only speak in simple sentences, but that was plenty for day-to-day conversations.

I told the driver that I was visiting from abroad, and that this was my first time speaking to a French person in French. He looked at me like I was pranking him. I guess he didn't believe me. That made me feel like I'd cleared the first checkpoint. Now I was really looking forward to seeing the person who'd told me to show him what I could do.

Though the person I was going to see right now wasn't Richard.

"You have good taste though, taking Rue de Rivoli to the tower. You've got a good view out the left side for the whole trip—the Louvre, Tuileries Garden, Palace de la Concorde. You can see all the big tourist spots on one road."

"Thank you very much. How long until we arrive?"

"About twenty minutes if we don't hit traffic."

My destination was the landmark everyone thinks of when you mention France. It's the Eiffel Tower in English and *Tour Eiffel* in French. When even proper nouns change that much from language to language, I can understand why people prefer to use their native tongue.

We got caught behind a line of tour buses, so it took me thirty minutes to make it to at Champ de Mars—the location with the best view of the Eiffel Tower. I paid my fare with the Euro bills I still wasn't used to using, and the moment I got off, a party of tourists clambered into the car like they couldn't wait another moment. This really was a tourist destination, after all.

At any rate, I'd arrived. And just as I was about to contact the person I was coming to meet, I heard a sound. Music.

The sound of flamenco-style music as fingers delicately plucked at guitar strings.

I appreciated how easy he was to identify. The vast expanse of grass spread out before me as I searched for the source of the sound, finally landing on an Asian man playing a guitar. I couldn't help cracking a smile. I was just so happy that someone I knew was waiting for me here on this lawn filled with tourists from all over the world.

"Shimomura! Shimomura!"

My shouts startled the people around me as I waved. The guitarist looked up at me, his red baseball cap partially shading his face, and smiled. He looked more tanned than before.

"It's Haruyoshi. Haruyoshi!"

He slung his guitar on his back and walked up to meet me—my friend from college, Haruyoshi Shimomura. He had a carefree smile on his face as he gave me a hug.

"Man, no one calls me Haruyoshi anymore. It keeps getting turned into 'Aruyoshi.' Even the people in passport control called me 'Aruyoshi.'"

"Oh, I guess it's not just French that doesn't have that 'h' sound but Spanish too, huh?"

"Yup. So people keep nicknaming me stuff like 'Aru' or 'Yoshi.' I wish they'd go for something like 'Harry,' to be honest."

"People have a hard time saying 'Seigi,' too. But there are some people where I live who know Japanese, so they tend to get it right, at least."

"Well, aren't we lucky."

"Now, now, let this Buddha bring you inner piece."

"I don't think most friends would come bearing Buddha in their backpack."

"I think having a friend come all the way from Granada to Paris to meet you is much more unusual."

"You really don't know the first thing about European geography, do you? Ignoring differences in elevation, the distance from Granada to Paris is about the same as Aomori to Yamaguchi.

It'd be a domestic trip in Japan. What fraction of the distance between Granada and Kandy do you think that is? It doesn't even compare. Admittedly, there's no Shinkansen here, so the trip did take a whole day," he laughed. As we chatted on the lawn, he never even looked inclined to part with his guitar.

Haruyoshi and I met at Kasaba University in Tokyo. We were both studying economics, but I somehow ended up apprenticing as a jeweler while he moved to Spain to study flamenco guitar in Granada. Kasaba likes to advertise itself as having graduates go on to work in a diverse array of fields, but I think we both exceeded expectations. Economics had absolutely nothing to do with where we'd ended up.

I had moved to Sri Lanka after I graduated, but Haruyoshi left to join his instructor in Spain in the spring of his third year. After studying for a year on a tourist visa, he decided to get serious about it, formally dropped out of Kasaba, and was currently living in Granada on an art student visa. He told me all about this on a video call.

I felt like we were much closer now than when we were in college, probably because we were both pursuing unusual fields outside Japan. But recently there was another, hidden reason.

"Haruyoshi, so...what happened with that thing?"

"Well, long story short..." He pulled a square case from his little shoulder bag and handed it to me. It was a plastic case with a photo for a cover. And the man on the cover looking wearily up at the sky, guitar in hand, was clearly none other than the very Haruyoshi I knew. Inside was a homemade CD.

"I can have it?! Thanks. I'll pay you back. Um...the title's, 'The Sound of Alhambra'? Is that song you play for me over the phone sometimes on here?"

"I dunno which one you're talking about, but my whole repertoire's on there, so it probably is. Take it. If anyone should be paying anyone money, it's me, anyhow."

Haruyoshi flipped the CD case over and pointed at one part of the back cover. There was another person credited behind Haruyoshi Shimomura on guitar.

Enrique Wabisabi.

It was obviously a stage name. But Wabisabi, seriously? What was that even supposed to be? Enrique was easier to understand at least, being a Spanish name. European names change depending on the country. Even if they're spelled the same way, they're often pronounced differently. For example, the English name "Richard" is spelled the same way in French, but you don't pronounce the "d." "Enrique," meanwhile, was the Spanish version of the English "Henry."

The word "piano" was written in parenthesis after the name. I guess it was the name of Haruyoshi's accompanist.

"Oh, so you ended up recording with him. That's incredible. Did you two ever have an opportunity to meet?"

"No, we haven't, but he's a really incredible person," my friend mumbled. He seemed a bit in awe. "I'm serious, man, he's incredible. He has such a gentle demeanor and keeps perfect time with me, but somehow he's a total perfectionist—you'd think he had eight hands when you hear him play."

"I-Is he really that incredible? Really?"

"What? You're the one who introduced us. Are you seriously telling me you've never actually heard him play?"

"Well, I, uh...I don't know anything about music..."

A certain finance talent whom I'd just parted ways with immediately came to mind. Oh, Jeffrey—I hear you've been really busy lately, but I hope you can get some sleep on the plane, at least. Henry had joked with me probably at least twenty times by now that Jeffrey would work himself to death if left to his own devices, meaning sooner or later, Henry was going to have to drug him with sleeping pills and throw him on a yacht heading to a tropical island.

It had been a long time since Henry first contacted me personally. It was right after I'd moved to Sri Lanka. I didn't have his contact information, so when I suddenly got an email from an unfamiliar address with the subject, "Hey, it's Henry," I just assumed it was spam and nearly deleted it. I was absolutely shocked when I saw the words, "Thank you very much for what you did regarding the Claremont family inheritance." I hadn't heard from him since I tried to smash their family treasure back in England.

I was completely perplexed as to why he'd be contacting me. Henry, being as polite as was humanly possible, apologized for his lack of contact and all the trouble I had gone through, and expressed his desire to get to know me better.

And his desire for me to help him learn Japanese if at all possible.

I was shocked. Henry and Richard had a pretty significant age gap. He was pushing forty. Why would a man who'd lived nearly forty years of his life not knowing Japanese want to learn a new language? It was often said Japanese was one of the hardest languages for English speakers to learn, too. But beyond that, his little brother and Richard had both learned Japanese from their Japanese governess. Couldn't he have asked his brother to teach him?

I asked as much in a reply after making numerous searches with key words like, "emailing an earl's heir example sentences," "emailing nobility examples," and "polite sentence composition examples," and received another extremely polite reply.

He didn't want to become more of a burden to Jeffrey.

He wasn't speaking out of some kind of self-loathing—just the simple fact that Jeffrey was always worrying about him, and he was fed up with Jeffrey spending all his spare energy and resources on him. Henry never wanted him to do anything of the sort in the first place, but when his condition got rather perilous—his own words—he found it difficult to reject his help. So, he explained to me, he wanted to try and start something new without Jeffrey's knowledge, to repay him for all the worry he'd caused him, in a way.

That was the first time that the heir to the title actually felt like Jeffrey's older brother to me. So he liked to surprise and delight people, and had a bit of a reckless side, too? Yeah.

Henry explained that he was looking for someone to teach him Japanese and would be willing to pay a fair wage for the service. He asked me if I had a friend or even a family member who might be up to the task. I asked him if I could do it, and he replied with another "no." He claimed he was worried about Jeffrey finding out through Richard, but I think he was more concerned with interfering with my studies.

That was when I suddenly remembered that he played piano. It helped that right before I'd gotten his email, a certain someone had been complaining to me over a video call about how he wanted to record his music soon, but it was looking like he was going to be forced to use a two-generations-out-of-date synthesizer for the accompaniment if nothing changed.

I looked up even more sample sentences to construct a reply, making a very gentle suggestion. And then I hurriedly contacted Haruyoshi and asked him if he had any interest in tutoring a forty-year-old English man in Japanese over the internet. He was always one to keep things in perspective, so I didn't think things would go badly. Even if it didn't work out, I figured it'd be an interesting experience for the both of them. That was what my gut told me at the time, anyway.

One thing led to another, and now we were here.

I let out a little sigh of relief as I gazed at the name "Enrique Wabisabi." I had never pried for more details on just how "perilous" his illness had been...but I did know how far human beings could push themselves. And thanks to watching my mother, Hiromi, I knew just how much effort it took for someone to stare down a precipice, decide to turn back, and retrace the path they'd taken to get there.

So I introduced Henry to my friend, and they got to know each other over the internet and even recorded a CD together.

I almost felt like crying. I was sure Jeffrey would if I told him about it, while Richard might smack me over the head. Both of them cared a great deal about Henry. I'd long since been prepared to get down on my hands and knees and beg for forgiveness. I would absolutely have to explain the situation in detail to both them and Haruyoshi at some point and just pray that no one got hurt in the process. But...

...right now, I felt pretty glad.

"I'm so happy. For the both of you."

"Enrique is a really incredible person. He apologized to me at the start, saying he was pretty sure a forty-year-old like him would struggle to learn a new language, but he was so motivated. His coursework is always perfect, and he's very concerned with learning correct pronunciation, and he even points out things about Japanese that I never noticed. It felt like a waste just to teach him to *speak* Japanese, so I tried teaching him some Japanese songs while I was at it, to give him something more to work with. And he can play piano so he picked it up so easily... He's just such a great guy," Haruyoshi gushed. "He's been paying me monthly, but one time, I told him that I was in a dispute with my landlord because I couldn't pay both my rent and performance costs, and asked if he could pay me in advance for the month. The next day, I checked my bank account and saw...three months worth of pay had been deposited into my account."

"Wow."

"I was actually pretty mad about it. I mean, doing something like that is dangerous. What if I was a bad guy? I could've passed his information along to some other bad guys and they could have extorted him for even more money."

"Y-yeah."

"I know I probably sound ridiculous right now. If I were in his shoes, I'd never want to work with someone who asked for an advance on a payment and then got mad at me for actually doing it. But then he told me, 'I'm very sorry, I didn't mean any disrespect. If it's at all possible, I hope you will think of it as a token of my appreciation for the sincerity with which you've treated me.' It's probably just because I'm not very good at English, but sometimes the way he talks reminds me of how lords in period dramas sound."

"Ha-ha, ha ha ha, ha ha..."

I broke out into a cold sweat as it occurred to me that he did know about wealthy-finance-guy Jeffrey's social media. But he didn't seem aware of the fact that Jeffrey was English nobility or that his older brother was the current earl's heir. Henry's physical appearance probably made him look too old to be Jeffrey's brother. I silently thanked him for being too kind to pry any further.

"Thanks, man," Haruyoshi said.

It startled me. I thought he had read my mind. But that didn't seem to be the case, as my friend continued.

"Not just for the extra source of income or finding an accompanist for me but for helping me meet someone like him so early in my life. We're vastly different in terms of age, social standing, and even the way we think, but somehow we understand each other, and that's such a rare thing. If I'd just kept on living a life of poverty in Spain without ever meeting someone like him, I think I'd have come to hate all older wealthy people."

"...Have you been struggling that much?"

"No, not really. I'm grateful to Enrique, of course, but any country or society is going to have those kinds of disparities. I mean, I'm Asian—that alone has given me a lot to think about. I guess it's just that whenever I think about the future, money trouble is always foremost in my mind."

Haruyoshi went on to explain just how good Enrique's piano playing was. He explained that when he played Enrique's accompaniment on his portable stereo on the street, it made more people stop to listen. The piano was a powerful instrument that could serve as a "one-man orchestra"—but, he explained, the biggest factor was how earnest his playing was.

"At my school and the flamenco bar I practice at, pretty much everyone is desperate for their moment in the limelight. Absolutely desperate. They want to succeed, they want people to like their art, they want that applause. But his music is like a clear stream. This is just me guessing, but I wonder if there was a long period where he couldn't play? The way he can play just about anything I request with a smile on his face kinda makes me feel like a little kid again, just awed by how incredible music is."

It was probably similar to the feeling of looking at Mt. Fuji or gazing at ocean waves. "I'm happy for you."

"Me too," Haruyoshi said with an awkward smile. "I'm grateful, of course, but I've been starting to feel frustrated with myself for just kinda doing whatever I want. I've decided to really throw myself into practice and get better. It's rough, but it's been fun."

He smiled again after that, but it only took a moment for me to notice how strained it was.

"If I'm being honest, though, there's a lot I'm unsure about. I considered trying to get a job in Spain without going back home to Japan, but the employment rate isn't as high in Spain, and it's not like I'm some extraordinary talent. But if I go back to Japan, I'll be a college dropout...and, I mean, I knew that going into this, but once I start thinking about it, I just can't stop."

"I totally get what you mean..."

"You're in better shape than me, aren't you? You've got your diploma. I didn't even finish."

"That's not gonna help me anymore, either. We've both missed our new graduate windows."

"Ugh, let's just stop. No more of this. This isn't the kind of conversation anyone should be having under the Eiffel Tower."

The two of us lay out on the grass and just laughed for a while. Haruyoshi joked that if securing employment in Japan used to be called "a life on rails," that meant our lives had clearly gone "off the rails." I thought back to all the time I'd spent in the library, studying for the civil service exam. I guess I really had "derailed."

Still, I didn't think it was a coincidence that the two of us had been in the same exam prep class. It really isn't that unusual for people to find their calling along a path different from the one they'd been walking so far. Untrodden paths had no rails to follow. They were the paths blazed by pioneers who had no choice but to break down any obstacles that stood in their way.

But I wasn't the only person doing that.

My friend, who had taught me that the distance between Granada and Paris was about the same as between Aomori and Yamaguchi, pulled his phone from his bag, as if he'd suddenly remembered something.

"Seigi, can we take a selfie? With the Eiffel Tower in the background."

"...A selfie? You mean to post on your socials?"

"No, of course not. I'd never post a picture of you or post your name without asking. I promise."

I'd told Haruyoshi a bit about the troubles I'd had before leaving Japan. He reacted with a "that sucks" and seemed to understand how concerned I was about protecting my personal information, which made me glad. Haruyoshi turned on his phone.

"You don't have to if you don't want to. It's just for myself. It's hard to explain, but when I'm living over there, totally immersed in Spanish, sometimes it feels like my concentration of Japanese ions starts getting low or something."

"Japanese ions...?"

"You know, like your internal source of identity? I start finding it hard to express who I am in Japanese, and it feels like the whole framework of my identity is on the verge of collapse. But I just know if I had a picture of you and me together, just having fun, I'd be able to laugh it off. So that's why I want one."

Oh. That I felt like I could understand. It reminded me of a time, deep in the mountains of Sri Lanka, when it hit me that I hadn't spoken Japanese with anyone for a whole week. It had made me suddenly feel very detached from myself...and I guess Haruyoshi knew that feeling as well. Having a picture to look at during times like that probably *would* be nice.

"Yeah, why not. Let's do it. Maybe I'll take one for myself, too. Umm..."

"Have you never taken a selfie before? Give it here. I'll take it for you."

We took a series of silly photos, just like all the other tourists doing the same. I spent the rest of the time until my train arrived listening to him play guitar and catching up. This was the first time since leaving home that I'd spent such a long time talking to one of my Japanese friends. I'd never had strong feelings about my nationality or where I was born, but when you try living just a step away from what you're used to, it really drives home how dependent you are on the culture and country you were born into.

Maybe this was the true meaning of Étranger.

That reminded me—étranger was a French word. As I practiced French pronunciation until my throat hurt, I couldn't help but think about how, despite being so far from Ginza, French wasn't quite as divorced from the life I'd been living as I'd thought.

I bade Haruyoshi, fan of massive towers, farewell as he decided to get in line to ascend the Eiffel Tower. For my part,

I headed to Gare de Lyon, a station the TGV—a high-speed rail system—operated out of. It was a big station, like Shibuya or Shinagawa in Japan. Richard and I hadn't managed to coordinate our schedules, so we'd be meeting up "on location" this time. At least I'd gotten to meet Jeffrey and Haruyoshi as a result. It had started my trip off on a happy note, though I did feel like I was overdue for a text from Richard right around now. I'd let him know when I'd landed.

I checked my phone while I was in a taxi on the way to the station. As expected, I had a single message. From Richard. But its contents almost seemed cut off.

"Be careful. Meeting you."

I wished he would stop. I hadn't had the best experience with mysterious messages lately. I typed up a reply, asking him what he meant by that, but it was hard to imagine Richard, of all people, sending something like that with no follow up if he was in a position to do otherwise. He should have finished up negotiations in Italy and been on his way to a local airport near our destination from Milano, so he might have still been on the plane.

But what or who would be "meeting" me that I needed to be careful about? I would soon be heading south on the TGV. We hadn't really discussed travel plans in that much detail, but if anyone was coming to meet me, it would presumably be at the station nearest to the destination. Which wasn't going to be a concern for at least another four hours.

Figuring I'd have more information by then, I paid for my taxi in front of the crowded station and got out. Elegant reliefs were carved into the station's white walls, and it even had a clock-tower, like a castle. It felt extremely French. The tourists taking photos really stood out, but I'd heard that pickpockets were really common in Paris. I'd have to be on my guard to make sure I didn't embarrass my legendary grandmother.

I surveyed the area and checked the ticket that I'd bought online. I wasn't sure if I needed to go underground or straight ahead.

But then...

I surveyed the area again, and this time, I noticed something.

It wasn't an "off" feeling. If I had to describe it, it felt like "hitting the nail right on the head." It was like looking for a particular character in a drawing of a crowd in a picture book and finding him in a second flat.

It was color and shape that tripped my sensors. Maybe the brilliant hair, the pale gold of a pale sunflower, or piercing blue eyes the color of an ever so slightly overcast sky. Maybe the skin, pale as milk, or the perfectly fitted suit. Perhaps one of those things caught my eye when they entered my field of view. I was pretty sure they had. At about two o'clock, roughly thirty meters in front of me.

I thought you were arriving by plane.

He slipped behind a sign and didn't seem inclined to move from there. He was probably planning to slip behind me and follow me once I entered the station. I wasn't about to let that happen. I could still see his legs peeking out from beneath the sign, clad in a charcoal grey suit. *I can't believe he's wearing a suit on vacation.* I'd taken him at his word when he told me not to worry too much about it and dressed in a casual shirt and chinos. I had made sure I looked well kempt and reasonably put together, at least, so I could probably make it work.

I decided to try using the crowd to circle around, hiding in the mass of people and sneaking up behind him to surprise him. I was still a little wound up from hanging out with Haruyoshi at the Eiffel Tower, and in a bit of a mood, almost like I was a junior high student again.

With my backpack still firmly on my back, I clapped him on his shoulder. I should have realized something was wrong at that point.

"Gotcha! Hey, Richard, uh...huh?"

"I found you."

The voice rang out, beautiful as the chime of a bell.

The figure in the suit slowly turned around before me. They slipped a hand behind their neck sweeping up their hair in one motion. A torrent of golden hair, which must've been tucked into the collar of their suit, spilled out down to their chest. I was greeted by a delicate neck, slender waist, gleaming lips, and the gentle fragrance of perfume.

I nearly let out a groan, but with a frantic effort, managed to hold it in. No one else would praise me for pulling that off, but I sure was. Good job, Seigi. Good on you for not losing your cool in this situation. Maybe you have grown a bit. Good boy. Well, enough of that distraction.

A smiling woman stood before me. A *woman*, not a man.

The woman, smiling like a goddess of sunshine, took my hand in hers and squeezed, announcing, "*Bonjour*, Seigi! I'm Richard's mother. I knew you'd find me. I've been so desperate to meet you."

She spoke fluent English. Clad in a masculine suit which, upon closer inspection, was clearly tailored for a woman's body, she shook my hand and continued cheerfully, "Now, let's get on that train. Don't worry, I've heard all about what's going on with you two. Octavia told me. I'm so excited."

Somehow, those last words sounded cold and distant to me.

Gare de Lyon Station connected Paris to Lyon, so it primarily served travelers heading to the south of France. If you took the long-distance train, the TGV, you could be in Marseille in four hours. We'd departed at three in the afternoon, so it was already past seven when we made it there, but the sun still hadn't set. It was the height of summer and sunset wasn't until close to 9:30. It made it hard to know when to have dinner. By the by, my understanding was that sunrise was at around 6:30 a.m.

"Were you planning to take the bus from here? You don't have to worry about that, I have a car. I will accept payment in the form of a 'thank you,' hmm?"

"Thank you very much. I appreciate it. And sorry for the trouble."

"You're very welcome, heh heh. You don't have to be so formal."

I felt like we'd had some version of that exchange about twenty times while on the train.

Her English had a peculiar idiosyncrasy that wasn't present in Richard or Saul's speech—she would occasionally end her sentences with a rising intonation, almost like a little bird chirping. She usually used it on phrases like, "I will accept payment in the form of a 'thank you,' hmm?'" or "Feel free to enjoy yourself, hmm?" or "You can share my earbuds if you'd like, hmm?" These phrases inevitably included a subtle command of one sort or the other: "thank me," "rejoice," "share my earbuds," and so on. It seemed to delight her when I reacted the way she wanted and we could communicate smoothly. I tried ignoring her "orders" and changing the subject to see how she would react, but she just looped the conversation back around to the same topic again. The script was set in stone.

Her orders weren't particularly onerous, and she didn't seem like she was trying to cause trouble. Honestly, it almost felt like I'd suddenly gotten myself a little sister who really enjoyed my attention. Her voice was always bright and cheery and playful, like a bird that couldn't help but enjoy the sound of its own song. She was a wonderful person.

And she was the mother of the boss who had done so much for me.

She looked incredibly, unbelievably, young—beyond even the scope of even nature's most incredible miracles—but even if she'd had her son at twenty, she'd have to be over fifty by now. She was the furthest thing from an adorable little sister. Even if she barely looked thirty.

I didn't quite know how to interact with her.

"*Madame.*"

"It's Catherine."

"...Catherine."

"That's me," she replied in a singsong tone.

She was seated in the driver's seat of her sky-blue car, while I occupied the passenger seat. There was no space in the back seat for me because it was packed full of sleeping bags and other cloth camping goods.

My plans had initially been to take a thirty-minute bus ride from the station. Instead, we were headed to Aix-en-Provence, or Aix as the locals called it. It was where Catherine was supposed to be enjoying her vacation to the fullest. As I understood it, there was a lot of demand for health resorts in the south of France, and as summer was said to be the best season to visit, that was when the tourists came flocking. It didn't take long in the car for me to understand why.

An entire field of lavender.

And when the lavender ended, a field of sunflowers.

And after that, vineyards full of vines covered in yellow-green leaves, trellised up with bunches of grapes dangling off them.

The lavish fields went on, seemingly endless against a backdrop of smooth limestone-colored mountains. The golden fields of wheat even looked divine. Catherine giggled whenever I let out a little gasp as we passed ancient-looking water wheels or churches.

"This is your first time in Provence, isn't it, Seigi? Welcome!"

"Provence?"

"The name of the region. This is Provence. Marseilles and Aix are the names of cities. It's like how in Japan, Tokyo City is in the Kanto region, right? Same thing here. And yes, I do know what the Kanto region is. My old friend, Chieko, has sent me letters. I even have photos of her daughter's wedding. The groom looks like such a charming fellow. Anyway, this area is called Provence. Make sense?"

"It does. Thank you very much."

"It's a wonderful place, so you won't want to forget it. It's a place full of wine and truffles and the refreshing sea breeze. I just know you're going to love it. No no, no need to wait—you can love it already, hmm?"

"I-I sure do."

"Wonderful. I think I'd like to put on some music—do you mind?"

"Go ahead."

Her white fingers pressed a switch, and the car was filled with the sound of a woman singing. I felt like I'd heard the same song on the train. During the train ride, she'd encouraged me to take a nap, saying I must be tired from the long journey. I think we barely talked for an hour, and for half that time, I'd had one of her earbuds in, listening to music with her. French songs.

"It's Dalida. I love her music."

"Is she a young singer?"

"Oh, no, she died a long time ago. Suicide. How tragic. Goodness, you really don't know the first thing about France! But I guess you are rather young, after all. You have so many things to learn to look forward to. How wonderful. I really love this part of this song," she said, before singing along with the late singer. *"Paroles, paroles."* I could hear a male voice speaking in the background, but with Catherine singing over the song, my French skills weren't enough to make out what he was saying. Sweeping fields spread out beyond the window.

Since she was in such a good mood, I tried asking her the question I'd asked her a few times now but never gotten an answer to.

"Um, so, how exactly do you know Octavia?"

Catherine remained silent for the length of a vineyard plot. The singer kept on singing. Just as I was about to give up on the topic, she suddenly opened her mouth.

"Now that is certainly a question. Perhaps you could say that she is a hostess, and I am in her employ."

Hostess? Like the lady of the house, entertaining guests? If she was claiming to be working for Octavia, wouldn't that make her Richard's enemy? She *was* an actress—was her behavior with me all an act? I guess it was possible, if also hard to believe.

I didn't say anything. Catherine smiled.

"It's okay, you have nothing to worry about. I'm your ally."

Ally. Didn't that imply the existence of enemies? I still didn't understand what she meant by any of it. She was my and Richard's ally, while working for Octavia? What was that supposed to mean?

The image of a certain someone with a brown undercut flashed through my mind.

I still didn't really understand where Vince stood in all this. His behavior was erratic and made me want to ask him just whose side he was on. He'd given me his email and phone number but never replied to me after that. Lately, I'd just been sending him emojis to annoy him. I wondered what he was up to now?

Pointless as it felt, I just told her directly that I didn't really know Octavia and was wondering if she liked or hated me because of some kind of misunderstanding. The beautiful singer's next song began. Catherine must have put on one of her albums, since all the songs were by the same performer.

The road undulated as Catherine shifted gears and smiled. She really did have the exact same dimples as a certain someone.

"She asked me for a favor. 'Please host Mr. Richard and Mr. Nakata this summer. I promise I'll help out,' she asked. And I replied, '*oui!*' Nothing more, nothing less."

"What did she mean by 'help out'..."

"In more concrete terms, she gave me the money to buy back the villa we'll be staying in this summer. It was several tens of thousands of euros."

That comment almost made me feel like I was about to puke up my guts. Several tens of thousands of euros? That could be anywhere from ten thousand to over a million. Regardless, it definitely didn't sound like a sum a normal seventeen-year-old should be able to move with impunity—not to mention that the person receiving that money was an adult.

I was left at a loss for words as Catherine continued speaking, turning her gaze to the window. Large trucks would pass us from time to time, so despite the peaceful scenery, the road required the driver's attention.

"Octavia is...a good kid. The kind who tends to overthink things a bit. I like her."

"I don't really know what to make of that. Could you be a little more specific, if you don't mind?"

"I'm sorry. She asked me not to talk about that, so I'm going to obey her wishes. She's still just a little girl, please don't bully her too much."

If anyone's getting bullied, it's probably going to be your son, I thought but held my tongue. Not everyone had parents with personalities so outrageous that it gave them a horrible headache, and anyway, Catherine seemed nothing like that. She seemed like a nice person who was maybe a little eccentric, at worst. She'd even made it clear that she liked me. If she were up to something, would it really be to cause harm to me or Richard?

Even if I assumed that was the case, for the sake of the argument, I didn't think it could be *serious* harm. At least, I hoped not.

"All right, I understand. It would make me very happy if you could tell me whatever you feel comfortable telling me about your dealings with Octavia, though."

"Your English sounds just like Ashcroft when you're unhappy about something. Oh, Ashcroft is my ex-husband. Do be a little more cheerful. Let your words sing—like you're on vacation, hmm?"

That was an order. I felt like I was starting to understand why Richard's governess, Chieko, had described her as a "queen."

I concluded that I wasn't going to get the answers I wanted if I didn't obey her order. Maybe this was the right time to use the trick I had up my sleeve.

I politely asked if she would answer me using the French I'd learned.

"My!" she exclaimed in a tone that was decidedly cheerful, singsong, and perfectly fitting for a vacation. "How delightful! I didn't know you could speak French. Then we shall speak nothing but French at the villa. Thank you. I'm not very fond of English myself. It's not that I struggle with it. It's just that French agrees with me better. Don't you agree?"

"I do."

"Heh."

She laughed and then started talking about something in rapid-fire French. I felt dizzy. I didn't think my listening skills had been put to the test this hard since I was sitting for college entrance exams. She was mostly using verb conjugations that I hadn't learned yet, so I was stumped on that account, too. I was hopelessly confused. But then it hit me.

"...Um, are you deliberately speaking in a way that I won't be able to understand?"

"Oh my, you really are a clever one. Heh heh heh. Now, now, no need to be so hasty. It's more fun to leave some mysteries for later. That's how all good relationships start, don't you agree?"

It was a deflating answer.

I was flabbergasted for a moment but then relieved. It felt like she was telling me it was okay to laugh. Getting angry right now was clearly going to get me nowhere, so I should just laugh, instead. That was the better option.

That said, I knew a young man laughing loudly in a closed space like this could be intimidating, so I stifled my mirth and gazed out the window.

"Everything here is so beautiful."

"Everything? Like what? Tell me."

"Like the flowers, and the fields, and the sky, and the buildings, and even the shape of the mountains," I explained as I gazed out at the countryside.

Catherine giggled. "True," she assured me with her bewitching voice.

Her every gesture was like a simple dance move, with no perceptible gaps in-between. I didn't know if I'd ever grow bored of watching her...though I had to be careful not to seem rude.

"It'll be all right, Seigi. Soon, you're going to be having so much fun, you won't know what to do with yourself. You don't need to worry, because I'll be there with you. I can't wait to get to the villa. I left a note behind."

"A note?"

"Yes. I just know my sweet son is desperate for you to arrive." She let out a long, dreamy sigh, "I'm so glad I got to meet you."

And so, we continued driving through the countryside for another thirty minutes. We turned off at the sign for Aix-en-Provence, and I watched the sunbaked brick streets go by as we approached a line of large houses with a decent amount of space between them. I was guessing these were holiday homes, set slightly apart from the heart of the city. The health resorts in places like Kamakura and Hakone must look similar, despite the vast difference in scale.

I recalled the word "villa"—French for "vacation home." Catherine had used it earlier, when she said that Octavia had loaned her some tens of thousands of Euros to help buy it back.

Wait, buy it *back*?

"Um, *madame.*"

"Catherine. Cat works, too. Although, I do prefer Catherine."

"Catherine, I had a question about the villa we're on our way to."

"I bought it recently, but it used to belong to my mother."

She explained in a dreamy tone that when Richard was little, the two of them would spend their summers here. Then things happened and she was forced to give up the house. Apparently, it was uncommon for villas like this to be sold.

So she owned the villa in the past. My memories were pretty vague, but I did recall the topic of Richard's mother having a lot of relatives with money troubles coming up when I met Chieko. Were those troubles in the past or still ongoing? If they were still ongoing, I could see how someone as wealthy as Octavia making an offer like that would be almost impossible to refuse.

I really couldn't let my guard down here.

The car slipped past a vineyard, arriving at the top of a small hill. We drove through a green iron gate and sped up to the front porch. The two-story stone building sat atop a hill overlooking the area. The sunbaked brick walls that I had seen so many of on the way from the station were adorned with seashell reliefs, and there were green storm shutters on the many windows. It looked like it could house an entire rugby team and still have room to spare. The long distance between the gate and the actual house didn't even seem odd. Despite both countries being of similar size, their architecture couldn't be more different.

As I got out of the car, I felt the afternoon sun against my skin. The golden sunlight filtered through the leaves, which were a deeper green than emerald and more refreshing than peridot. There were hardly any flowers in the garden, but countless trees seemed to have taken their place, branches waving in the wind. The breeze rustling through the trees had a woody smell to it, though different from the scents of Japan or Sri Lanka.

"We're here," Catherine sang. "Welcome to my summer villa. Our delightful little treasure hunt starts now."

Richard dropped his heavy bags on either side of him as he stood before the front door. He wore the same expression he'd had in Sri Lanka—the one that suggested he was suffering from a massive migraine.

Reunited with her son, Catherine greeted him with a big hug. And then a second and a third. She pretended to cry when he slipped out of the fourth, but Richard just smiled and ignored her, ushering us into the house.

The inside of the estate, to be blunt, looked like a haunted mansion. It was full of dust and spiderwebs. The storm shutters were closed and everything smelled like mildew. There was no

LE PREMIER JOUR: DAY 1

light. It looked beautiful on the outside, but the inside looked like it had been abandoned for years.

"Richard, Catherine told me something about Octavia earlier..."

"Hold on a moment."

Catherine seemed to dance into the mansion. There were centimeters of dust on the stone floor. There were no signs of recent activity. She ignored the steps to the second floor and moved down the hall into a larger space that was presumably a dining room, kicking up clouds of dust as she walked. If she'd only just bought the house back, it must have been abandoned for a while before that. I hoped it had electricity and water, because I was getting concerned about whether we'd actually be able to stay here. Then I remembered the camping gear in the back of her car. Was that what it was about? It couldn't be, right?

Catherine led us into the unnaturally tidy dining room, stood us in front of the long table, and went, "ta-da!" The only light came from the gaps in the storm shutters, so the room was quite dark. The big grandfather clock ticked away, its contours only vaguely visible under the layer of dust sticking to it.

In the center of the table, which could have easily seated ten people for a meal, sat what looked like a wooden tray.

It was circular, and about the size of a mouse pad. It had a number of small, circular hollows carved into it, which were surrounded by a sort of track also carved into the wood. I had no idea what it was for. Was it a tray for, like, lining up a bunch of quail eggs or something?

I glanced over at Richard to see how he was reacting, but he hardly seemed to notice me at all. His expression was grim. I wondered if he was okay. Maybe he was feeling ill or something.

"Now, boys, observe closely. What do you think this is?"

"Catherine, I demand an explanation. I saw the note you left for me, but I know you didn't invite us here of your own free will."

"Ugh, please let me finish my explanation first. It's rude to interrupt an amusement park employee's explanation of how a ride works with unrelated questions, wouldn't you agree? It's important to stick to the program."

"You are decidedly *not* an amusement park employee, you are the mistress of this estate and the person responsible for inviting us here. I would prefer you do your actual job."

"If you would just hear me out first before criticizing, maybe you'd know! You always have this look on your face like you know everything. I don't like arrogant people like that."

"All I'm saying is that you have a responsibility as someone who's invited a stranger here."

"Seigi isn't a stranger. We're already friends."

"Don't be ridiculous."

"All right, all right," I cut in. Richard must have been exhausted from traveling. His tone was much more pointed than usual. And Catherine must have felt similarly.

"Let's try this again. Hmm...no, the mood just isn't right. Seigi, maybe you could give me some encouragement, hmm? Make sure it really comes from the heart."

"You can do it."

"Seigi."

It'd be a lot easier on everyone to just go along with her. The boss I depended on so much should have known that, too, but when I looked over at him, I felt a jolt run through my whole body.

I suddenly felt like there were *two* Catherines in the room.

Richard looked like an abandoned child, wondering why I was listening to someone else and not him. When I recoiled, he seemed to realize that something was off about himself. He looked away, frustrated, and let out an irritated sigh as he rubbed his brow. At roughly the same time, Catherine replied, "I'll give it my best shot," in a cheerful tone.

"This is a game board. Are you familiar with solitaire, Seigi?"

"That's a card game you play by yourself, right?"

"It is, but in France, Solitaire is a game played with marbles. It dates to around the eighteenth century. It's said that the game was developed after the French Revolution by a noble awaiting execution in prison, to keep themselves entertained. And this is that game. I imagine they came up with it using whatever pebbles they could find, since they weren't allowed cards. Romantic, isn't it?"

Was that really romantic?

"There are, of course, many theories about its origins," Catherine added. Her son, who still looked like his head hurt, ignored her and began inspecting the walls and chairs. I was worried about how things were going to go from here. It seemed like the job of finding out any information was going to fall to me.

"Um, so you said this game is played with marbles, right? Where are the marbles?"

"Bingo! You really are a clever boy, Seigi. Take a look right here." Catherine searched the many pockets of her jacket, found nothing, and moved to patting herself down. By the time her hands got to her butt, she seemed to find something, which she offered to me. "Here!"

It was a round stone. A beautiful sphere about the size of my thumb.

An orange piece of chalcedony. A charming, vividly colored stone that was typically used in pendants, bracelets, or other low-impact pieces of jewelry. Part of the quartz family, just like agate and amethyst. I knew agate without stripes existed, but it wasn't something Saul's business often dealt in. It wasn't a very expensive stone, after all. But up close like this, you could see it had a charm that far exceeded its monetary value.

"And if you put that in here—see? It fits!"

I did as Catherine urged me to and placed the chalcedony onto the board full of divots. The marble fit perfectly. But there was more than one divot. There were thirty-three in total. And with one filled in, there were thirty-two left. She had mentioned a "treasure hunt" earlier.

Did that mean...

"Thirty-two marbles have been hidden in this estate. I'm not sure if it's too late or too early for an Easter egg hunt, but they're not eggs, so you needn't worry about damaging them. Do you think you can find them all? If you do find them, I just know that a wonderful treasure will appear somewhere in this very mansion. Exciting, no?" she said with a smile.

She really was an incredible actress. I'd heard she starred in movies, though I'd never actually seen any. She was the kind of person who could conjure any expression to entertain people. I, who had a tendency to let whatever I was thinking show on my face, felt like I could learn a thing or two from her.

Richard flatly ignored Catherine's dazzling smile, maintaining his sour expression.

"You're saying you hid marbles all around this estate?"

"Yes, I did! I tried my very best."

"And you want us to find them?"

"Exactly! Isn't it exciting?"

"Well, that makes things simple. Retrieve all the items you hid, and we'll be done here."

Richard's words were blunt. His logic certainly was extremely logical and expedient, but...

An ambiguous smile appeared on Catherine's face, like she'd just been told something she didn't quite understand. She seemed to know her son wasn't about to say another word, because her eyebrows drooped right after, and she shook her head. It was bizarre to watch the real Richard and his mother, who looked like him in a costume, standing before me.

"But Richard, then all my hard work to hide them will be for naught!"

"By that logic, won't our efforts be even more wasted by being conscripted into this asinine game of yours? Why must we go out of our way to do this? What are you even getting out of this? If you need money, you can always come to me."

"I'm doing quite fine financially, thank you very much. I wish you would stop belittling me. I'm an independent woman who can support herself. Why are you nagging me over every little thing just because I'm making friends with Seigi?"

"His presence has absolutely nothing to do with my concerns. I don't know what's gotten into you, but you should know that I would struggle to forgive even my mother if she insulted my friend."

"Insult him? I would never! I just want to have fun with both of you! I even made us lemonade—it's in the fridge. Admittedly, that's the only thing I know how to make, so I don't have anything else for you, but I assure you it's delicious. I'm telling you the truth... I thought you loved my lemonade... It's the only thing I'm any good at..."

Catherine burst into tears. It had been a while since the last time someone cried in front of me. The people in Sri Lanka were generally mild-mannered, rarely showing their emotions or getting into shouting matches. Maybe because Kandy is a quiet little town in the mountains, everyone there was polite and reserved. Like Richard usually was.

I gently slid between them, placing my hands on Richard's chest, and pushed him back out into the entry hall to get some distance from Catherine.

"You don't need to worry yourself about this. It seems we have a means to resolve this much faster than anticipated."

"Richard."

"You can stay outside."

"Listen, Richard, I don't like the way you're acting right now."

Richard made a face like Catherine had when I said that. He didn't seem to be aware of it. I had to wonder if he'd reverted a bit to the way he'd been when he was living with her—a child, living with his queen of a mother.

"Are you okay? You're not feeling unwell, are you?"

"I'm surprised that *you* would take issue with the way I treat my mother."

I had to wonder how much of this Octavia had anticipated happening. It might have been another vector for her to torture him, just like the sexual harassment cruise from hell. But if that was a component of the situation, I was in a better position to counteract some of those effects this time.

Richard's attitude in that moment reminded me of a cat with its back arched and fur standing on end. "Hey," I said to him in Japanese. "What do you want for dinner tonight? Meat? Fish?"

"...What?"

"If we're going to be staying here, I'll have to go shopping. She said there wasn't anything in the fridge but lemonade. That's crazy. Do you know the hours of the supermarkets around here? Like how late are they open?"

"You seriously intend to stay here with her?"

"I don't think we have any other option today. I can't speak for tomorrow or the rest of the trip, but there isn't really time to leave or find a hotel right now. I'd also like to get some cleaning supplies, but I'm not sure if I'll be allowed to expense that."

I said that last part in a jokey "Seigi-the-part-timer" tone, and Richard straightened up like he'd abruptly awoken from a dream. Good, what a relief.

The beautiful man brought his hand to his chin at just the perfect angle and mumbled a thoughtful, "You might be right. I believe the big chain grocery is usually open until about nine, but it is vacation season, so don't be surprised if they're closed. Mom-and-pop stores and farmer's markets are more common in this area. Take Catherine with you. She should be able to guide you around. But I'll have to placate her first."

Richard still looked sour, but it didn't take long for him to collect himself and put on his jeweler face. He was in work mode. I felt a little bad about it, but there was nothing else to be done. I encouraged him to return to the dining room, but before he did, the blond man looked me right in the eye.

"Have you decided what you want for dinner?" I asked.

"Whatever you'd prefer, chef. Good lord, what a ridiculous reunion this has turned out to be. But I'm very glad I get to see you," he added hastily, looking slightly anxious. That phrase had become something of a habit for us lately.

Right now, the main priority was getting his mother to stop crying. I patted him on the back to encourage him, and he looked at me like I'd forgotten something. I know, I know.

"I'm really happy to see you, too. I would have said so earlier, but I figured it was more than obvious. You look as beautiful as ever today."

Just hearing that put a smile on his face as he hurried back into the dining room. I felt profoundly relieved. I didn't have the first clue how to comfort a crying woman. I didn't even know if I should *be* here. Selfish as it might be, I was really glad that our resident specialist in that arena was back in working order.

"Goodness, he always gives me trouble, no matter how old he gets. I'm so sorry, Seigi. I've been very rude to you. I can't believe I lost my composure in front of a guest like that."

"Don't worry about it, please. If anyone should apologize for being rude, it's me, because I have to ask you for a favor."

"Oh, no, no, it's no trouble at all. Quite the opposite in fact. I didn't know you were such a talented cook. If you come to Provence, you just have to visit a *marché*. But now isn't a good time for that. You have to visit the *marché* in the morning. We'll save that for tomorrow."

The sky-blue car drove nimbly along the bumpy road. The sun was about to set, but Catherine showed no sign of slowing down.

Earlier, Richard—looking like a handsome actor who had just stepped off a theater stage two hundred years ago—had exhausted all his words and switched to gestures to comfort the crying Catherine. It was all in French. "It's all my fault. Please cheer up. Your smile is like the twinkling of the stars," and so on. That was about the extent I could pick up with my language ability, but Catherine's cheer quickly returned, like a deflated balloon being pumped full of air once more. She enthusiastically hugged her son and kissed both his cheeks—four times per cheek. French culture sure was different.

Richard went on to acquiesce to the treasure hunt for the time being, before asking the most important questions about the state of the villa. Electricity, water, and gas were all operational. The property had been returned to Catherine while the contractors were working on it. It was just everything else that was a problem. The house had been abandoned for at least a year, if not longer, and was absolutely coated in dust. The upholstery in the sunroom on the first floor was being eaten by insects beneath its covers. The back seat of Catherine's car was loaded with fresh sheets and pillow covers, but the place wasn't really suitable for people to live in immediately. And, of course, the refrigerator was empty... though the ice-cold lemonade was super sweet and delicious.

I went on a shopping trip with Catherine before the supermarket closed. I'd spent more than enough time living on my own to know what was needed to thoroughly clean a house. Richard stayed behind to work on the "treasure hunt." It felt like both of us were doing exactly what we should be.

To my eye, the city of Aix was a quiet place with a lot of history, and an even mix of tourist attractions and wealthy residences. A historic district remained inside of what must have been castle walls in the past—fairly typical for Europe, based on what I recalled from studying for the civil service exam. There really was a huge difference between memorizing things for a test and actually seeing them in person. It was like a feudal Japanese castle town had been frozen in time, unchanged.

"If you follow this road, it'll take you right to the *Place de la République*. It should be just coming into view...oh thank goodness! That supermarket is still there. The last time I was here was a decade ago. Oh, how I missed this place."

Catherine drove into the parking lot and got out of the car, leaving me to back the car into a spot. I guess she really had been quite disconnected from this place until she bought the house back.

Inside the massive store, I picked up a bucket, soap, and mop that were all far too big by Japanese sensibilities, and put them in the cart as I attempted to engage Catherine in small talk. How she spent her summers, what kind of work she was up to right now, and so on. I threw in some details about my time in Sri Lanka, and she responded in surprisingly good humor.

"Summer is, of course, the season for vacation. It's an important opportunity to recharge from a year's worth of exhaustion, so I try to have as much fun as possible. When I still owned the house in Provence, I would spend my summers here, but lately, I've been all over the place. The last few years, I've only gotten two months—or just one, in the most awful cases—of vacation. Even though I'd prefer three. Can you imagine anything ruder? Last year I went to Majorca, and I think the year before it was Capri. I was invited there by someone I'd worked with on a film, but thinking back on it now, it wasn't much of a vacation. I had to pose for so many photos..."

Which meant she wasn't working on a movie right now. I tossed some bottled water, soap, and plastic wrap into the cart, and she brought over some delicious chocolates, macarons, and cake, piling them on top of the soap and plastic wrap.

"My current job is Columbine."

"Columbine?"

"It's a classic theater role. The performance itself is mostly pantomime, so I don't have any lines, really. It may be old and full of history, but it's very entertaining. Do you know what kind of story unfolds when Columbine and Harlequin are on stage together? ...You don't, do you?"

"Sorry, I don't really know much about this sort of thing. What exactly are you talking about?"

While we were waiting in the checkout line, she pulled out her phone and showed me a photo of herself, face painted white with splotches of red and black makeup. Even examining the picture closely, I couldn't tell it was Catherine. Of all the things I was familiar with, this most resembled clown makeup. It completely blotted out the most prominent features of this family of breathtakingly beautiful people. And yet, Catherine was smiling wholeheartedly in that white makeup.

"It's extremely fun. Both children and adults can laugh at it. If only you knew a little more French."

"So you're a comedy actress right now."

"*Oui.* The word 'comedian' is French, after all."

She made some silly gestures. The woman sitting at the register waved at us to hurry up and put our items on the belt, and I began to unpack our cart while Catherine greeted the cashier with a dazzling smile.

Our haul barely fit into the back seat of her car. Catherine laughed at how the mop was sticking out a bit and went to sit down in the driver's seat when I stopped her.

"I have an international driver's license. I think I remember the route, so I can drive back."

"You don't need to worry about that. You're my guest."

"But you drove all the way from the station, too."

I insisted and Catherine looked relieved, asking me to go ahead with a smile. Her driving was a little aggressive and tended to put the fear of death in whoever was in the passenger seat when she went around curves. I was grateful she'd driven me here, but sometimes you need the right person for the job.

My first time driving in France was up hill. It was hard to accelerate. It was fifteen minutes by car to the nearest supermarket. It had occurred to me on the trip from the station, but this really was a car-centric society. A city of this size in Japan would probably have a bunch of rail stations, but I guess that's more of a Japan thing, huh?

"I wonder if Richard's found any stones already. He's such a smart boy."

"He really is. I really look up to him."

"Oh, do you now? Has he been a good boy? I hope he's not causing you any trouble."

I almost burst out laughing. I guess there really was one person on this earth who could think and say those things about Richard, of all people. Parents seeing their children as children, no matter how old they got, was probably pretty universal. But wait...

There was something I was curious about.

"Richard grew up in England, right?"

"Yes, with the Claremont family. The family home is marvelous. Everyone speaks such perfect, aristocratic English. How's the earl doing? I hear he's all but on his deathbed. Of course, it would be insolent of someone like *me* to express concern for him. That family gave me the same level of respect as a French feather duster."

Catherine's voice suddenly dropped by about half an octave. She really was easy to read. I was privy to the circumstances of the fight that led to her split with Richard's family, including how she'd instigated some fake family drama to facilitate the split out of fear of becoming a financial burden on Richard. I also learned that Richard's father was a talented scientist whose energies went primarily to his research with little left over for his family. Richard had probably kept his parents at arm's length ever since.

Maybe that was what it meant to "be a good boy." I'd had people like Grandma and Hiromi, around whom I could drop my mask and complain about being tired or fed up, even if I was only being half-serious, just to get some attention. Without people like that, Richard would have had no choice but to keep the mask on. I mean, I guess he had Jeffrey? But cousins weren't really the same as parents in this regard.

Which was why it felt a little weird to hear the parent of a kid like that ask if he was being "a good boy." Even more so when that kid was nearly thirty years old and a man I owed a deep debt of gratitude for looking after me.

"What's wrong, Seigi? You're making a dreadful face. Is driving around here that stressful?"

"Oh, no, I'm fine. Sorry. I imagine it's fun to drive around here once you get used to it."

"You and Richard really are so much alike." She added, voice dropping to a mumble, "You're both such good boys."

Her tone lacked its usual singsong quality. Just as I was wondering what that could possibly mean, a large truck suddenly appeared in the oncoming lane, and I abruptly turned the steering wheel. Catherine screamed like a child on a roller coaster. She was back to the playful mood she was in earlier. Maybe I misheard what she had mumbled.

"Richard really is a good boy. Trust me, I know that."

Catherine looked at me. I may not have been able to take my eyes off the road, but I could talk.

"...Then why did you take Octavia up on her offer?"

"You find that suspicious? She's just as good a kid as Richard is."

I grimaced. How was someone who threw your own son to his perverted "uncle" on a cruise ship to get sexually harassed a "good kid?" It didn't make any sense. I just had to assume that there was some very important piece of information being concealed from me. Jeffrey *had* just told me that they weren't pursuing legal action for now. I'd initially assumed that they wanted to go easy on her since she was a minor, but even I knew Jeffrey wasn't that naive.

What kind of situation was Octavia in, really?

"Madame."

"Catherine, please."

"...Catherine. What exactly is your relationship to Oct—"

"Wait! Over there! Stop. Right now! Stop this instant!"

"Yes, ma'am!"

What was that about? I didn't see anyone around, but maybe she'd spotted someone she knew?

Catherine immediately got out of the car in the empty area and encouraged me to follow her. The place looked like an olive grove or a vineyard or something. Residents of a nearby villa were looking at us, wondering what we were doing, but Catherine was unconcerned. Since these were summer homes, neighbors probably didn't interact much. Why on earth had she made me stop here?

I stepped out onto the rough gravel road and was left dumbfounded when she struck a pose like at the end of a stage performance. She held her arms out wide, one leg extended and a cheerful expression on her face. Was she trying to tell me to look at her? No, wait, *behind* her.

A white mountain towered over the seemingly endless fields. It was the color of limestone. While it may not have been a particularly tall mountain, it demanded attention. Its irregular, trapezoidal shape made quite the impression, irrespective of whether you considered it a mountain or a piece of art.

"Look, it's Montagne Sainte-Victoire."

"Sainte-Victoire... Is it a particularly famous mountain?"

"Ugh," Catherine sulked, dropping her arms. "You aren't really an art person, are you, Seigi?"

"What do you mean?"

"Cézanne loved that mountain. The painter, Paul Cézanne. The father of modern painting. Are you familiar? 'These boulders were on fire. There is still fire in them.' Cézanne was known for painting apples, but he painted a lot of stone, too."

Now that she mentioned it, the name did sound familiar. I remembered seeing his paintings hung with great care in an art museum in Marunouchi, alongside other impressionists like Monet and Van Gogh. He was famous.

Catherine went on to explain that Cézanne had set up his studio near here, that he'd had geologist friends, and that he would go to the quarry to feel inspired. Provence is a region rich in limestone, and the high-drainage soil makes it very suitable for the production of grapes and rock salt. It had probably been a seabed at some point in the distant past. The asymmetrical Montagne Sainte-Victoire was clearly not a volcano. It was the result of a geologic fold, but from a geological perspective, the land was still formed by the movement of "fire."

This place must've been heaven for someone with an interest in geology.

"You know...one of my friends from college would love this place."

"A college friend? How lovely. Is he handsome?"

"She, actually. She loves stones."

"Oh I see."

Catherine's voice rose sharply as she pummeled me with questions. I remained confused about what was going on. She asked what she was like, what kind of stones specifically she was interested in, how long we knew each other, whether she was cute or pretty, what she liked to eat, et cetera, et cetera, et cetera. I was uncomfortable giving out personal details about my friend, so I just kept things vague. She continued asking questions until she was satisfied and finally withdrew.

"Really? She sounds like a lovely friend. Yes. Hmm. How lovely."

"Y-yeah."

"Having friends is important. So very important. People really love you, don't they, Seigi? I wouldn't know what that's like."

And with that, she got back in the car. She was silent the rest of the way back to the villa. Maybe she was just tired, but I worried that I'd said something wrong. I debated about apologizing to her later as we walked into the house.

"You sure took your time."

The beautiful jeweler was waiting for us, having removed the jacket he'd worn on the trip and rolled up the sleeves of his off-white shirt. I couldn't blame him for keeping his shoes on—if you changed into slippers right now, you'd be up to your ankles in dust.

The board on the table caught my eye. There were now *five* chalcedony marbles. In addition to the orange one, there was a pink, a black, a clear, and a pale yellow one.

"My! How wonderful! That's my beautiful boy! You already found four. Good job, Richard."

"I incorrectly assumed the marbles were just hidden as is, which made the search more difficult."

"Oh no, silly me. You see, the marbles aren't the only fun we're to have here."

Catherine turned away from me, giggled, and held out her hand to Richard. Richard, who seemed to be trying his best not to make a rude expression, placed a piece of paper in her hand. It was wrinkled and about the size of a candy wrapper. Just the right size to wrap up a little marble. It had something written on it.

One line written in western script. French? No, it was English. It was so small, I couldn't get a good look at it, but the structure seemed odd. What was it? Scripture? Or poetry maybe?

Before I could make heads or tails of it, Catherine returned the paper to Richard.

"All of the marbles hidden around the estate are wrapped like this. And these wrapping papers are *very* important. They form a treasure map when you collect them all."

"A treasure map?"

"Yes! I did as I was instructed and wrapped the paper I was given around the marbles before I hid them. I don't know where the treasure is or how to solve the code, but I do have certain duties as the lady of this house, so I made sure to check what was written on the papers."

Catherine swore that nothing bad was written on them, holding up her hand like she was taking an oath. I guess she was Christian? I didn't know what Richard's religious beliefs were, but I didn't recall him ever mentioning going to church on Sundays. It was interestingly novel to see how naturally his mother struck a pose like that—I'd spent so much time speaking to him in Japanese, but this made me realize the obvious: that this man belonged to another culture entirely.

Unaware of the awe I was feeling in that moment, Richard looked once again like he was suffering from a terrible migraine.

"...I take it you didn't think to take photos or notes before you hid them?"

"Of course not. That wouldn't make the treasure hunt very fun, now would it?"

"So, what's the plan if we can't find all of them before this vacation is over? Do you have a cheat sheet of their locations somewhere?"

"Huh? Oh, fair point... If I forget, then...I'm sorry. But Richard, I'm not worried. You're a very bright boy. I know you'll find them. It'll be all right," Catherine said, smiling like a dahlia blossom. Her smile was like a weapon of war, blasting us with the sheer force of her aura.

Richard ignored it completely and replied with a simple, "If you say so." The air was heavy.

Maybe it was about time I cut in.

"Uh, um, I thought I'd make a seafood stew for dinner. The market was closed, but I did get some delicious looking ingredients. I mean, this dish is from around here, right? Bouillabaisse, I mean."

When I said that word, the beautiful mother and son looked at me like they'd just gotten a glimpse of hell. They even moved in sync. The sheer intensity of it was impressive. Huh? What? What

LE PREMIER JOUR: DAY 1

did I say this time? Did I make a mistake with the menu? Or did someone have an allergy?

"Bouillabaisse...wow."

"'Wow' what?"

"Oh, Seigi, bouillabaisse is...it is a dish from Provence, but it's very difficult. I was curious what you were planning with the fish you bought, but I never expected..."

"The shrimp and fish have to be dressed just right, and the vegetables require preparation as well. It also needs to simmer for an extremely long time. At any rate, it is an unavoidably difficult path."

"Don't worry so much. I can handle something like that."

"Just the thought of preparing a meal that takes so much effort makes me want to pass out. So that's why you wanted to see the pots before we left. You should rethink this. Even locals don't make it. It's too much of a bother."

"You didn't come here to hone your cooking skills. I strongly suggest you save your energy for other tasks."

"Ah..."

The stereo-surround-sound argument that bouillabaisse was too hard seemed like it would go on forever if I didn't relent. I told them that there was no point in making it if they didn't like it, so I'd have to think of something else. They sighed in unison before saying that they hadn't meant it like that. So they *were* just concerned for me? I see.

Neither of them seemed to be very skilled at basic household chores. Admittedly, "chores" was just a catch-all term for odd jobs you had to do around the house, so if you lived the kind of life that didn't require you to do those things, I didn't think lacking those skills was actually an issue. But that gap creates space for people like me.

"Give me two hours. And do not, under any circumstances, open the door to the kitchen during that time. Just like in 'The Crane Wife.'"

"The crane what?"

"Seigi. Using the wrong words can be fatal. I believe he's referring to the mythological taboo of looking."

"Whoops."

In response to Richard's criticism, I explained to Catherine that in the Japanese folktale I had alluded to, if the protagonist waits and doesn't open the door before he's told, he gets clothing and food and so on. I made a joke about how it seemed like a fitting tale for the country that invented instant meals that can be prepared with three minutes and a little hot water, then went to sort out the food from the cleaning supplies and carried just the food into the kitchen.

This house's kitchen was decidedly much friendlier than the one in the house back in Sri Lanka. There was no wood-burning stove and no bowls for grating coconut. It was still covered in dust, so I took a dust cloth—that I had literally just bought—and cleaned up the areas I thought I would be using, made sure I knew how the stove worked, and spread out the ingredients.

Big shrimp with the heads still intact. Beautiful fresh fish with silver and scarlet scales—three different ones, in fact. I knew one of them was sea bream, and though I wasn't sure about the other two, they looked so delicious that I didn't think they could be a bad addition. If I could get fish of this quality for a few euros a kilo, I'd be eating fish every night. I was a little confused about how that was the case, considering Aix wasn't on the sea, but Catherine explained that it was because Marseille was so close. Apparently, it was a massive fishing port.

I opened the second reusable shopping bag emblazoned with the French supermarket's logo and pulled out onions, tomatoes, celery, carrots, saffron, butter, bottles of herbs, and a local white wine. The kitchen was flooded with a sea of color from the vegetables I'd bought while looking at the recipe. I felt almost like I was looking at a spread of tourmaline, the queen of many colors. There were a lot of misshapen vegetables, but that seemed to be the fashion in France lately. I guess it made the food feel closer to nature. I wondered if it might catch on in Japan soon.

I let out a little sigh as I looked at the mountain of food.

"I'm really going to use *all* of this..."

I was kind of amazed. Both in Japan and Sri Lanka, about 80 percent of the cooking I did was for one person. I meal-prepped ahead sometimes, but preparing a meal for three people was a novel experience. I never had the luxury of enough free time to make a big meal like this, anyway.

At any rate, I figured I'd make a little extra in case we had to make it last for a couple days, so I rolled up my sleeves, put on the apron I'd just bought, and clapped my hands. It was time for Chef Nakata to take center stage. If solving the treasure hunt was going to require cracking a riddle in the form of an English poem, I wasn't sure I'd be able to contribute much at all as a native Japanese speaker. What I *could* do was make sure that a certain somebody playing the role of Holmes had a clear head.

I actually thought it sounded pretty fun. Maybe I had the right personality for the job.

It took me two and a half hours. Nearly an hour of that was spent on processing the shrimp and fish.

In really simple terms, bouillabaisse is a seafood and vegetable stew. I knew that, and it said as much in the recipe. Thank you internet. I tasted it, and it wasn't half bad.

The shrimp were left whole, the fish filleted, the vegetables tossed in. A bay leaf was added to remove any unwanted fishy flavors, and then it was finished with parsley. The golden color imparted by the saffron almost seemed to glow in the big red pot. It almost made me think I must be some kind of culinary genius at first, but it was really just a result of how good the ingredients were.

I came out of the kitchen saying, "It's ready," and found Richard in the dining room. There were seven round balls on the wooden tray and more little scraps of paper. Things seemed to be going well on his end. But it had already gotten dark today, so it was probably time to call it quits.

"Where's Catherine?"

"She said she went to check the hours of the pizza place that delivers here, just in case."

"I appreciate having a backup plan, but I really don't think we're going to need it."

"So it seems..."

Richard offered to clean up and began wiping down the dining table and setting it. The utensils posed a different problem. While they had all been wrapped up neatly in cloth in a cupboard, they were unpleasantly sticky to the touch. Best not to think too deeply about it. They definitely needed washing, but that was only to be expected of anything left abandoned in a house like this.

I left Richard to wipe things down as I started bringing out the food. I was thankful that the table was so massive that we could leave the solitaire board on one end and still have plenty of space to eat.

Catherine walked in through the front entrance as I was carrying the pot out.

"Richard, the pizza place is on vacation so—oh."

I set the red pot down on the red trivet and pulled off the lid. The bright red of the shrimp and the yellow of the saffron came into view beneath the orange-tinted electric lights. I couldn't imagine how all three of us could possibly resist.

I lifted my head and asked what they thought. Both Catherine and Richard had the same look on their faces. What was that supposed to mean? You could have cut the tension in the air with a knife. The two of them peered into the pot, hardly moving from where they stood.

Was it admiration? For me? No. For the bouillabaisse.

"What on..."

"*C'est magnifique!* I can't believe it."

The two of them cautiously approached the table, almost like they were unsure if they should get closer to a crashed UFO. *I didn't put anything that bad in it...*

I encouraged them to dig in before it got cold and started portioning out servings, filling the room with the delicious aroma. It may have been summer, but summer nights in the Mediterranean were chilly. This would never work in summer Japan, but we were currently in the perfect environment for such a stew.

I served three plates and set them down along the edge of the table with each of the table settings. The flatware all seemed to be made of silver. They were a bit tarnished but felt heavy and comfortable in the hand. I let Richard pour the wine. Everyone but me was so beautiful, I felt almost like I'd gotten lost and wandered into a film shoot.

I encouraged everyone to dig in and picked up my spoon when Catherine aggressively stopped me.

"No, Seigi, wait. There's a word one must say at times like this."

I asked if she meant *"itadakimasu,"* and she shook her head.

"*Bon appétit!*" she said, shouting more than singing.

It did sound familiar from my French studies. But I hadn't prioritized learning it as much as things like *bonjour* and *bonsoir*. What did it mean again?

"It literally means 'good appetite.' In practical terms it's an invitation to enjoy the food. It's the phrase you should be saying," Richard said, staring at me intently.

"Yes, yes!" Catherine said, jostling me.

I didn't really get it, but it was clear to me that the words needed saying in this place, almost like it was a required incantation.

"...All right then, *bon appétit.*"

"Merci," the two beautiful people said in unison, before their typical expressions returned: Richard's vaguely awkward pout and Catherine's dazzling smile.

It occurred to me that the two of them may have done something like this in this very spot ages ago. When Catherine originally owned this house and when Richard was much younger.

I watched covertly as the two of them took their first bite. Surely it would be okay? If there was anything off about it, it might be that it had a slightly more Japanese flavor profile. But look, that just made it bespoke.

I asked what they thought and Catherine let out a little moan that was difficult to describe. It sounded almost like emotions just spilling from the back of her throat. Her son gave her a scolding look, and she apologized with a bashful smile. She looked a little teary-eyed.

"It's very delicious. You have a wonderful talent, Seigi. It tastes like eating happiness itself. Oh no, I'm going to cry."

"...Well, he always has been a good cook."

"Richard, you're being so rude. Thank Seigi this instant."

"……"

Richard looked mortified but regained his composure a few moments later and turned to me. This felt like a standoff between East and West. But that would make me his opponent, and I'd be knocked out before I even got a swing in. It would never even occur to me to pick such a fight. I'd just wind up on my knees, begging for mercy for all eternity.

The most beautiful man in the world was staring at me with a bashful expression that still hadn't quite crossed the line of politeness.

"Seigi, I've known for quite a while now that you are a talented cook, but it seems I must acknowledge your skills once again. Bravo. Perhaps you could open a restaurant if you felt so inclined. But I have to ask, when did you learn to cook this?"

"What an arrogant way to say that. Does that even count as a compliment?"

"Stay out of this."

"Ah, hah, humm, ah. Thanks, Richard. Where did I learn this? Good question."

Struggling to change the subject, I ended up confessing that it was my first time making it and I'd just followed a recipe. They both told me to stop joking. They even had the exact same expression as they waved their elegant hands in front of their half-open mouths, which was honestly a bit dizzying.

"Cooking is so much harder than that. Like if you cook an egg on too-high heat, it'll burn, but if the heat is too low, it stays all liquid. It's so difficult."

"You can even cause explosions with a microwave if you run it for too long, and yet you succeeded in making a stew from scratch in a kitchen you've never been in before. The odds of that happening are astronomically small."

"Maybe there's some kind of secret to it. Or maybe this is just something all Japanese boys can do? Probably not, right? One of my Parisian friends married a Japanese man who couldn't even fold his underwear. They divorced two months later."

"Seems plausible. I think it's about time that you taught me the secret of your skill. What sort of tricks do you employ?"

"Is this really how you talk now? Why can't you just say, 'thank you, I love it'?"

"I don't know how many times I need to tell you, but you have no right to interject here."

"Oh, it's fine, I'm, um, used to it! Yes! Let's dig in!"

This was an unexpected insight into the source of Richard's poor cooking skills. I didn't think it's genetic or anything, but children did learn from the adults they're closest to, and in Richard's case that must've been Catherine.

Though that did make me wonder...who had influenced me to learn to cook? Hiromi? I don't think she ever had any strong opinions about cooking, positive or negative. She was just too busy. Part of the reason I decided to go to Sri Lanka was because Mr. Nakata, my stepfather, was finally able to move back to Japan from his work in Southeast Asia and live with Hiromi. She was going to turn 60 soon. She was probably starting to think about leaving the night shift to the younger nurses, and when she should seek retirement. But I couldn't even imagine what she'd be doing once she retired. Work had always been the center of her life, and she'd always been working hard. For my sake, for Grandma's sake—always for someone else.

I think part of why I learned to cook was so I could give her an opportunity not to work so hard sometimes. I think it had started in junior high.

Thankfully, the quantity of bouillabaisse had been reduced by a healthy amount. No problem there. I moved about half of it into another pot to save for later as is. I planned to add some fancy rice with the baffling name of Milanese Koshihikari to the rest of the remaining saffron-yellow soup, let it simmer, and make a Japanese-style rice gruel, so I returned to the kitchen to get started on that.

It didn't hit me until after I finished that this wasn't a pub where male college students congregate but a small household consisting only of a lady, her son, and his friend. This was clearly *way* too much food.

While I was struggling to figure out if I should put both the pot of leftover bouillabaisse and the gruel into the fridge, which really wasn't all that big, someone arrived at the villa. Catherine got the door. I left the kitchen and went into the dining room, discovering that the visitors seemed to be the couple who had seen Catherine and me at that random stop on the way back. I listened closely and heard them invite her to join them for an *"apéritif."*

Apéritif? I looked at Richard. What was that? The beautiful man took a seat that was out of view from the entryway.

"It's an alcoholic drink had before dinner. It's a custom in France to have drinks with neighbors before a meal. Not that I've ever participated before."

Oh, that's what it is. But that didn't make sense to me. Why did those people come here? I tilted my head a bit, and Richard slowly mouthed one word to me: swingers. Oh.

I quietly moved around the dining room so I could see into the entryway. The visitors both had slightly darker skin than Catherine: a very cheery older woman and an older man who must've been her husband.

Catherine regretfully declined their offer but then turned around like she'd suddenly remembered something. She ran over to me when she noticed I was there, kicking up dust as she moved. The guests didn't seem bothered by it. They must've been very understanding people...or maybe they just didn't care.

"Seigi, you made some soup risotto, right? Would you mind if we offered them some? You did say that we had far too much left over, and surely we have a bowl or two that we didn't use. Right?"

I told her "yes, of course!" before Richard could scold her for being selfish, with that frustrated expression on his face. I saw no issue with sharing with them. Richard looked away from me with a "hmph." *Don't worry, there will be plenty left over for us to eat.*

Catherine winked cutely at her son, reminding him that they should be nice to their neighbors. I briefly made eye contact with the couple standing in the entry hall as I headed back to the kitchen to help Catherine. I bowed slightly to them and they both looked at me, confused. Right, bowing wasn't the custom over here. A smile was more than enough as a casual greeting. I thought I'd gotten used to doing that in Sri Lanka, but my old habits reemerged when I relaxed.

Richard's eyes had sharpened, as if he had something he wanted to say, but he ultimately remained silent and just looked disappointed. I'd have to remind him that I could make him as much as he wanted later. The supermarket was just a few minutes away by car, and it was an absolute heaven of cheap and delicious seafood.

I scooped out a decent portion of the gruel, filled an unused soup bowl, covered it with plastic wrap, and brought it out into the entry hall. For some reason, they wouldn't take it from me. Catherine took the bowl from my hands and handed it to them with a smile, and almost as if time had suddenly started up again, they began smiling and chatting. I could understand wanting to talk to a beautiful person you just met, but the stark contrast in treatment had me a little confused. I decided not to worry about it.

The couple left, saying they'd stop by again sometime. They didn't seem to know any English, so they spoke to Catherine entirely in French, but the first-meeting small talk being exchanged was at a level I could understand just fine. Just as I was thinking I should have said something, Catherine let out a sigh.

"...Speaking to strangers is so exhausting."

"Huh?"

I was surprised. Catherine had seemed to be enjoying herself, like she'd just come from a party, when she was speaking to them. She suddenly donned her sparkling smile again, as if she'd remembered something.

"Hey, Seigi, let's all enjoy a *digestif* together. We have to show our appreciation for our wonderful chef. I bought some cheese and dried fruit earlier, too."

"Are you regretting turning down their invitation for a drink?"

"What are you saying? This is Seigi's first night in Provence. We have to celebrate!"

Catherine patted me on the shoulder and returned to the dining room where her still-frowning son waited.

Our drinking party didn't last all that long. Catherine got drunk almost instantly and was scolded by her son for bothering me. Her son being who he was, wasn't the type to drink much himself. I'd heard that a long time ago he'd practiced how to not get completely wasted, but his tone when he talked about that sounded a bit pained. He probably didn't want to remember it. After sipping at my white wine for a bit, I used washing up as an excuse to slip away. Richard stared daggers at me, insisting that he would do it, not me. I turned him down, saying I was only doing it because I wanted to. Holmes should stick to his job.

After deciding to buy some bread tomorrow morning and what to make for lunch, I returned to the dining room to find Catherine in a nightgown, excitedly reporting that there was hot water in the shower. She looked like a pearlescent princess from the land of the stars, in full regalia in her long-sleeved, white nightgown. It almost made my head spin. Her cheeks must've been red from the wine. She was so unsteady on her feet that she seemed about to fall asleep at any moment.

Her son scolded her, saying she was in no state to be in front of company. She withdrew to one of the bedrooms on the second floor, but then it hit me—I hadn't even thought about cleaning the second floor. Was she going to be okay?

"She got here before us and spent the night here already. Her bedroom was perfectly clean."

"That's a relief..."

"This is no time for relief. All of the other rooms have been essentially untouched. I mean, what is wrong with her? This place has six rooms, but she only got her own sorted out."

"Oh."

I guess that meant there was nowhere for us to sleep.

Just out of curiosity, I tried opening the door to the salon next to the dining room, which had yet to be touched since we arrived. That was probably the room you'd use to enjoy an *apéritif.* I shut the door again in three seconds flat. We had made the right choice not opening it earlier. With its storm shutters closed for such a long time, the room smelled of mildew, and if I wasn't imagining things, it looked like sheets and sheets of lace were hanging from the ceiling. *Spiderwebs.* And I was pretty sure the fluffy grey something covering the floor wasn't a carpet. I pretended not to have seen anything.

Aw man, I should have spent some more time checking out the rest of the house before I got carried away with cooking.

"Catherine did have some sleeping bags in the back seat of her car."

I suggested sleeping here with an awkward smile on my face. Richard hesitated for a moment before announcing that she had, apparently, cleaned up one room. I understood what he meant without him having to explain further.

"Okay, I'll use a sleeping bag then. I'll try cleaning up another room if there's time, but I don't want to make too much noise because Catherine's probably already asleep."

"You don't want to sleep with me?"

Come again?

I needed a second to take a few deep breaths. I had probably misheard him, but it was also possible that I hadn't. And if I hadn't misheard him, I might have misunderstood him. In times like this you have to make sure you say the right thing. The right thing. What *was* that though? What would be right? Umm...

"...Wouldn't that be a little cramped?"

"What on earth are you talking about? The guest rooms in this villa are massive, and they all have two beds, one of which you're welcome to if you'd like."

"Oh, sorry, my bad. I guess I was imagining being crammed in like sardines in a box, like on school trips. They'd make us sleep three to a bed sometimes."

"I'll just pretend I didn't hear that. The shower is over here."

Richard showed me to the bathroom at the back of the first floor and disappeared upstairs. it was a very typical bathroom with a shower next to the toilet. The room was decorated with gorgeous white tiles with a blue floral pattern, but there was no bathtub. Maybe to compensate for that, there was a large pool in the middle of the now-dark yard. I guess swimming was your only option if you wanted to take a bath?

Not for the first time, I was surprised at how different my priorities for bathing were. To Japanese people, a "fancy" bathroom didn't mean lavish tile so much as an extravagant tub. I guess that was cultural differences for you.

I checked for any hidden "treasures" just to be safe, as I rinsed off with some hot water and changed into my night clothes before going upstairs, where I realized that it was absurd of me to have expected a regular guest room. The room that had been prepared was basically a high-end hotel suite. I knew I'd just have to get another shower if I opened any of the other doors, so I gave them a wide berth, deciding to save exploring for tomorrow.

While it didn't have a mini-fridge or TV, the room was furnished with a seating area and writing desk. The beds were huge, too. It made me think whoever had originally furnished the villa had probably wanted to be able to accommodate families with small children as guests. There was even enough extra space between the two beds to fit a third bed if necessary.

I didn't see Richard anywhere.

I flicked on the light on the nightstand and started looking up old movie information on my phone—with a particular name in the search terms: Catherine de Vulpian. I was surprised when I got a hit almost immediately. The page wasn't a comprehensive overview of her career, but it did list four of her roles from films from the 1980s—two supporting roles and two leading roles. None of them were big studio productions with famous directors. They seemed to be films focused on putting raw human emotion on the screen, rather than highlighting an actress's beauty. None of them seemed to have made much of a splash, but I had more or less expected that. If they'd been big hits, someone as beautiful as Catherine would have a much harder time living her life out of the public eye.

The thought had occurred to me, back when she was talking about classical theater, that she didn't seem to have sought movie roles out of a desire for the attention of the masses. Occasionally, there were names in the credits with the same surname as her. I wondered if other artists in the family had gotten jobs through her or if she'd been pressured to help a relative get a job. Just as I found a review complaining that the director had gotten so infatuated with a certain actress that he'd lost his mind, I heard someone coming up the stairs and quickly shut off my phone.

Richard knocked and came in. This was my first time seeing him in sleepwear. Seeing him with unkempt hair and wearing floppy pajamas felt even more scandalous than seeing Catherine in her nightgown, but mostly because he was a very private person who preferred to have his own room when traveling. I made a comment about how I wouldn't mind using one of the sleeping bags after all if he'd prefer it, keeping my back turned to him, and the courteous English man politely ignored me.

With everything that had happened today, we were surely both exhausted. Best to forgo the chitchat and get some shut-eye... or so I thought. Richard seemed to be feeling unusually talkative.

"In very broad strokes, we have three questions right now."

He must have been talking about the treasure hunt. *That's the great detective for you.* I rolled over to face the other bed and saw Richard sitting up against the headboard, looking down at his lap as he spoke, rather than at me.

One. Richard held up a finger. What was the point of this treasure hunt? What was the treasure, and why did we have to search this estate for it?

Two, why had Octavia recruited Catherine? She was Richard's mother, so if Octavia's objective was psychological torture, she was probably the right choice in that regard...but if that was really what Octavia was after, there had to be a better way to utilize her. I grimaced, saying that I understood what he was trying to say, but it was an awful way to put it. Richard let out a knowing sigh.

He really seemed to struggle to maintain his composure where Catherine was concerned. I didn't want to intrude or anything, but I *did* want to cover for him where I could. I supposed I'd just have to do my best.

The last question was the third one.

"How was it possible for Octavia to give Catherine hints about a 'treasure' hidden on this estate?"

"...Oh, now that you mention it."

Catherine had hidden a bunch of marbles in the house, but that was it. She didn't know how to solve the riddle or anything about the treasure. How *was* that possible?

And what exactly were we searching for?

Catherine had sounded very confident when she explained that it should be a fun treasure hunt. That meant there was a treasure hidden somewhere in the mansion. So who hid it? And who had told Catherine about it?

It had to be Octavia, right? She'd been described as a very enthusiastic shut-in. Would she really travel from Switzerland to the south of France to do something like that? It could have been one of her loyal servants. Like a certain somebody with an undercut. But what was the point of doing that?

Richard was fiddling with something in the other bed. It looked like scraps of paper—the ones Catherine had warned were important, the ones the marbles were wrapped in. I was guessing he'd transcribed the contents of the notes and which stones they had come with in the notepad on the dining room table, so carrying them around shouldn't have been an issue.

"Are they poems?"

"So it appears. You may not have noticed this, but some of the letters are bolded."

"Oh."

I could only glance at the text from a distance, but I noticed letters like "c" and "f" that were occasionally bolded. There was at least one character like that on each sheet, so it seemed like it had to be intentional rather than a printing error.

The obvious solution was that once you collected all the pieces, you'd have to take the bolded characters and rearrange them in the right order to get the answer. And somehow that would make a treasure map? Or maybe the writing itself was the "treasure"? Hiding something malicious in a collection of sentences that seemed innocuous at a glance was pretty easy. Especially if you had confidence that the final, intended reader was clever.

With Catherine having been so upset this evening and Richard not being himself, either, I was totally preoccupied with keeping the peace and never had the opportunity to ask if we should even continue looking for the treasure.

"Richard."

"Leave the deciphering to me. I'm pretty good at it. You could say it's something of a curse placed upon those of us with a love of languages."

"Are you really going to keep going at this?"

"That ship has already sailed. I don't think you have anything to worry about this time."

"I mean, we only have seven out of thirty-three so far, right? Surely you can't figure it out yet."

"All the more reason to thoroughly check everything."

Richard went on to say that Catherine had neither relatives nor a romantic partner to look after her, meaning he wasn't sure what would happen if she were left here alone. We were stuck with her until we had the full picture of what was going on.

I understood. Okay, I would see it through. And for the time being, that mostly meant chores.

"Hey, what do you want to eat tomorrow? Meat or fish?"

"......"

He didn't respond. I guess it was too abrupt a shift in subject. Or maybe he was tired. Just as I was about to say good night, Richard suddenly opened his mouth.

"You know, you..."

Richard wasn't looking at me. He was still looking down at his lap.

"...Never mind. Just be mindful of your surroundings."

"What's that supposed to mean?"

"Exactly what I said. This isn't the heart of Japan or the mountains of Sri Lanka, it's a rural city in Europe. People are much more ignorant than you might imagine. I just hope nothing happens."

He burrowed under his blanket, the shapely back of his head facing me. I needed to turn out the light.

"Wake me if anything happens. Good night."

"Night. Wake me up if I snore."

"You snore?"

"Sorry, I don't actually know. I haven't slept in the same room as someone since I was a kid."

"Will do," he said, with what sounded like a faint chuckle.

I took another look at his blond head before I turned out the light on the nightstand. His golden hair fell gracefully along the gentle curve of his head. I knew I shouldn't stare; it was rude. But I wanted to look just a little longer. My fingers scratched at the air in a strange way until I turned out the light.

Our stay at the villa had only just begun. Our situation was enviable—beautiful scenery, delicious food, and it wasn't costing a thing. And yet, I hoped that we could end this treasure hunt thing as soon as possible.

Laughable as it might be, I really did care about him. If anyone tried to do him harm, I was going to do everything in my power to get between him and the source of that harm.

I quietly reminded myself not to forget the role I came here to play. The curtains were pretty thin, so once my eyes got used to the dark, I could faintly make out the shape of the windows behind them. I closed my eyes, thinking I'd probably wake up with the sunrise.

Le Deuxième Jour:
Day 2

T HE MARBLE HUNT TRIP was going almost too well, thanks to the work of one Richard Holmes. As the sun approached its zenith, the seven stones had become twenty-one. There were only twelve left. It was some truly excellent work.

Richard, however, was a monster the next morning. I woke promptly and easily around 7 a.m. with the light of dawn, ready to get started cleaning the estate, but a blanket creature slipped from the neighboring bed and frantically grabbed me by the leg. It ordered me not to clean anything yet, because it could use the marks left in the dust to figure out where things were hidden, and that was it. The man was covered from head to toe in his blanket, so I couldn't even get a glimpse of his face. He probably didn't want me to see him right after he woke up.

I agreed to hold off on cleaning and chased the creature back into its bed, encouraging it to get some more sleep. I decided to wander around early-morning Provence instead, phone in hand. I took pictures of the vineyards and the mountains and returned to the villa in about thirty minutes. Sure enough, Richard was there in the dining room in his usual spot. His hair was ever so slightly wet, but perfectly coifed, and his vertical-striped shirt fit the resort vibe just right. Seeing him sitting there, legs crossed and sipping his royal milk tea, it made me think I'd imagined the blanket creature from earlier.

"Good morning."

"...Morning."

His sparkling smile commanded me not to ask any questions about what happened that morning. I felt like he took after Catherine a bit in this respect. I almost let out a laugh but covered it up by clearing my throat.

I was granted permission to clean some areas of the house, which took until about noon. After that, I borrowed the car and headed into town to restock on the cleaning supplies that were running low. On my way back, loaded down with supplies, I coincidentally ran into the neighbors from the previous day and said hello. They seemed to be on their way into town by car but had stopped on the road to look something up on their phones.

I stopped my car, too, and asked them in English if they were going shopping, and they replied in French, asking me which supermarket I used. The conversation was already awkward, but I told them about the shop Catherine had showed me in my broken French, and they headed down the hill in their car without another word.

When I got back to the villa, Richard and I made and ate sandwiches with the ham and cheese I'd bought in town. There came a sudden clamor from the second floor, and a woman ran down the stairs like Cinderella when the clock struck midnight, blonde hair streaming behind her. I guess Catherine had woken up at about noon.

"Good morning, boys! My, you're up early. Hunting for treasure is all well and good, but you should get some rest, too. Oh, Seigi, you cleaned? Richard, you should be entertaining Seigi. It's so hot out today. What if you two go to the river?"

"We have sandwiches. Would you care for some brunch, my lady?" Richard offered in a cool tone.

Catherine turned up her nose and thanked him with a bow, like the resident of a medieval castle. Clad in a summer dress, she seemed to be flaunting her legs at her son, who summarily ignored her.

"The marble collection is going well. Just to confirm, you aren't the kind of woman who would do something so foolish as to bury them in the garden, are you?"

"I'm not allowed to give you any hints. It's more fun to find things on your own, after all. But I guess I can say that I've never been very fond of getting my hands dirty."

That settled it. Richard drew a slash through the vast garden section of the villa map he'd drawn on his notepad. No need to search there, essentially. His notes included all of the rooms on the first and second floors, and even the mailbox and fence around the place. It looked a bit like a treasure map, actually.

There were twenty-one pieces of paper on the table, held together with a large clip. He'd let me look at them, but they all appeared to be poetry about love. Richard had written down the bolded letters and tried rearranging them in various orders, shifting them around one letter at a time, but still couldn't seem to come up with anything.

Richard announced that he was taking a break and rose from his chair to head into the room next to the dining room. The sunroom, which I'd cleaned up somewhat, currently had the door to the garden standing open. That door would take you directly to the pool, which still needed cleaning, though the fish-shaped fountain was working without issue. It was perfect for dipping your feet in to relax.

The villa's garden seemed like it must've been a vineyard in the past, to me. The house built up on the hill looked like its walls and furniture had been renovated several times over, but the foundation was fairly old, and the stone walls by the entry porch looked similar to the walls of the monasteries we'd passed on the way from the station. It seemed like a structure with quite a bit of history behind it.

Catherine got my attention as she ate one of the egg, ham, and watercress sandwiches I'd made and sipped at a glass of orange juice.

"Seigi, I had an idea. Why don't we go out today, just the two of us?"

"Huh? But why?"

"Because I want to surprise Richard. He's such a stick in the mud."

Catherine explained with a smile that she wanted to hold a garden party tonight. I wondered what kind of party she had in mind. A feast for the three of us? She seemed to take my question as a suggestion and clapped her hands together saying, "That sounds just wonderful! What does he like, I wonder? Do you know, Seigi? Does he like Japanese food? Or Sri Lankan food? Goodness, this makes me look like such a failure of a mother— it's almost like I don't know the first thing about my own son. Well...I guess I actually don't."

Catherine cast her eyes down sadly, knocking back her orange juice as if it were alcohol. I was pretty confident that I knew what Richard liked to eat—he was the Emperor of Sweets, after all—but I didn't think it would cheer Catherine up to hear that. Deciding to go along with the party idea for now, I suggested we go out shopping.

"The ingredients we have in the fridge aren't really ideal for a party."

"...Yes! It's still morning, well, early afternoon? The *marché* should still be open. We need to hurry, Seigi! I do love shopping."

It seemed like the princess's good mood had been restored. Catherine hurriedly finished her sandwich and ushered me into the car, excited to buy some tasty treats.

But where had Richard gone?

I looked for his striped shirt in the yard. The greenery had had such a calm, mellow hue in the twilight yesterday, but the intense midday sun transformed it entirely. The garden was flooded with light, almost like it had its own personal sun illuminating it, and the whitish ground was covered in the tasteful ruins of what looked like an old marble wall. Other than the occasional red wildflower, everything was unbroken green.

There, sitting on the edge of the pool, which stood out from the rest of the garden with its thick coat of paint, was Richard. Based on how quickly he was typing on his phone, I figured he must've been communicating with a client. I was a little relieved to see a more normal expression on his face.

"We're going out! Call me if anything comes up!" I shouted, leaning halfway out of the sunroom. Richard leaned back and waved in acknowledgment. I spun around and headed for the car. There was barely any—or rather, absolutely no—pedestrian traffic in the area, so the front door probably didn't need to be locked as long as Richard was there.

"Sorry to keep you waiting. So we're headed to the *marché*?"

"No, the river."

"Huh?"

"Going to the *marché* is important, but this lovely afternoon is perfect for enjoying the water. Come on, I want to go to the river with you. Okay?" Catherine said with a smile that was like being shot at point-blank range.

I was at a loss for words for a moment, searching my brain for the appropriate polite response. It eventually occurred to me that I didn't need that in this situation, so I just let out a little grunt and nodded.

"Thank you," she sang in response.

I vaguely recalled that Europe had a legend about beautiful mermaids with equally beautiful singing voices. The mermaids would sing as they brushed their hair atop rocky outcroppings, leading ships down the river to their doom.

The river was in the opposite direction from the supermarket. Catherine had me drive, but concentrating on operating the vehicle was quite the struggle, as she regaled me with memories of Provence over the familiar sound of the female singer's voice flowing from the stereo. Regardless, the stream was beautiful. It wasn't so much a river as an irrigation canal, but the water was so clear you could see the riverbed and the shore was covered in white stones. The only other things in sight were trees, fields, mountains, and the sky. The sheer scale of the environment here was so great it was almost terrifying. It was like Hokkaido but if no one spoke Japanese.

"Goodness! I'm so happy. It's been years since I was last here during the summer," Catherine said, throwing off her designer sandals right in front of me and splashing around in the river in her bare feet. I could hear her exclaiming how cold it was. I was planning to remain on standby on the shore as her driver, but when she came back, she hurried to roll up the hem of my pants.

"Seigi, this is your first time in Provence, right? You can't sit around on the sidelines. That's no fun. Come! Come, come!"

"All right, maybe just a little."

I gently pushed her hands away, rolled up my pants, and took off my socks, before taking a step into the clear water. I let out a shout in Japanese the moment my feet touched the surface.

"It's ice-cold! I thought it was supposed to be summer!"

I just kept letting out quick shouts, and Catherine giggled like a little kid.

"Surprising, right? All the river water in this area comes from springs deep underground. Just like the gemstones you and Richard love so much. On days when the heat of the sun is scorching, it makes you feel like a fish. I missed this feeling so much."

I asked her if she used to come here to swim with Richard. Catherine scooped up her wet hair and giggled.

"We did. That was such a long time ago now, though. He would have been six or maybe seven at the time. Or maybe it was before that? It was after Ash and I had divorced so...no, maybe it was before that? Grandma was still alive back then—my mother, that is. Richard's grandma." She smiled. "That villa used to belong to her. I think I told you about that yesterday. That reminds me—she was the one who first established a connection with the English side of the family, so it goes quite a ways back. For them, too."

Catherine's voice dropped about half an octave again. I guess she didn't have many positive memories of the Claremonts. I knew a bit about Richard's cousins, but I was out of my depth when it came to the earlier generations. It was a bit surprising— I had always assumed that her connection to the Claremonts began with Richard's father falling in love with her at first sight.

I said as much, and Catherine smiled.

"A fair point. I don't think Ash would have had the slightest interest in me had I been human at the time. But I was a dragonfly, so he loved that."

"A dragonfly?"

"It was a performance piece. Have you never seen something like that before? I wonder if I can still pull it off. Oh, it would be perfect for the party! I'll have to think about it."

Catherine's voice rang like a bell as she performed some mysterious dance steps. I offered her my hand, worried she might fall, and she spun around, landing in my arms. She was so slender and graceful. Were all movie stars such dainty creatures?

"Seigi, what do you think of me?"

Catherine looked at me with sparkling eyes. Her eyes seemed like twin replicas of the summer sun—almost like sphene. They were truly dazzling. I felt like I should be wearing sunglasses.

"You remind me a lot of Richard."

She burst out laughing. Well, I should have expected that. What else was I supposed to say when asked for my impression of a parent and child who were *this* similar? It was a pretty laughable answer, sure, but I hadn't just been talking about their looks when I said it.

"Like how you care so much for other people. It reminds me a lot of Richard."

"Oh."

Catherine gently pulled away from me, and I retreated to the shore. We didn't have any towels, so I just kind of shook myself off on the rocks before putting my socks back on.

"I think that might be the first time anyone's ever said that to me. You mean I'm capable of being a civilized person who cares about others? You see, people often call me a 'queen.' They say I'm never satisfied unless I'm on top. What a rude thing to say. But if I'm being honest, they're probably right. Sorry. Heh heh heh."

"What do you mean?"

"Well...if I see a much younger, prettier girl at a party, for example, I suddenly get all anxious and want to steal all her friends away. Or if some man I don't even care for doesn't like me, it makes me want to *make* him like me. It makes me uncomfortable if I can't be sure everyone around me likes me. I was actually diagnosed with an anxiety disorder, but during my treatment my therapist fell in love with me and I couldn't bear to go back to the clinic. I have a lot to answer for."

It all sounded a bit ridiculous, but I was more surprised by her confiding in me than by the actual content of what she had said. This wasn't the sort of thing you should be telling the young male friend of your son, whom you hardly knew, right? At least not without knowing his background?

If I had to take a guess, someone might have told her about my background. About how the situation with my biological father had made me afraid of people for a while and about how I was still scared to walk among crowds of people in Japan.

Someone who wasn't Richard.

I could feel myself getting defensive, much like a porcupine with its spines standing on end, ready to prick anyone who approached if they made one wrong move. I needed to calm myself down. I didn't think Catherine meant me any harm. She was Richard's mother. And she had just confided in me about her own struggles. What was the safest way for me to react? Without being rude.

"...That must be difficult."

"It is. It's very difficult. Thank you, Seigi, you're very kind for a young man."

"Are young men not typically kind?"

"Not in the slightest. They are some of the cruelest creatures in the whole world. They draw on my dresses with crayons and slobber all over their wooden blocks. Absolutely dreadful."

Before I could say that it sounded like she was talking about infants, not young men, she shot me an impish look and chuckled. I guess she was teasing me. I smiled awkwardly, begging her not to give me such a hard time, and Catherine laughed like she was having even more fun.

"Hey, tell me the truth. Do you like me, too?"

With the sun at her back, she leaned over, putting her hands on her knees as she peered into my face. Her face was dizzyingly close. There was only one thing to say at times like this.

"I admire you."

"How exactly can you admire a woman you've only just met?"

"Because I think anyone who could move into a house like that all by herself and set up a whole treasure hunt for her summer guests is a wonderful hostess."

"...Goodness. Yes, you may have a point," she mumbled to herself.

She twirled around in the cool water. I worried that she might fall, but her footing seemed steady.

"Yes," she repeated, looking at me again. She had a radiant smile on her face. "When you put it that way, I think you're right! Maybe I *am* a wonderful hostess. I do have a talent for entertaining, and I can pick up just about anything with ease. I *am* a woman deserving of admiration. I deserve to have both men and women gossip about just how wonderful I am. You're welcome to think of me that way, too, you know."

"Good thing I already do."

"Thank you. You really are ruthless," Catherine said, smiling like an innocent child again.

When we went down into town, I was first surprised by how big the city was, and then surprised by the *marché* itself. Either side of a large street was lined with street stalls like you might see at a festival in Japan. There were shops selling lavender bouquets, fresh fish, ham, cheese, gardening accessories, lacework, truffles—anything you can imagine. That reminds me—*marché* was French for "market." Maybe this was what markets used to look like?

Catherine shopped, indulging her every impulse to eat something, while I focused on selecting several sweet treats that looked like things Richard would enjoy. They weren't on the level of the stuff we had in Ginza, but they were way more modern and elegant than the Sri Lankan pudding or baked sweets I would make. Catherine suddenly stopped just as we were heading back to the car. Right in front of a street sign that read "Rue Mirabeau."

"This street is named for a person. You could say he's one of the more prominent figures from this region. He was a count during the French Revolution and very famous for his face."

"H-his face?"

"Yes, he was said to be *very* ugly!" she said, giggling like a child. She looked around, like she'd just said something she shouldn't have, then continued talking, both hands full of bags. "But he was very popular. He may have been a member of the Second Estate as a noble, but he represented the Third Estate—the commoners—in the government and gave many impassioned speeches. He changed the social order."

She went on to explain that while there were many blood-drenched stories from the French Revolution, the count had died of illness before the guillotines of the Revolutionary Tribunal were put to work. Perhaps he was lucky, in that regard. All I knew about the French Revolution was what I had studied for my exams, but I had the gist of it. It was the beginning of the modern era, when political power shifted from the hands of the nobility to those of the people, but the monarchy was later restored by Napoleon. Posters of paintings depicting him and his family members had been all over Charles de Gaulle. I specifically remembered one of him wearing a crown. I wondered if the original was somewhere in the Louvre?

I mentioned knowing about Napoleon, and Catherine looked at me grumpily.

"I can't deny that Napoleon was a great man, but Mirabeau was a good man, too. I think his popularity with women proves

THE CASE FILES OF JEWELER RICHARD

that. Even though he wasn't a soldier, just an ugly man. That's
something you should know now that you've visited Provence."

She chuckled again. An ugly man and an orator. I guess it's
not that surprising that he was popular. His face had nothing to
do with his personality. If anything, I'd learned from my time
with a certain someone that having too pretty a face often made
people keep their distance.

"When it comes down to it, your face doesn't really matter all
that much—especially not compared to what a person thinks and
how they behave. Heh, I always liked that notion. But faces do tend
to lead people astray," Catherine mumbled self-deprecatingly.

We put our things in the car and took off to return to the villa.
We hadn't even gotten ten meters down the road before I noticed
something strange.

Someone was following us.

It was a man. His unkempt white hair was crammed into a
hunting cap, he wore overalls that were covered in white powder
for some reason, and he was really running after us. But he'd never
be able to catch a car. What was going on?

"Um, *madame*, I think someone's behind us."

"What?"

She was in a cheery mood, humming, as I pointed behind us
with my chin. She just needed to look into the rearview mirror. She
followed my lead, looking in the mirror, and even turned around.

"What? You saw someone? There isn't anyone there."

I looked again. All I saw in the mirror was the cobblestone
street stretching out behind us.

"Sorry. I saw an elderly person chasing us... Do you have any idea who it could have been?"

"Not a clue. Goodness, who could it have been? We didn't forget anything."

Catherine and I both looked back again one after the other, but the suspicious old man was nowhere to be seen. I wondered if something had fallen off our car or something. Just to be safe, I made a circle around the fountain in the middle of the main street before returning to our original route, but there was no old man in sight.

"...What was that?"

"Don't worry about it. It happens sometimes. Rude people chasing after me. I'm just too beautiful," Catherine said without a hint of hesitation. Well, she wasn't wrong about that. Even from a distance, her smile exuded a kind of energy that attracted attention and her voice sounded like sweet birdsong.

But if it were up to me, I wouldn't want to live such a terrifying life.

"Shall we go home?"

"I think so. We have a party to prepare, after all. I wonder if Richard is still hard at work looking for treasure."

"Don't worry. If any weird people come chasing us again, I'll do something about it."

"...Oh, I'm not worried. I'm an ever-cheerful hummingbird. What makes you think I'm worried?"

"Oh, um."

I wondered if I should say it. When Richard got nervous, the rhythm of his speech changed ever so slightly, as did the gestures he made while speaking and the places his gaze would settle. Assuming the same went for Catherine, she was probably a little flustered right now. She and her son were very alike in the way that they didn't like to let that show, and I didn't want to go out of my way to draw attention to it.

"Sorry, I just kind of got a feeling."

I feigned scratching my head. Catherine watched my expression for a bit before flashing a strange smile—the corners of her mouth were tense, almost like she couldn't decide if she was going to laugh or not. She let out a little sigh.

"You really are a kind boy, Seigi. *Merci, mon chevalier.*"

I thanked her and stepped on the gas.

Thankfully, when we got back, Richard was out. He'd left a note saying he'd gone to the library, which I was guessing meant the Aix library. We must've just missed each other.

Just as I was wondering how he'd gotten into town without a car, Catherine explained that you could rent bikes here. Apparently, Provence was popular with cycling enthusiasts—which made sense to me, considering how popular it was in Hokkaido, too—and all the big cities had bike rental services. Under normal circumstances, Richard would have taken a rental car, which would have allowed him to not be so visible, but just looking up where the nearest car rental place was made me exhausted. You'd need a car to rent a car! So a bike was the obvious answer. I was sure he'd taken a taxi all the way from the airport to the villa.

He'd left a second note. One was addressed to me, saying that he had finished searching the first floor. There were now twenty-eight marbles on display in the game board. He had practically finished already. The slips of paper and his notepad were missing.

I guess he'd been making good progress on the riddle. Maybe that's why he went to the library.

Well, whatever. Right now, my job wasn't to think about stuff—it was performing the manual labor necessary for us to go about our lives. Catherine withdrew to her room on the second floor. I could hear the sound of footsteps as she practiced something—maybe the dragonfly act she had mentioned down by the river? It was clear that her idea of entertainment was different from the Japanese norm, but I was struggling to imagine what this "dragonfly" thing could even be. Like a mime, maybe? I had no clue.

I prepared myself not to be shocked by it—whatever *it* was—and focused on getting dinner ready.

We'd had seafood yesterday, so I thought meat would be nice today. I consulted with the butchers at the *marché* in both English and French, and they unanimously recommended lamb. That meant sheep, specifically a young sheep. All the locals in the vicinity echoed the recommendation. If everyone was that enthusiastic about it, it couldn't be a bad choice, right? I bought a large quantity of lamb, and they even threw in some herbs to eliminate the gamey smell and some quail pâté. I was very pleased.

And that's why we would be having lamb tonight. Specifically, a bone-in leg. I'd only ever had lamb in *jingisukan*, but I found plenty of recipes when I searched. It made me wonder if there were more parts of the world where people ate sheep than pig. You could hardly ever find pork in Sri Lanka, but boneless pork rib was a real treat in Japan.

I'd decided to roast it, having read that lamb was well-suited to roasting and wouldn't take too long that way. I could use the leftover vegetables from yesterday to make a salad, and that, along with the pâté, should be perfect for a festive dinner.

I didn't know when Richard would be back from the library. He wouldn't be answering his phone right now, either. I figured I'd spend another two hours cleaning before getting into dinner prep, so I grabbed a hand rake and went out into the garden, where I ran into one of the neighbors again. Just the woman this time. Maybe here to extend another drinking invitation? Unfortunately, the lady of the house was currently busy preparing for a party.

"I'm sorry, the owner isn't available right now."

"You paint walls?"

It was so sudden. Paint walls? What did that mean? We were struggling to communicate again.

I asked what she wanted, and she just repeated the same phrase in French again. It sounded like she wanted to ask me to paint some walls for her, but I didn't understand why. Why would she ask me that? Maybe she and her husband weren't native French or English speakers? I wondered how best to facilitate some kind of mutual communication with her.

"Can you come now? We'll pay thirty euros an hour."

"Is it an emergency? I can help look up the number of a contractor for you."

She let out an annoyed-sounding groan. I guess the important part was whether I'd come with her or not. I figured I should get Catherine's permission first. I asked her to wait with a little nod and went back inside to call Catherine, but she just brushed me off, telling me to save it for later. She wouldn't even let me in the room.

I didn't know what to do, so I went back outside, and the neighbor asked me another question.

"Where do you live?"

"Me? Sri Lanka."

"Will you come for forty euros? It won't take long."

I was even more confused. Did I look like some kind of housekeeping demon to her? Could she not see the potential disaster that could result from challenging a total amateur to a speed painting competition? It did feel odd to have someone so insistent on asking me to do menial labor...but it could be an interesting experience, so I figured, why not? I left the mower in the corner of the yard for the time being and went along with her.

The neighbor had come by car. Their villa was closer to town than Catherine's, and smaller, too, but it had its own pool. I guess the pool was a summer necessity. The couple exchanged some angry sounding shouts in a language I didn't understand before the woman came over and handed me a roller and a can of white paint. The man was in the back of the house painting the walls blue. It looked like they were doing a massive remodel of both the interior and exterior.

"Looks like a lot of work. Are you sure you wouldn't be better off hiring some more people?"

"You paint these walls."

"You mean the entire exterior?"

"All of it."

It was a much bigger area than I had imagined. It was the entire exterior of the house. If you asked a professional, they wouldn't quote anywhere near forty euros, let alone be able to do it in an hour. It made sense to me now—they wanted help to save money. I told her that I'd do as much as I could, but I had work to do, so I'd have to leave after an hour. "Good," she replied.

I didn't really understand what was supposed to be "good" about that, but she went and put on a rain poncho and went inside to help her husband. I recalled a college friend of mine from an area in Hokuriku where rice was grown. Though I didn't know if he'd been telling the truth, he'd said that during planting season, everyone would get together and plant the fields as a group—like they weren't just neighbors but more like people invested in a common cause. I guess that's probably just what happens in places where hands are in short supply.

Well, whatever. I'd just have to see how much I could get done in an hour. It'd be worth it to get a funny story to tell at the party later tonight.

At least that's what I thought.

Painting wasn't actually very hard. And no one complained about the job I was doing. The windows had been masked off with tape, so I could just keep painting with the roller without issue. But it really was a massive area. Too massive. It was two stories. I hadn't been told to paint the second floor, but once I finished the first, the woman came out carrying a stepladder. I asked if she meant for me to use that to paint the upper floor, and she nodded and said yes. The second floor was about five meters off the ground, so it would be pretty serious if I fell, and there was no safety line. But if I didn't do it, either the husband or the wife, both of whom looked to be in either their forties or fifties, would end up doing it. Just the thought was a bit terrifying.

I'd already agreed to the job, and only had thirty minutes left, so I got on the step ladder and started painting the second floor. Not long after I had started, I heard a squeak from the road in the direction of the villa. It was a bike. I looked over toward the hill, wondering if it might be who I thought it was, and saw a man wearing sunglasses riding a bike. A man with blond hair and wearing a striped shirt. A polo shirt or something probably would have been better in this weather, but this beautiful man always wore a proper button-down.

Richard had already noticed me before I could wave to him with my roller. He took off his sunglasses, looking utterly stunned.

"Welcome back. I'm just helping out a little. Catherine's back in the house."

"That's so dangerous! What are you doing up there?"

Well, he wasn't wrong. I couldn't exactly explain myself from up there, so I awkwardly started climbing down just as the woman came out of the house.

I would never forget the way Richard looked in that moment for the rest of my life.

"What the *hell* are you making him do?" Richard demanded in English. It was clearly not a question so much as an accusation. When the woman hesitated to respond, Richard shifted gears and began speaking in another language I didn't understand. Surprised by the fluent attack, the man came out of the house. By the time I reached the ground, the man seemed to be apologizing for something to Richard, but that just made him even angrier. The couple fell completely silent...which was only to be expected. This was probably their first time seeing Richard, and having this beautiful man who looked like he'd just stepped out of a movie screen spitting fire at you all of a sudden must've been completely unreal. His eyes blazed with blue fire, and I couldn't help but marvel at how their color seemed to deepen when he was worked up as I set the roller and paint can down.

Richard spoke like a machine gun spitting enough bullets to take out ten people before letting out a big "hmph!" about thirty times grander than any Catherine had made. He wrapped an arm around my shoulders and pulled me away.

"They think you're our servant."

"What, me?"

"They apologized for borrowing our hired help while we were out. Preposterous. I'm not even going to ask what you were thinking, but I find the way you've been treated inexcusable. And what was the mistress of the house doing? Did she just obediently loan you out, like a toy?"

"No! Nothing like that!"

I explained that I'd come here on a whim all my own and insisted that Catherine didn't know a thing about it, but Richard only seemed to be half listening. He'd abandoned his bike and started walking, for some reason, so I had to push it along. As the setting sun gradually enveloped Montagne Sainte-Victoire, I kept apologizing to Richard for my incompetence, and he kept rejecting my efforts, saying I didn't need to apologize.

He was right. I really couldn't imagine how ignorant people could be here.

There were three residents of Catherine's gorgeous villa. It was obvious to anyone at a glance that the beautiful mother and son were related, but me? What did I look like? Who did people think I was to them? The two of them were white and I was Asian. Catherine spoke French natively and my French was broken and awkward. They'd refused to accept the food from me yesterday—she'd had to hand it to them. And the first time they saw us, she was in the passenger seat and I was driving.

I don't actually think it was that odd that they mistook me for a servant.

"You are a very considerate person. So much so that it isn't simply a matter of your being raised in Japan. You really ought to learn that there are many people who seek to take advantage of people like you. I don't want to see you being used by vacation home flippers for their own gain."

"Flippers? You mean that's not their house?"

"The buying and selling of vacation homes in this area isn't exactly unusual. People often commission renovations to get more favorable pricing. Those people are probably intermediaries of some sort. Catherine was mistaken to be so friendly toward them. She's always willing to smile at anyone."

"Sorry, but I'm fine, really."

"Don't apologize. This isn't your fault."

I went silent—not because I didn't have anything to say, but because I was pretty sure that he would understand even if I didn't say it out loud.

Then whose fault was it? Who needed to take the blame for this to be resolved?

Richard suddenly realized I was pushing his bike for him and cast his eyes down. He took the handlebars from me and began plodding along with it. When Richard's spirits were down, he had this peculiar pitiful quality to him, almost like a dayflower in the rain. It packed a punch—I wasn't especially vulnerable to it or anything, but his pained face was completely outrageous. I could hardly stand it.

After I'd choked back the words in my throat two or three times, Richard opened his mouth again.

"...This is true of any country, not just France, but the farther you get away from major city centers, the fewer non-local residents there are. There are a lot of immigrants in France, and while Asians are not uncommon in any region, the way locals in places like this perceive and treat outsiders is very different from Tokyo or Paris."

"So they all think that any foreigner is a migrant worker?"

"You're not wrong. No matter the country, you'll find people who make broad generalizations about immigrants and struggle to see them as fellow humans. They said they thought you were Sri Lankan, but if I had said you were Indian or Mongolian, they would have believed me. That's roughly the level of awareness Europeans tend to have of Asian cultures."

"Unless they have friends in each of those countries, that is. It's my fault for not knowing that."

"...I thought that knowing that myself would be enough to protect you. But I was naive for thinking that. How can I possibly apologize to you?"

"Oh, don't apologize, you're just going to make me feel bad. Plus, I just helped paint a neighbor's house."

"They didn't consider you the same class of human as them. It's intolerable," Richard said, sounding like he was struggling to get the words out.

You are not to hold prejudiced views on the basis of a person's race, religion, nationality, sexual orientation, or any other quality. I recalled the clause in Étranger's employment contract. It wasn't about being impeccably ideologically pure but more about being conscious of your own prejudices and biases and taking great care not to let them hurt our clients, right? To take it one step further, it was saying you shouldn't act without thinking or allow harmful stereotypes to be perpetuated. It would be pretty bad if they encountered another Asian person who had been invited here by a friend to relax in their villa and treated them the same way as they'd treated me. I could see that happening.

Or at least, I should have been able to.

"Sorry."

"Don't apologize."

"I'd appreciate it if you'd tell me what I should say then."

"……"

Richard went silent for a bit, continuing to push his bike along. Then all of a sudden, he said, *"Shiritori."*

"What?"

"In Japanese."

"Why now?"

"Come on. You start," Richard decided on his own and stood there waiting for me to go. All I could do was laugh. But man, *Shiritori*, I hadn't played that in years.

"…Rhodochrosite."

"Emerald."

"Danburite."

"Egyptian jasper."

"Rosinca."

"Isn't that just another name for rhodochrosite?"

"W-were we playing with that rule?"

"Then why did you make it all gemstone names?"

"Well, when you said 'emerald,' I just kinda rolled with it."

"Are you trying to make me remember *every* gem name that starts with E?"

"Oh, you know, now that you mention it, a lot of them end with '-ite,' don't they?"

We started over from "Egyptian jasper" with R, and I pondered what word to use next. Just talking in Japanese really did make me feel like all my cares were melting away. What a strange feeling. It took no effort to put my thoughts into words. It felt warm and secure, like drinking tea at a *kotatsu*.

I had probably been making a slightly scary face earlier, which was why Richard had suggested this.

"R...red bean mochi."

"Ice cream parfait."

"The kind with banana, right? T...t...tiramisù éclair."

"Your pronunciation got a little French-sounding at the end there. Rice pudding."

"G... What starts with g? G, g...a food that starts with g..."

"You could dispense with the food restriction. You sound like a machine that's run out of oil."

"Gratin! Oh, lemme take that back."

"Not a chance."

Richard laughed and said "tough luck," a phrase I'd only heard a few times in my life, to announce my loss. I felt relieved. I already really, really, really, really liked his face as it was, but I think I liked this particular expression of his most of all.

I hammed up my frustration over the loss, and Richard snickered.

"Another feather for my cap—I beat a Japanese person at *Shiritori*."

"You're basically unbeatable. You could conquer the whole of Japan with ease."

"I will humbly refrain. I'm sure it would do wonders for expanding my vocabulary, but it does sound dreadfully exhausting."

Richard let out a chuckle as we walked another few meters up the hill in the slowly setting summer sun, before abruptly stopping.

"...One of my most painful childhood memories was the day I brought a group of my classmates to that villa shortly after I'd started school."

"You had friends over here? Wait, but wasn't that when—"

"In both France and England, when parents decide to get divorced, children have the right to live with either of their parents, and parents have a duty to care for their children. Catherine wasn't exactly living a life of luxury at the time, but she did at least own that villa."

For summer vacation, Richard had invited three boys to come to the countryside of Provence with him. Catherine was delighted to have the opportunity to entertain some of her son's friends for the first time. She was a very attentive hostess and charmed them with her dazzling smile. But at the end of their two-week visit, Richard's three friends were no longer Richard's friends—they had all become Catherine's groupies.

Richard reluctantly explained that they were like completely different animals when they were at the mansion and when they were outside. From the moment they woke up, they tried to curry favor with her. In the afternoon, they'd fight over who would get to walk with her, and in the evening, they would compete over the order in which they got to dance with her. She had turned them into such desperate creatures.

"This may sound a bit harsh, but irrespective of whether she's dealing with children or adults, she cannot feel secure until she's exerted her influence over everyone in her orbit. I seem to be afforded special dispensation as her son, placing me outside the effective range of her charms, but where anyone else is concerned, she will mercilessly lay siege until she has dyed them thoroughly in her colors."

At the end of that vacation, Richard announced to his mother that he would never again bring his friends over to her place. Catherine had seemed hurt, but also seemed to understand his reasons, and laughed it off saying that perhaps it was for the better. The fact that she didn't apologize felt telling. After that, Richard really did never introduce his close friends to her ever again. Not even the woman he was determined to marry.

"I have a lot to answer for." Catherine had said that in a joking tone, but I guess it was a lot more serious than I'd suspected. But on the other hand, that slightly—ever so slightly—put my mind at ease.

"...I'm glad."

"For what?"

"Well, I was just worried I might have to grab you and make a run for it at some point."

"Run away? Why?"

"I mean, you gotta be prepared for trouble, right? Like if somebody decides to, you know..."

I groped at the air with my hands. I couldn't bring myself to say it, but I was pretty sure he would understand.

The most awful parent-child relationship I could imagine was the worst of the worst. The type of dynamic where if you locked the two of them in a room together, only one would come out. I knew that sort of thing was extremely rare and that nothing good would ever come of hating someone so much you were willing to destroy your own life, but one of the annoying things about blood relatives was that sometimes logic didn't apply. They can make you want to kill, or die.

So what did a silly treasure hunt or other people's problems matter if the man who'd pulled me from the pits of hell more than once was struggling with something like that? This wasn't a little island in the middle of the ocean. We could just run away. We'd both booked return tickets with flexible dates, and if we couldn't escape France because there were no open seats, we could rent a room in Paris and I'd treat him to pudding and royal milk tea every day again.

But based on what I'd heard, that didn't seem like it would be necessary.

Catherine could be reasoned with, so it would be fine. If words worked, there was no need for other tools.

"I'm glad it didn't come to that," I said, and Richard sighed and walked in silence for a bit before calling me a worrywart under his breath. It didn't seem like he was trying to push me away. He sounded more worried about me.

I couldn't help but remember the way Catherine rolled up the hem of my pants when I watched him fidget with the handlebars. They really were alike. I mean, they were parent and child. It only made sense that they'd resemble each other even when they weren't making an effort to *imitate* one another. If that weren't the case, there wouldn't be so many people suffering from these too-close relationships.

"Maybe I am a worrywart, but I can't help worrying about things that I care about. So, what's actually going on with this Octavia thing? I heard about your meeting with Jeffrey and Henry. Is everything okay?"

"I'll have to save both the apologies and explanations for another day. But I am confident that we're slowly getting closer to the heart of the matter."

"...Well, that's good. Is there anything I can do?"

"I need you to be patient. I don't need a gun that will fire at anything on my word. All I want from you is a friend who will stand right beside me and look at the world in a slightly different light."

"Huh? Oh...oh..."

"Seigi, are you all right? I know I've made you walk quite a distance, and they didn't have you wearing a respirator or anything while painting—are you feeling unwell?"

Paint? Feeling unwell? *You know, maybe that did do something to me. But I'm okay. I'm feeling great.* I wanted to say as much—in English or French or Japanese, it didn't matter. But no words would come out.

I suddenly stopped and went silent. The man pushing the bike also stopped. The wheels of the bike squeaked. I pulled my phone out of my pocket, and Richard looked at me quizzically.

"What is it?"

"No, I uh…I just suddenly got the urge to take a picture. Just one."

I used the panorama mode I rarely ever used to take a 270 degree shot of the area, trying my best to keep Richard and the bike out of the shot. Provence's sky, the fields of olive trees, the dry fallen grasses, the plastic bottles carelessly tossed aside, and the white stone paths—*listen to this. Well, don't actually listen, because I can't say it out loud, but just guess.*

My dear boss called me his friend.

He said all he wanted from me was a friend. Which meant I was his *friend.*

I was so happy.

So happy. Too happy, even. So happy that I didn't know quite what to do with myself.

I know, I know. I know it's a little late for this. Our strict employer-employee relationship had only lasted until, at most, the fall of my second year of college. We'd grown very close for the relatively short time we'd known each other. Deep down, I'd been pretty sure that made us friends…but I mean, what *were* friends in the first place? Was friend just a promotion from acquaintance? If that were the case, surely you would know what rank you were at and why you'd been promoted? Had I advanced in that way? Had I made some great leap forward since my second year of college, in terms of our compatibility? I didn't really think so.

Maybe that was why, even though I knew we were getting closer, I told myself not to get a big head. I convinced myself that it couldn't possibly be that simple.

Now, presented with something like this completely out of the blue, I was utterly helpless—like I'd just taken a body blow to the most tender part of my heart. I was so happy I felt like singing and dancing and screaming and doing cartwheels, but that would definitely result in me hurting myself, for one, not to mention making me look suspicious and probably scare people, and then this man would have no choice but to say he didn't want to be friends with me anymore. And that would suck. It would be embarrassing enough for him to notice how happy those words had made me. Richard liked to keep things cool and rational. I should find a way to follow his lead.

But I was just so happy.

As I kept walking, trying to keep my mouth in check, Richard accidentally kicked his bike three times. That might have been my fault for not walking straight. I should straighten my posture a bit.

Wait—straightening up exactly what part, again? And how should I do that? Would tensing my abs work? I wasn't sure, so I just decided to walk with my whole body tensed. Before long, my right hand and right foot swung forward at the same time, and I started freaking out a bit. Just be normal. *Just walk normal.*

"...You're easy to read."

"Huh? What's that mean?"

"Nothing at all."

"The feeling is mutual," he added hastily.

He went on to smack his leg into the bike's pedal another six or seven times until we arrived at the villa. Odd behavior for a man who seemed fundamentally incompatible with the word "clumsy," but I guess everyone had days like that sometimes.

"Welcome home! Oh my, Seigi was with you? Did Seigi go to the library, too?"

A beautiful dragonfly came out to greet us when we arrived.

She wore four large wings on her back and a blue knee-length dress. Her hair was tied up tightly into a bun. It looked like a real stage costume—it was definitely too elaborate to be a Halloween costume. The wings, made of wire and cellophane, gleamed blue, the color shifting between greenish and greyish with the viewing angle. They fluttered as Catherine walked. She looked like a real fairy queen.

When I looked over at Richard, he had that look on his face again, like he had a splitting headache. "...What are you doing?"

"I'm preparing for the dragonfly! I was practicing in the garden. And I'm still going strong. Welcome back, Seigi, I wish you would've said something if you were going out. I was so worried. Aren't you a little late? Dinner isn't even started yet."

"Sorry, but there is salad in the fridge."

"Seigi."

Oh. Crap. He just told me not to apologize, too.

Richard stepped forward to stand before his mother in her cute costume and straightened up, though a thin wrinkle formed on his brow. "You know you haven't the slightest idea of what he's been through, and yet you insist on relentlessly putting our guest to work. He is neither your personal chef nor your driver."

"What's wrong, Richard? Why are you suddenly scolding me? Seigi, did something happen? Did the two of you get into a fight?"

"Listen to me. I am talking *to you.*"

"Please! Don't speak to me like that! It reminds me of speaking to that awful butler in the house in England. Those people hate everyone. They pretend to be so polite, all the while looking down their noses at me, like I'm nothing."

"That has absolutely nothing to do with this. I just want you to understand what I'm saying."

"Oh, but it does! The way you talk, it's like you're a king trying to control everyone and everything around you. I am not your subject. It isn't right. And neither is the way you treat Seigi."

"What are you trying to say?"

Catherine was on the verge of tears, but there was fire in her eyes, too. I was sure that if I tried to cut in now, I'd just be pushed away...but I had a bad feeling about what was to come. About what she was about to say.

"You're not mad at me because I'm treating Seigi inappropriately. You're mad at me because I'm treating Seigi the same way *you* treat him, and you can't stand to see that. The two of you don't even look like friends. You look like a king and his underling. He just says 'yes' to everything you say. That's not a friend. All you want is a Sancho Panza who will smile and nod, captivated by your beauty, and shower you with praise. If anyone's treating Seigi like a cook or a driver, it's you."

That was the moment I witnessed, up close, what it looked like for someone to silently snap. Everyone hit their breaking point in different ways, so maybe I was lucky to be able to tell when it happened to Richard. His usual aura of graceful beauty flipped in an instant, becoming something else entirely—an air of intense intimidation that made all your hair stand on end. Pretty people being terrifying when they're mad is a bit of a cliché, but this went so far beyond that. *This* was a whole other level. This was the divine wrath of a dragon.

Richard was boiling with the kind of anger that shouldn't be directed at a lone woman, and Catherine wasn't backing down—so I slipped between them. Thank you, karate training. I did have a decent idea of what defensive stance to take to deal with an opponent in this situation.

"Hold on."

"Release me."

"Wait! Just wait!"

"Seigi!"

"I know—just give it a moment. Count to twenty."

It was Jeffrey who'd taught me that you were much more likely to get someone to actually wait if you gave them a specific number to count to. He knew all sorts of anger management tricks. It was him I was thinking of as I turned to Catherine.

"I'm sorry, but would you amend what you just said?"

"...What do you mean?"

"Exactly what I said," I explained.

Catherine remained confused. She probably hadn't expected Richard to get angry with her or for me not to be on her side. Sorry to add insult to injury.

"I'm not his driver or his chef, I'm just trying to be a normal friend to him. I am a foreigner, so the way we interact might look a little odd, but I'm happy and comfortable with our dynamic, and I've never felt like he was taking advantage of me. If anything it's the reverse. He's done a lot to support me—an awful lot. You just don't see it."

"It's only right that he does. Everyone in his family has enough money to never work a day in their lives. But that doesn't mean you need to just accept his arrogant behavior. It's not a good thing."

"My words are failing me. I don't just mean financial support but intangible things, too—giving me his free time, his concern, and affection. I think I might die of embarrassment if I have to get more specific than that, so I hope you'll forgive me for not doing so—but at any rate, your 'king and underling' assessment is wrong. That's the truth. That's not the kind of relationship we have. Even if it doesn't look like that to you, you're wrong about this," I said, scratching the back of my head and smiling.

Catherine was decidedly not smiling. She looked like a child who was at a loss for what to do. She bit her lip, then made a noise like a displeased cat.

"...I'll be impressed if you can say that to me after you spend twenty years living like that!" she said, slipping past me and running out into the entry hall. A few moments later, I heard the sound of the car's engine. Before I had a chance to go after her, the car had taken off at high speed toward town. The beautiful, gem-like dragonfly wings lay discarded on the ground.

"I was too slow. This isn't good. Richard, do you have any idea where Catherine might have gone? Richard...Richard?"

Richard sat down in the dining room and covered his face with both hands. I was pretty sure this was the beautiful-boy-cooling-his-head pose, but weirdly, he wasn't moving. He was hunched forward, fingertips firmly gripping his hair, and if you listened very closely, you could hear him groaning softly.

"Are you okay?"

"...I want to take a panorama shot of this scene."

"Did you hit your head or something?! Sorry, I kind of pan-icked earlier."

"You're fine. I lost my temper. I sincerely apologize for the inconvenience."

"You sound like you've practiced that one a lot..."

"It's all in your head."

His movements were stiff and robotic as he made his way to the entrance and confirmed that the car that obviously wasn't there was, in fact, gone. "I wonder where she went," he asked out loud in a tone that reminded me of a train station announcement. Then he loudly cleared his throat and, for some reason, went crashing into the salon that I still hadn't finished cleaning.

I heard the sound of cushions getting the tar beaten out of them. Following that, the jeweler returned, looking like his usual self.

"Good lord, how embarrassing for both my mother and I to lose ourselves like this at the same time. I'll go looking for her. What a bother. Seems I still struggle to maintain my composure around her. I must have some pent-up anger left over after all. Seigi, you should stay here."

"You have spiderwebs in your hair."

"...Thanks."

"I'll go."

The beautiful man looked me right in the eye. He seemed to be okay—I could tell. He wasn't the type of person to drag out conflict longer than necessary, and anyway, I hadn't jumped in only because I was worried about him.

"Didn't you just say you lose your temper easily with her? Plus, I'm the one who actually made her run off. I need to apologize first. I don't think anything I said was wrong, but I think I went too far. Plus, we only have one bike."

"...Do I look *that* emotional?"

"You don't, and I have a lot of faith in you, too, but everyone's got their exceptions."

When I said that, Richard gestured like he was brushing spiderwebs from his hair again and cast his eyes down to the floor.

Could anyone blame him? There was only so much you could do against someone who knew everything about you—from the moment you were born, from even before you knew yourself. When you were suddenly sucked back into a mutually dependent dynamic like this—like you were adult and child again—emotional, defensive reactions like getting physical tended to win out over rational thought. That was how my seriously disgraceful rows with Hiromi had gone, anyway, if I were to describe them objectively. Richard and Catherine didn't seem that bad, but all parent-child fights had the possibility of going that way. It was an outcome best avoided, obviously, but you also couldn't really blame the people involved when things got like this.

"I'm borrowing the bike. Why don't you work on solving the riddle while you're waiting, great detective? I'll figure something out."

"That's not funny. I'm calling a taxi to head to the nearest rental car place. I've already made a reservation, so I just need to sign for it and pick it up, and then we'll have four wheels at our disposal. I should be back in thirty minutes. If she isn't back by then, I will start my own search for her. But until then, I'm counting on you." Richard looked at me intently.

I got it. You can trust me. I guess I'd said some pretty rash things, too. I mean, his own mother had driven off after an emotional outburst. I'm sure he was worried she could have gotten into an accident or something.

I read the instructions for the rental bike and made sure the lights worked. It was cold out, so I ran upstairs to grab a jacket from my luggage. When I got back, Richard was waiting for me by the front door. I guess he wanted to see me off.

"I'm gonna head to Aix first and check the places the two of us went to. If I can't find her, I'll go to the police."

"Thank you," Richard said, bowing his head deeply before a faint smile appeared on his lips, "We should have dinner together again somewhere, sometime soon."

It was a bit of a strange phrase to send someone off on, but I was happy to have the invitation. I told him I'd look forward to it and stepped on the pedals.

The Tour de France was like the French cycling version of the Hakone Ekiden. In English, you might translate it as "one lap around France." Cyclists, with their massive thighs, ride around all of France astride their bikes' slender wheels. There are teams and strategy and a lot of very passionate fans. If you mention France and cycling, the Tour de France is the first thing that will come to any sports fan's mind.

That evening, I felt like I was taking on the challenge of my very own solo tour.

I started off by heading to what looked like Aix's police station and showing them the picture of Catherine that Richard had given me to ask if they'd seen her, but they just asked me if I was her manager or something. I guess they thought I was an employee looking for an actress. They all had the wrong idea. When I explained that she was a relative of a friend—I don't think they would have believed me if I said she was his mother—who had run off after a disagreement and that I was looking for her, a woman police officer showed me some sympathy, saying "it happens." I hadn't memorized the villa's address, so I just gave them her name, asked them to tell her that Seigi and Richard were looking for her if they found her, and then headed back into town. Even the older part of the city had a lot of hills. If she was hiding out in some spot only locals knew about, I was totally screwed.

I got a map from the tourist information center and asked people to let me know if they'd seen her, all while planning a cycling route around the city. The map had the rather dramatic title, "The Former Capital of the Kingdom of Provence" but it did feel fitting for a former castle town. Maybe the difference in scale of castle towns between here and Japan came down to the size of the country, but I had to wonder if the influx of different groups of people had been so commonplace that the castle didn't really need to be able to withstand a siege.

I came out by the square fountain featuring three goddesses on Cours Mirabeau and hit the post office, city hall, and cathedral. I traced the northwestern edge of the city before turning around and returning to Cours Mirabeau, where I'd started, and looking around the supermarket we had gone to. It had easily been an hour, and I had struck out everywhere I tried. My only word from Richard had been a "disappointed" emoji. I guess she hadn't come home.

The stone-built town was beautiful in the twilight, though I didn't really have the time to enjoy it while on the hunt for someone. There were cafés all over in spots with good lighting, filled with both locals and tourists at leisure—such a quintessential European sight—but it did feel a little odd to see kids running around on roller skates and scooters. The old and the new mixed together, like it was only natural.

I wondered how Tokyo would look to my eyes now if I were to go back.

Oh no. I was getting tired, and my thoughts were starting to wander. I had to focus on finding Catherine. This went without saying, but she was a beautiful woman. So beautiful that you'd want to ask her how she was doing, even if you had no real reason to do so. Just thinking about the kind of people she might attract when alone and upset was scary. This wasn't a city with a lot of gang activity, and she was an adult who could speak fluent French, so I wanted to believe she would be fine...but unlikely things *did* happen.

I only got more worried once the sun had completely set. My shoes didn't seem like they were up to the task of cycling for hours, and the soles of my feet felt like they had tiny cuts all over them. It hurt a little. I had to hurry. But where to go? It was too dark to read the map without any light.

I decided to go somewhere where there was light, to start. People are attracted to light at times like this.

As I rode around like a madman, the glow of neon caught my eye. It was quite a way from the city center, but I guess it was some kind of attraction? If it was a place where it wouldn't be weird to park a car, it might count.

I went to check the parking lot. Not only was it dark, but there were a lot of cars here. I didn't think I stood much chance of picking out her little blue car from the rest, so I decided to check inside.

Through the glass doors, I heard a familiar "thunk" sound, followed by the sound of things going flying.

It was a bowling alley. I could see a sign with a logo featuring white pins and a yellow arm.

Maybe she went bowling to cheer herself up? It didn't seem that crazy. I didn't know her well enough to rule anything out. If Richard had been the one to run off like that, I was sure I could have found him by checking each and every notable dessert shop in the area, but with Catherine, I had no idea. There were a lot of young men at the bowling alley. Aix was home to a university with a famous law school, so there were probably a lot of students here.

Figuring I'd take a look around, I eventually left the space with the bowling lanes and found myself in a smaller room with crane games and racing games. There was one person there who caught my attention.

An old man in dirty overalls.

There was no doubt in my mind that he was the one who had chased after our car that afternoon. It looked like he was playing some kind of shooting game—at least, he was holding a gun and pulling the trigger. I'd seen something on the news about games being good to keep the mind sharp in old age—maybe he was a believer, too?

And should I try talking to him?

If he'd just thought Catherine was some kind of celebrity, he might have already forgotten what had happened that afternoon. But what if, just what if, he knew something that might give me a clue to work with? I felt a little bad for interrupting his game, but surely I could be forgiven if I kept it quick.

"Excuse me."

My voice didn't carry over the music playing in the background of the bowling alley and the sound from the game itself. The old man was facing the game screen, so I went around behind him to get his attention. He let out a "whoa" and jumped back. I must have startled him.

"Sorry, I..."

"You're Japanese, aren't you? How about a round?"

I was once again caught completely off guard. A round? I had no idea what he meant. I really wasn't up for a repeat of the painting thing.

I slowly and politely replied, "No, not that. I don't think you know me, but we may have run into each other this afternoon. Did you chase after my car?"

"Ohhh." The old man nodded, squeezed my shoulder, and smiled. "I remember. You were the one with Marie-Claude's daughter. You were driving."

"Marie-Claude's daughter? Do you mean Catherine?"

"Is that her name? She's just as beautiful as her mother. Wasn't she just here? Did you come to pick her up?"

"Huh?"

Well, I'd just hit the jackpot, if I did say so myself. The old man said he'd seen Catherine here. I thanked him and asked where exactly he'd seen her, but he seemed to think what I was saying was odd and wouldn't cooperate. Before I could explain that she had run away, he dragged me over to the game case facing his. It was the same kind of game he'd been playing, just directly across from his unit.

"Let's play. I always come here after the shop closes. Woulda rather been talking to the girl, but you'll do."

"Sorry, but I—"

I just said what I needed to exit the conversation and ran around the facility, but I didn't see anyone who even resembled her. Not in the bowling alley, not in the food court, not in the underwhelming arcade—that presence that was like a large flower was nowhere to be seen. It wouldn't have been strange for her to have a whole gallery of onlookers, but there was nothing of the sort.

I wondered if maybe the old man had just been mistaken. I checked one more time before returning to the old man, and he greeted me with a smile like he'd been waiting for me to come back. Crap. I feel like there's been a misunderstanding.

"This is a Japanese game. You're Japanese, right? I can tell from your eyes. We get a lot of Japanese customers. Pick up the light gun. You'll get the hang of it in no time. Don't worry."

The moment he said that, the old man put a coin into his machine. The game had begun. It looked like it was probably at least ten years old. Though based on my gaming experience, the screen seemed nice and there was a lot of information. I couldn't even follow the instructions on the case. The left-hand controller was kind of like a ball, functioning like a mouse, and the right hand one was like a toy gun with a cord attached. I guess that was the light gun he was talking about. At a glance it looked like the type of shooting game where you fire at the screen. I'd never played one before. And looking at the screen, it seemed like it involved shooting at people.

The figures presented as targets moved unsteadily behind obstacles. The old man peered out from his cabinet, pointed at me, and smiled.

I understood. This game let you engage in a virtual death match against the person across from you.

Was this really okay? Like, give me a break. This is an old man. I just wanted him to listen to me, I didn't want to do something disturbing like this. But while I was thinking, the game began, and in mere seconds I had become Swiss cheese, slaughtered all too abruptly by the old man. Agh. I had no idea how to dodge. I couldn't even tell if I was shooting or not. The soldier-looking character on the screen, who was taller than me, lay unmoving on the ground. Agh. Now if this were a racing game where you threw bananas and shells, I think I'd have had more of a chance.

The old man looked a little disappointed as he lamented, "and it's a Japanese game, too," under his breath.

Well, sorry. I'm truly sorry. Sure, Japan and Korea are big countries for video games, but that doesn't mean all Japanese and Korean people are good at games. The word *Retry?* hung on the screen as a countdown timer until the next coin started.

Should I try again? No way, right? I mean this was the last thing I should be doing. I needed to ask him about Catherine. Wasn't this the perfect time to end the game, too? But I felt bad. The old man sounded so happy when he encouraged me to give it another shot. He was *really* excited. So maybe I should give it another go? But I didn't think my skills were going to improve much in a second round. I'd just be instantly murdered a second time, wouldn't I? But—

Just as I was starting to lose my mind between the fatigue and creeping feelings of guilt, someone gently grabbed my hand. Well, it wasn't really my hand they were grabbing but the light gun.

A slender, angular hand.

"Are you really Japanese? Didn't you go to a university where the nearest Akihabara station was just one stop away? You didn't have any friends to go to the arcade with? Your performance was hilariously bad from back there, but maybe the view was better from your perspective."

A chill ran down my spine, and I let out a weird squeak.

When I turned around, I saw a young man who was a little shorter than me standing there. He had brown hair in an undercut and wore pink sneakers, distressed jeans, and a jacket embroidered with a phoenix. Where did you even find clothes like that?

His pop-star aura hadn't changed. And neither had his Japanese, as slippery as the icy surface of a frozen river, or the sharp gaze looking at me.

"Give it here."

"...Okay."

It was Vince.

He took the light gun from my hand and said something to the old man in French. The old man happily clapped his hands and inserted another coin. Another round on him. Was he really okay? The word *Ready* appeared on the screen.

I folded my arms and looked for signs of Catherine.

Or at least that was the idea, but—

The moment the word "start!" appeared on the screen, Vince and the old man began a sort of incomprehensible dance. From my perspective off to the side, they were engaged in some kind of life-or-death match that involved them both making intricate movements with their lightweight guns. They seemed evenly matched, too. While I'd had no idea what to do and died almost instantly, Vince had his opponent at his mercy. The old man kept shouting "oh ho!" and *"merde!"* He must've been enjoying himself. The game clearly wasn't state-of-the-art or anything, but maybe it was really good, even by the standards of a casual gamer?

Probably not. Vince's interests sure were broad.

They went into a third round with one win to Vince and one to the old man. Vince grumbled about "no off-screen reloads in this day and age" and how "terrible the lag" was. He was speaking Japanese, but I only understood half of what he was saying. Every so often, I'd hear people cheering "strike!" in the background as I watched the conclusion of the heated battle.

Vince won.

After the bloody game was over, the old man set his gun down, looking satisfied, and walked over to Vince with his arms wide. Vince looked a little uncomfortable as the old man pulled him into a hearty hug, getting the white powder on the belly of his overalls all over the phoenix embroidery.

"Thank you! I thought I'd never get a good match in this place, but tonight has been incredible. Plenty of people play fighting games, but fans of this stuff are practically an endangered species."

"Hm. Well if you're into FPS, you're probably better off playing online."

"Yeah right! I can't win with my crappy connection. And I don't wanna get flamed by elementary school kids for latency. Tell me, how did you move up and down like that?"

"You just point the gun down and you'll crouch."

"What the... I've been playing this damn thing for five years and I didn't know that."

Vince had somehow squirmed away, but now, the old man pulled him into another hug. Vince seemed to give up and hugged him back. I took the opportunity to ask my question.

"I'm sorry, did you say you saw Catherine earlier?"

"Oh, her? She was bowling. She got three strikes. Just like her mother. I'm too much of a coward to speak to someone as pretty as her."

I heard a *ka-thunk!* from the bowling alley behind me. Well, this was just perfect. But where was she now? I hung my head, and the old man looked confused.

"If you didn't come to get her, I think she already went home. That was like thirty minutes ago."

I hurried to check my phone. I had a missed call. And two texts. From Richard. They had just arrived two minutes ago.

"Catherine's back."

"Sun has set. Dangerous on the road. Hurry home."

He was writing in Japanese again. The way he wrote reminded me a bit of Meiji-era telegrams: concise and easy to understand. My legs still stung from pedaling so much. He was right though, I should get back as soon as possible.

But.

I glanced at Vince before firing off a quick reply.

"I'll be a bit late. You don't need to worry."

I put my phone back into my pocket. The old man looked at the two of us quizzically. Maybe it was unusual to him to see two Asians in one place.

"Are both of you friends of Marie-Claude's daughter?"

"No, um."

"I am an acquaintance of her son's. This fellow here knows her as well, but I do not."

"Wait, she isn't old enough to... Well, I guess I am eighty now. Blood sure is powerful stuff. She really looks just like her."

A thin film of tears formed in the old man's eyes. Maybe he had chased after the car because he was surprised to see a girl who looked just like someone he used to know. Maybe I hadn't needed to talk to him at all, but it turned out all right in the end. I thanked the man, apologized for taking up his time, and bowed.

Then, I turned to Vince. I tried to change my tone. Just like Richard would when he was in business mode.

"It has been far too long. Do you have a moment to chat?"

"Only if you keep it short. I'm starving."

"Then why don't we get something to eat here, so we can talk?"

"I can see it in your face that you have no intention of letting me leave. If you get too used to playing guard dog, you're going to have a rough time when you're on your own, Mr. Nakata."

"I am neither a guard dog nor a servant. I can't say the same about you, though."

"Ooh, aggressive aren't we? How about a duel?"

"Absolutely not. I'm just gonna die again anyway."

"Hmm."

Speaking in English was probably the wrong call. The old man slipped between us and asked us, with the aid of some hand gestures, if we were getting something to eat. Unfortunately, when Vince responded that we were and asked if he knew any good restaurants, the old man's face lit up just like it had when he realized I was Japanese.

"Let's go out to eat together now! I know a great place. They've got great wine and delicious truffles."

"Ooh, now that sounds just perfect. Let's do it, Mr. Nakata. Your treat."

I didn't know what to say. Ignoring the issue of who would be paying for now, I had been hoping to get Vince alone so I could interrogate him relentlessly. That was going to be difficult with a random third party in the mix...which was probably his strategy. I shouldn't let him get one over me. "Shouldn't" being the operative word there.

The old man already looked like a little kid impatiently waiting for an upcoming school trip as he started walking out of the bowling alley. He sounded excited as he urged us to follow. I'd already disappointed him once, I couldn't bear to do it again.

Oh well. I guess the three of us were having dinner together.

The old man had a light pickup truck in the parking lot. It was only thanks to that truck's headlights that I was able to notice that the bike had a flat tire. Vince pointed and laughed, saying I must have ridden it a little too hard. Even as he laughed, his expression hardly changed. I don't think I'd ever seen someone who could laugh with such a blank face before. It was kind of interesting, even if I wasn't on friendly enough terms with him to feel comfortable laughing with him.

After all, he was the person who slipped that piece of jewelry into my pocket on that cruise. I don't know what motivated it, but Richard wouldn't have gone through all that if Vince had just had the wherewithal to refuse to do it because it was immoral. Obviously I had suffered because of it too, but it was nothing compared to the emotional torment he went through.

The old man loaded my bike into the back of his truck and looked around, asking where my friend had gotten off to. That was when we heard an engine roar like a howling wolf.

It was a black motorcycle. Vince sat astride the bike, wearing a black leather motorcycle jacket over his now rather dusty embroidered one. He reminded me of Richard, in the sense that he knew exactly what clothes would look perfect on him...though all those clothes had to be fairly recent purchases. I wondered if he'd thrown out all his old clothes? The ones he wore back when he was still chubby and working for Richard.

"Where to?"

"You'll see when we get there. This is your first time in Provence, isn't it? I can tell from the way you're dressed. You should be wearing grubby shirts, sandals, and straw hats with a glass of wine in hand. It helps you forget the gloom of the big city."

"Ooh, I think I like that." Vince replied politely, not sounding remotely like he believed what he was saying, and the old man responded enthusiastically. I believed him when he said it wouldn't take thirty minutes and hopped into the passenger seat of his truck.

"Sorry about that earlier. I suck at games…"

"What are you talking about?! You saw my second match. That friend of yours is a blood-soaked angel. If I were Count Mirabeau, he'd be Saint-Just. You might be pitifully weak, but I always play alone, so you gave me the opportunity to actually beat someone. Thank you."

He looked like he was almost about to cry.

I took the opportunity to tell him about the misunderstanding with the neighbors that afternoon and how I ended up having to paint their house. I wanted to think of it as just a silly misunderstanding, but gradually the shock of it was hitting me— they believed I was less than simply because I was Asian and they were white. I was grateful to live in an era where international news was readily available, and I of course knew about racial discrimination from reporting and stuff, but having been the victim of it myself, I was astonished at how little hatred or malice was in their eyes—it just came naturally to them. I felt an unreasonable anger belatedly welling up within me. I couldn't talk about this with Richard. He would get even more angry on my behalf than I was myself. And I didn't want to make him worry any more than he already had.

The old man listened and nodded as this person he just met complained to him. He drove confidently even though it was dark. I couldn't help thinking that he might be more talented with a *real* gun than a light gun. But maybe that was just because of my visit to the Musée de la Chasse et de la Nature earlier.

"There are people like that, sure—but there's all *sorts* of people here. It's a pretty town, but not everyone's doing as well as appearances might make it seem. They're poor and struggling. And I don't mean poverty of the financial variety but poverty of the soul. That's the problem. Bad things happen everywhere, so everyone's inclined to think that they're the most unfortunate people in the world. That's what I mean by poverty of the soul. When you start thinking that way, hurting other people is easy. It's a hard pill to swallow, but it's true that everyone suffers. That's why they want someone to help them. But when they hurt people in pursuit of that, it causes even more suffering. It's awful."

"……"

I told him I couldn't stand that thought, and the old man smiled as if to try to cheer me up. It reminded me a bit of Catherine. Come to think of it, her smiles always had a reason behind them—to welcome someone, to encourage someone; it was always for someone else.

"You're going to go to lots of countries, aren't you? Promise me you'll become a strong man. Love is what matters. Make sure you carry lots of love with you. Despite everything, this is a country founded on love for one's fellow man. Those of us who can nourish our own hearts are strong. And people like that will never be poor."

"...I'll try my best."

"Good answer. Look! We're here!"

The truck came to a stop with a mighty *thunk*. Without my even realizing it, we had ended up on Cours Mirabeau. I guess there were no penalties for parking on the street.

The old man jauntily exited the car onto the cobblestone road. In front of me stood a tall plane tree and a restaurant. It had outside seating, but it was a little too chilly to eat outside, so the old man ushered me through the doors.

The inside of the restaurant was so lavish it seemed like a different world entirely. Mirrored walls and glass chandeliers, and a painting of a man in a clown costume made up of delicate brushstrokes.

"You know Cezanne? He's famous for painting apples. He used to come here a lot. And a bunch of other famous people like Picasso, Piaf, and Churchill. They're open late, so no need to worry. I'll take you home, too. Eat and drink to your heart's content. It's on me."

"I-I don't know if I—"

I flinched, because the restaurant looked expensive—but then Vince came in. He plunked down on a sofa in the back, raised a finger to call over a waiter, and ordered some sparkling water. I didn't understand how he could be so imposing, despite not being that much older than me. It was starting to make me feel an irrational sense of competitiveness. After all, it wasn't like I *didn't* have money in my wallet.

I decided to sit down across from Vince for the time being, flipping through the menu like him. I was relieved to discover that the prices weren't nearly as high as I'd imagined. I guess it *was* a café, not a place that serves elaborate multi-course meals. It seemed relatively casual, with à la carte ordering. It was just the place's interior that was over the top, with the pricing a welcome contrast.

Vince and I placed our respective orders for meat and fish with our waiter, and the old man added several things, along with some wine. I was reminded that France's drinking and driving laws were much looser than Japan's. Yet another cultural difference.

The restaurant seemed to be popular with the locals. Several customers who seemed familiar with the old man called out to him, saying "Pierre! Pierre!" I guess his name was Pierre.

"I run a *boulangerie*—a bakery. Marie-Claude was one of our regular customers during the summer. Men would line up at ten in the morning to get a look at her as she came in to buy bread."

"I guess she was really beautiful, too."

"Oh, but of course. She was so beautiful she'd make the goddesses of the fountain green with envy. Someone told me she was a model for some designer brand I've never heard of. She had a certain edge to her, too, as I imagine anyone *that* beautiful has to, and her little daughter was adorable and sweet enough for the both of them."

That must have been Catherine. I guess her father wasn't around? Pierre never mentioned him, at least. But the conversation was interrupted there.

A whole, grilled ocean fish. A piece of bone-in meat covered in a wine sauce and sprinkled with dill. Green tagliatelle in a lemon cream sauce. A salad with tomato and egg and Caesar dressing. Pâté. French fries. Sparkling water and a bottle of wine. Steam wafted off the packed table.

"Bon appétit!" the waiter sang and left the table.

We had a lot to talk about—but maybe we should eat first. We'd been given small plates for sharing, so I grabbed some of the fish, meat, and salad and brought a bite to my mouth with one of the slender forks.

Urgh.

"Ngh..."

"What's wrong, Mr. Nakata? You're making a very strange face."

I couldn't respond.

It was delicious. *Extremely* delicious. Something about the taste of high-quality protein just really hit when you were exhausted. But I couldn't stand the idea of smiling and eating in front of Vince, of all people. I didn't want to accidentally become friends with him. There might be a time for that in the future, but that time wasn't now.

He was Octavia's pawn. A willing tool of the person trying to torment Richard.

And yet, Aix food was delicious. I tried not to look at Vince as I smacked my lips with enjoyment. It was pretty simple for the price, but the flavors were solid and made me feel like mimicking them would improve my cooking a bit. Broadening my flavor horizons was always welcome.

"It's delicious, isn't it, Mr. Nakata? Mr. Nakata? Are you enjoying your food?"

"No comment."

"You sure are unsociable tonight. I'm so sorry, Pierre. He may be making some strange faces right now, but I assure you that at his core, he's a good and kind guy."

"I'd appreciate it if you could forego running commentary like we've been best buds for decades."

"Aw, you wound me. I'm so hurt!"

Vince's bland expression clearly communicated that he didn't actually feel that way in the slightest. He skillfully ate his pasta, staring at me all the while. He must've been hungry, too, because we were both scrambling to get our share of the meat and fish. Pierre, who couldn't stand to watch this, ended up ordering another plate. I felt bad, but it was *really* good.

Vince and Pierre had reached a pause in their conversation about video games (which was hard for an outsider like me to follow). Vince said he needed a moment and held up his phone before stepping outside. I guess he needed to take a call. But from who? Octavia? It might be a chance for me to make contact with her.

I tried to get up, pretending I was going to the bathroom. Pierre grabbed my arm.

"Listen. I got a letter."

"Huh?"

"I got a letter from Marie-Claude. It was probably twenty years ago now. I received it shortly before I heard she had passed away in Paris."

There went my opportunity to get up.

He explained that while the letter had opened with her heartfelt admiration for Pierre's delicious bread, he didn't know what to make of the way it ended.

"She wrote that there was something in that villa. 'There's something very dear to me there, but there's nothing I can do anymore,' she wrote. She was already very ill by then, so she probably couldn't retrieve it."

There was something very dear to her there, but she couldn't do anything about it? What did that mean? I asked Pierre, and he shrugged.

"I always figured she found something but was too scared to take it back home with her. France is a country littered with history, everywhere you look. Old buildings are a dime a dozen here, but that villa is especially old. In the time of Saint-Juste and Count Mirabeau, that house belonged to a wealthy aristocrat or farmer. But when the revolution came, people like that were despised. They basically had two options: go into exile with only the possessions they could carry or run for it without a penny to their names."

LE DEUXIÈME JOUR: DAY 2

Pierre added softly as he sipped his wine, "It wouldn't be strange to think they may have left something behind."

"I dunno about your friend, but you're staying in her villa, aren't you? Could you ask Marie-Claude's daughter something for me? Could you ask her if she's found the source of her mother's anxiety yet?"

I was speechless for a moment.

I thought back to last night. Richard's three big questions about the mystery. How could Catherine have us search for a treasure that she didn't hide herself? And then, who hid it?

Could it be...

"...Do you think Marie-Claude told anyone else about that?"

"Beats me. All I ever was to her was her baker in the summer. I don't even know what her family was like. She never said anything about only telling me, nor would she have any reason to, that I can see. But there never seemed to be anyone else at the summer house other than her and her daughter."

Apparently, he would drive his three-wheeled truck up to the villa to deliver bread once every three days, because she complained that it was too hard to get up in the morning. He said it was an extremely quiet home, up on a hill that no one visited, which seemed at odds with how ostentatious Marie-Claude was.

Catherine's comment about finding talking to people exhausting rang in my ears.

"Do you still have that letter?"

"Of course I do. It still smells of her perfume, too."

I asked him if he'd be willing to let me show it to Catherine, and he said "of course" with a nod, explaining that that was the reason he had chased after our car in the first place. He promised to come by the villa tomorrow afternoon. I shook his hand without really thinking about it.

I was glad I'd talked to him. I felt like we might be able to make some progress now.

"Have you concluded negotiations for your petit France-Japan friendship treaty? What a champion of world peace you are, Mr. Nakata."

A certain someone seemed to have finished his phone call, as he was now teasing me in an oddly serious tone. I shot him an icy glare, but he was unbothered.

Once we had finished off the food on the table, and Pierre had sobered up enough, we concluded our dinner. Pierre moved to pay like it was only natural. I tried to go for the check, but he insisted it'd be putting all the men of Aix to shame if he let a young guest like me pay. A true gentleman.

The bill was paid, and I bid Pierre farewell until tomorrow. I waved until his little truck—driving completely straight, I might add—vanished into the night, before turning around. I thought he might have tried running away while my back was turned, but I guess not.

"...Finally, just the two of us."

"Oh, don't say such unsettling things. Are you going to try to shake me down?"

"No, but I do have a lot of questions. How did you know we would be here?"

"Huh? That's where you're starting?"

I wasn't talking about getting information from Octavia but the rough schedule of our summer stay in Aix. I mean, even I didn't know where I'd be going or what I'd be doing today when I woke up this morning. And yet, how did he show up at the bowling alley right when I got there?

Were there listening devices planted around the villa? Or had my phone been infected with a virus? That didn't seem likely. It was a burner that I got a sim for at the airport. Were we being watched? Regardless, any of those possibilities was disgusting.

Vince brazenly shot off some text on his phone before finally looking at me. He was smiling, but there was a hint of surprise on his face that betrayed his true emotions.

"You're as diligent and hardworking as ever. You're so Asian, it hurts. Are you sure your head isn't 80 percent full of Richard? The old man's taking advantage of you."

"That again? I wonder what Saul would have to say about that. He was your former employer, you know. He told me that he was never once late paying you."

"You just went and asked him? Huh, you really do do everything by the book."

"Also, you should amend that 80 percent figure. On this vacation it's been more like 97 percent. You got a problem with that?"

"I'm not a fan of unfunny jokes. Are you trying to do your best imitation of Mr. Jeffrey? I think you should give it a rest. He only gets away with it because he's obscenely rich and the potential payoff is worth the annoyance."

His mentioning Jeffrey made me recall all the information I'd just gotten in Paris.

"I heard all that from the horse's mouth. Including how you were working as his spy."

"Gee, thanks. I do think it might just be my calling. I am very good at keeping my feelings to myself."

"I'd like to see you say that in front of Richard."

"I think I could, but are you sure you wouldn't punch me if I did?"

"You'd be fine, wouldn't you? You must know some defensive stances from your Jeet Kune Do training."

"God, you're annoying. I thought I told you to stop talking like that."

"What you think of Richard, or whatever grudge you have against him is none of my business, but you don't get to take it out on me. If you have something to say, say it to him."

"I don't really have anything to say to him," Vince said curtly.

Fine. If he didn't have anything in particular to say, then I'd get right to the point.

"Why are you doing this?"

Why had he put the jewelry in my pocket? Why was he cooperating with Octavia? Why had he followed us all the way to Provence? All of it.

What was the point of it all? Was he getting something out of this? I didn't really think so. But then…

What was he trying to *accomplish*?

Vince gave me a blank look. Old men, apparently unbothered by the cold, occupied the café's outdoor seating area and discussed soccer. It reminded me of the pubs back in Japan. Vince gently touched the trunk of the plane tree and smiled faintly.

"I don't think you would understand, even if I explained it to you now."

"I don't really care what you think or don't. I just want to end this charade as soon as possible."

"How about I repeat the advice I gave you earlier? I told you not to get too infatuated with that man. It seems you didn't listen in the slightest."

"Don't get too infatuated with him?"

Was this about the same nonsense he'd told me earlier? About how it was "safer" to hate Richard? I ranked the importance of his words right around the same level as separating recycling from trash, but the fact that I'd remembered them so easily probably meant the unpleasant feelings they roused were still lingering in my heart.

"I've had quite enough of that from you. Worrying about a friend isn't 'being infatuated' with them."

"A 'friend,' huh? Wow, you really do run hot. Total opposite to me."

"Are you sure you should be wasting time like this? Isn't your wife worried about you?"

There were two surprising things about the old photo of Vince that Richard had shown me. The first was his physique and the second his adorable wife. Richard said that they were married. It was hard to imagine him bringing someone he loved along on these stalker trips. So what was she doing now?

Vince didn't seem particularly surprised. He just muttered, "So *he* told you about that?"

I couldn't help but bristle whenever I heard him allude to Richard in that tone. *If you want the right to talk about him like that, you should have made the effort to maintain your relationship.*

But maybe they never had much of a relationship to begin with? If he had to take Jeffrey's offer so he could afford medical treatment for a family member, and if that was why he'd passed on information about Richard, then maybe their relationship had never progressed far enough along the path to "friendship."

Vince seemed to notice something about my gaze, because one side of his face twisted into a smile. I could tell it wasn't a smile of pleasure.

"My reasons are my business. Judge me all you like. But there are some things I can't compromise on."

"Like what?"

Vince didn't respond. I was getting nowhere.

"Could you tell me a little more about what your reasons are exactly? Maybe I can help you."

"If there's someone who's trying to make the two of you suffer and I'm working with them, what makes you think I'm going to explain anything to you? The answer is no."

Maybe it had something to do with the Swiss girl. She had been cheering for Richard and Deborah to get married, and she couldn't forgive Richard, or the two cousins of his who forced them to break up. But what was her end goal? Why was she doing this? If she just wanted to make them suffer, the whole thing with the cruise and this treasure hunt seemed like a really roundabout way of doing so.

Why would she be doing this? Maybe there was a reason she *had* to. But what objective did she have other than torturing Richard and his cousins? What other reason could there be?

Vince just gazed out at Aix without saying anything for a bit, then pointed to one end of Cours Mirabeau, like he'd just remembered something. He was pointing west. What was that supposed to mean?

"If you bike about an hour that way you'll come to a town called Arles."

"What?"

"There's a famous café there, too. It was frequented by a certain painter, and it has these atrocious yellow walls. It's still in business."

"What?"

"The painter who was so fond of that café greatly revered another talented painter. They became so close that they even lived together for a time, but ultimately the painter sliced off his own left ear, ending their relationship, and that was that. It's a famous story. Surely you're familiar."

A man who cut off his own ear. Even I knew that one. I had read in one of those tourist brochures that the south of France was loved by the impressionists, but I guess this was also the area where Van Gogh and Gauguin stayed. Gogh had cut off his ear in a bout of madness.

It's not like I didn't know what he was trying to insinuate with that. But he was completely off base.

"You know, now that you mention it, I think I know what you mean. That painter of yours sounds like he was rather aggressive, but that's about it for similarities. I don't think you have anything to worry about. I am Japanese, not French, after all. If I ever get so angry I can't contain myself, I'll cut open my stomach rather than slice off an ear."

Vince replied with a loud click of the tongue. What? He'd ignored all my attempts at provocation so far, so why was this getting to him? He turned away, as if in annoyance, then looked back at me with hate in his eyes.

"I don't care what she says, I'm never going to like this side of you."

She? Octavia maybe? What did she say about me? Before I got the chance to ask, Vince combed his fingers through his hair and started walking toward his motorcycle. *Wait. I'm not done talking to you yet.*

"You can just wait there. Your ride will probably be here soon."

"My ride?"

"Did you not notice? That FPS-obsessed old man drove off with your bike in the back of his truck. Unless you were planning to walk all the way back."

"Huh? Oh, oh no!"

"I'm gonna skedaddle before I cause problems. I'm not staying in Aix, so you're wasting your time if you try to follow me."

Vince popped on his full-face helmet, zipped his motorcycle jacket all the way up to his throat, and melted into the darkness like a black horse. He wouldn't have waited, even if I asked.

I hated how emotional I was getting, but I couldn't stifle my anger.

"Do you enjoy wasting your life trying to ruin other people's lives? Because I'm not enjoying it!"

"I'm not, either. But it does make me feel better," he murmured as he kickstarted his bike. With a muffled roar, the bike vanished.

In its place was a little blue car, running down the long stretch of road. Richard was driving, with Catherine in the passenger seat. Why were they together? Where was I gonna fit? Upon closer inspection, it looked like the stuff in the back seat was gone. I guess it might be possible, with some effort, to wedge another person in there.

"...I found you."

"Oh, Seigi, thank goodness. It was so late, and you still weren't home. Richard and I were so worried! Are you okay? You're not hurt, are you?"

"I'm fine. But I may have lost the rental bike... I do know where it is though..."

"That's not what you need to be worrying about right now. Did you eat at that café? What a relief. I don't know what I would have done if you had been hungry and in distress."

"We brought lots of sweets with us. The thought of you hungry and crying was too much to bear. Seigi, I'm so sorry. I should have given you my phone number, too. I'm so glad we found you. Even Richard was on the verge of tears."

"I believe you're speaking about yourself, Catherine."

"Oh, I wasn't on the *verge* of tears, I was crying. I'm no good at holding back tears."

I apologized over and over, and Richard kept telling me not to apologize. He just stared daggers at Catherine, saying it was her fault anyway. Catherine, who was focused on me, didn't seem to get angry when he said that. This was entirely my fault for not keeping in contact, but maybe it could be our lucky break? That was probably too generous.

Catherine crawled into the back seat and insisted I take the front seat. I slipped into the car, whispering to Richard in the driver's seat.

"Richard, if you're here, does that mean—"

"He contacted me. What did you talk about?"

He didn't say his name, but I knew exactly who he was talking about.

I shook my head, thinking about Richard's former assistant.

"Nothing much really."

"...I see."

"Now let's go home! Richard and I had pizza, so you have nothing to worry about. Having pizza once in a while is delicious. As long as I don't break out tomorrow, it'll be perfect."

Neither of them seemed to have even considered just throwing the lamb I'd bought in the oven and eating that. I'd expected as much. I was relieved to hear they'd eaten…which reminded me. I had something to tell her.

"I am terribly sorry to have worried you, *madame*. But I have made a discovery. I have something I need to tell you about this treasure hunt."

"Goodness, what a coincidence! Right, Richard?"

"Indeed," Richard nodded. I wondered what that meant.

The man in the driver's seat looked over at me and smiled faintly.

"I wasn't just waiting for you to come home, after all."

"Does that mean—"

"But first, seat belt," his slender finger pointed at my waist. Oops.

Richard added that we would talk when we got home and removed his foot from the brake. Catherine hummed happily, leaning out of the window and sighing about how beautiful the starry sky was tonight. Starry night. That was the title of a painting. One by the painter who had painted that yellow café.

It was just a coincidence, of course—but it suddenly occurred to me that the painter who burned himself out in his dedication to the fire of art was also named "Vincent."

Le Troisième Jour:
Day 3

THE CASE FILES
~ OF ~
JEWELER
RICHARD

IT WAS THE MORNING of my third day in Provence, and the birds were chirping enthusiastically. I hadn't had time to clean any of the other rooms, leaving me sharing a room with Richard for another night, but I was too tired to even care if the other bed was occupied by a person or a monster. I fell asleep almost immediately after we made it home.

When I woke at eight, the neighboring bed had already been neatly made. I quietly made my way downstairs, and sure enough, Richard was in the dining room. He was wearing a loose shirt and pale brown pants—a familiar outfit by now, though upon closer inspection, both pieces were different from what he had on yesterday. The god who dwelt in the details of his beautiful face was looking as divine as ever. That said, his face might have been a little redder than usual. Maybe he got sunburned?

"Good morning. When you're ready, we can discuss what we didn't have the opportunity to last night."

There we go.

I took a shower and had some of Richard's expertly made royal milk tea, a hard piece of bread, and some slices of tomato. Then, I stood next to Richard and looked down at what he was examining.

It was the solitaire board, with every slot filled.

There were marbles of all colors—quartz, blue, green. It was a grand spectacle in its completed form. The grey, pale green, and light pink stones didn't exactly have the poppy color of ruby, sapphire, and emerald, and they weren't remotely translucent. Most of them were what we'd call "semi-precious stones." They were much cheaper than precious stones like diamonds, selling for far more affordable prices. Sometimes, unexpected demand made prices shoot up, like with carnelian or green chalcedony— but those were typically more targeted at collectors.

Seeing all the round stones neatly lined up like that made me think of the numerous blades of glass in the villa's yard, for some reason. Like a cadre of friendly young people, just begging to be played with. If you considered how minerals were formed, precious stones weren't that much older than the concept of the aristocracy—but you couldn't just *play* with stones that could be worth hundreds of thousands of yen per carat.

Then it hit me—this was a game board. Maybe I should have looked up how to play.

Naturally, all the pieces of paper had been collected, too. Thirty-two sheets, all lined up. At first, I didn't understand why they were arranged the way they were on the massive table. The text was aligned in all sorts of directions. I knew there had to be some reason for it, but what that reason was, I couldn't tell.

It wasn't until I looked down at the paper itself, rather than the words written on it, that I realized that they were all printed over some kind of map. Not on the *back* of a map but over it—and it didn't look like a printing error, either. The paper was old. Once the little slips of paper were carefully assembled like a jigsaw puzzle, a bigger image was formed.

It was a map. A familiar looking one—the floor plan of this house, with several partitions dividing up a rectangular box, and a big open space to the south. It seemed to include the yard, so maybe it was a plan of the entire estate.

There was one impossible-to-ignore point on the map. It seemed to be in the garden.

"A hidden map? Did the lines of poetry not mean anything?"

"I think they must mean something. They were written in a number of different codes. But they seem unrelated to the map, so we can discuss them later." Richard tapped the map with his finger. "Look here."

A real treasure map. I'd never seen one before. Would we find something if we dug in the marked spot?

Wait—I had to give him the information I'd learned first.

"I have something I didn't get to tell you yesterday, too. I met an old man who knew Catherine's mother. She was a beautiful woman named Marie-Claude. Apparently, he has a profound letter she sent him. He promised to bring it here this afternoon."

"Is that somehow connected to this treasure hunt?"

"Having seen this map, I have some confidence that it does."

I would have liked to tell Catherine about this, too, but she was asleep, so there wasn't much to be done there. I'd just have to go over it again with her later.

Just before her death, Marie-Claude had written a letter to an acquaintance in Aix. I explained that among the letter's mysterious contents had been a mention of the villa containing something very dear to her—something she couldn't do anything about. It had sparked my curiosity.

I asked Richard what he thought. He went silent for a while.

"...That settles it."

"Settles what?"

"The identity of this map's author: Marie-Claude."

Now that he mentioned it...I guess only someone who knew where the treasure was could have made a treasure map. Assuming there wasn't someone *else* who knew where it was, of course. But if there was someone else who knew the location of the treasure, surely they would have dug it up already? It didn't seem very likely.

What was really bugging me was the third question Richard had raised, earlier. How did *Octavia* know where Marie-Claude's treasure was? Were they related? I felt like Catherine would have at least mentioned if they were distant relatives. So if they weren't related, then how?

Professor Richard seemed to have picked up on why I had gone silent, but he didn't say another word. Was there a reason he wouldn't just answer my question?

"...I wonder if Octavia knows that Marie-Claude is the one who hid this treasure. Maybe she just got her hands on the map, somehow, and then she reached out to Catherine?"

"Of course she knows."

There wasn't an ounce of hesitation in Richard's voice. I guess he knew that for certain. How, though?

The beautiful man held up one finger, as if to ask me to wait a moment. He took all thirty-three of the marbles he'd found so quickly and poured them into an empty salad bowl, leaving the board empty. The game board was filled with little dimples that seemed perfect for eggs.

And then, with both pale hands, he cracked it in two.

"What the—you broke it!"

"Excuse you. This was made in two pieces. The base and the part where the marbles sit are two separate segments, joined together. I may have been a little too aggressive in separating them though."

"So you did break it..."

"I simply disassembled it with the method I had available to me. And between the two pieces..."

Were three pieces of paper, just like the ones the marbles were wrapped in. What on earth? Richard must have put them back inside once he'd found them.

They didn't seem to be part of the papers Catherine used to wrap the marbles when she hid them. And it wasn't poetry written on them, either. These pieces of paper were larger and packed with dense text. A letter?

"I've already taken photos of it. It's a very strange letter."

"Why did you go to the trouble of putting it back in there?"

"It might cause trouble if Catherine laid eyes on it at this stage."

So the letter had something to do with Catherine? I asked if it was okay for me to take a look, and Richard gave me a calmly encouraging look, probably telling me to read it if I could.

From what I could make out of the squiggly writing, it was in English. And judging from the signature at the end, which read "Marie-Claude," it was from Catherine's mother. The first line was addressed to, "Dear Comtesse." Comtesse? Was that a woman's name?

"I'm impressed you figured out that there was something in there."

"I had a hunch."

Huh? I looked up at Richard, who hesitated for a moment before announcing, in a tone that suggested it was unimportant, "I was fairly confident there was something in there once Catherine confirmed for me that this board was given to her by Octavia. Octavia and I used to pass notes to each other using little tricks like this...although we used letter boxes, not game boards."

Their usual correspondence was inspected, making it hard for them to be honest in their letters. So they'd come up with a workaround, Richard explained. The wooden box he would send her letters in had a double bottom where the *real* letter would be concealed.

I guess that meant the game board itself was a message from her to Richard? Was that really a thing? It wasn't what stood out to me most, however. Their correspondence was inspected?

"Um, I know this is going a bit off topic, but maybe you could answer this for me. Is Octavia a 'very motivated shut-in' who lives in Switzerland?"

"Did the walking, talking credit card tell you that?"

"If you mean Jeffrey, then yes."

Richard nodded. A very motivated and extremely wealthy shut-in whose written correspondence was inspected...and who was committing borderline crimes. Judging from that video message, it didn't seem like anyone around her was trying to get her to stop. What did it all mean? How did a seventeen-year-old girl end up like that?

"...Would you mind waiting a bit longer? I said I would never lie to you, but I think it would be better for both of you if I waited until the situation was clarified a little more."

"You mean for me and Octavia?"

Richard responded with silence. Got it. I guess I should just think of her as a troubled and somewhat annoying young lady. I was starting to have trouble viewing her that way, but if that would be better for Octavia, too, I would just have to believe him. I could look into her more on my own once this vacation was over...though I *had* at least searched her name online and found nothing that looked like it had anything to do with her. What would the next step even be? Going to Switzerland? That was too much ground to cover. I'd have to think of something else.

I nodded. Richard seemed ready to change the subject. He pointed at the letter from inside the board again.

"Note who it's addressed to. Can you read it?"

"It's to a Ms. Comtesse."

"Absolutely deplorable. *Comtesse* is French for 'countess.'"

Countess?

Richard continued as I stared blankly, dumbfounded. "Countess Leah. Leandra Claremont. The countess from Sri Lanka and my *other* grandmother. A letter from Marie-Claude to Countess Leah was hidden inside there. And as for the rest, well, you read it."

"S-sorry, I can't read it yet."

"……"

Richard raised an eyebrow and flashed a slightly cruel sneer. His beauty was terrifying. When your teacher smiled with such wicked beauty upon discovering new homework to assign you, it made even giving the wrong answers enjoyable. Maybe it was for the best that he wasn't actually a teacher.

"I see you still struggle to decipher cursive. Perhaps it's more than natural considering how many English speakers also struggle with it, but how delightful it is to have a new topic to explore."

"Don't worry, I know full well that you delight in assigning me homework. But that aside…"

I was surprised to learn that Richard's grandmothers had had a connection, but that wasn't the only thing I was curious about. What I really wanted to know was how Octavia had gotten her hands on a letter Marie-Claude had sent the countess.

"…Is Octavia somehow related to you?"

"I'm not sure I'd call her a relation. There certainly were connections between her family and the Claremont family in the past, but that was all high society maneuvering, not the sort of connection that would result in her coming into possession of my grandmother's letter."

Then how? I was about to press the topic when Richard raised a single finger. This was a different gesture from before. Silence. But why?

"By the way, would the beautiful lady eavesdropping over there mind showing herself? Life is far too short to spend it not gazing upon you."

"Goodness, what more could a mother want than to hear her son call her a beautiful lady?"

Catherine sauntered out, dressed impeccably once again. I guess she had paused on the stairs to listen in to our conversation.

"Good morning, Seigi. Good morning, *mon petit Richard*. I heard what you were talking about. You found the treasure, didn't you?! How wonderful! I can't believe you actually found it!"

Richard looked a little annoyed but calm. At this point, there was a massive line of questions that needed to be asked and he didn't have time to think about anything else.

"Catherine, I know it's rather impolite to pose a question like this to you first thing in the morning, but I hope you'll be willing to answer. Did you know that Marie-Claude had hidden a treasure somewhere in this estate?"

"No, I had no idea. Not until dear sweet Octavia contacted me. And I no longer owned this villa at the time, anyhow."

"How did Octavia request your cooperation in this, exactly? Did she ask you to 'entertain Richard' or something to that effect?"

"Oh, you sweet, innocent boy. You're going to get burned if you keep assuming girls are always kind and gentle. The details are just for us girls to know, so I can't tell you, but..." Catherine briefly turned her head toward me, smiling like a flower in full bloom, then turned back to her son. "It's a secret."

"...She wants something with Seigi? What on earth could he have to do with this?"

"Like I said, that's a secret. Oh, don't make that scary face. She never said anything bad."

"I understand. Then I would encourage you to please tell me the moment you feel so inclined."

Catherine smiled when Richard let the issue drop, looking a little disappointed, like a child whose game was interrupted. Her expression warmed, however, when she noticed the royal milk tea we were drinking.

"I'd like to try some. Is that caramel chocolate? I love sweets."

"I'm terribly sorry, but this beverage isn't suitable for people with lactose intolerance."

Richard explained that it was a kind of tea, but Catherine wasn't listening. But she wasn't just ignoring him, she was frozen with her eyes open wide. When the beautiful man raised an eyebrow and asked her what was wrong, her reaction lagged behind, too.

"I can't believe you remembered. We haven't seen each other in what? Ten years? How can you remember such a small detail about someone you haven't seen in such a long time?"

"It was nine years ago, actually. But no matter how many years it's been, I could never forget a single thing about you."

I couldn't understand the exact nature of the emotion flowing between them in that moment. Catherine looked ready to burst into tears, but Richard wasn't reacting at all. He wore his cool, collected, all-business expression, as if to say, "All right, on to the next topic." Still, I knew him well enough to know that he wasn't giving her that cold look because he enjoyed doing it. He was just very full of a certain feeling he wouldn't be able to suppress, otherwise.

Catherine gritted her teeth for a moment. Then, a faintly satisfied smile graced her full lips.

"Now you just have to find the treasure, right? Where is it? You should tell me, too. Also, would you mind letting me read that letter as well? It is from my mother, after all."

"With all due respect, I think we ought to save that for after we dig up this 'treasure.' There's nothing terribly significant in the letter, but certain parts of it are yet to be entirely clear in their meaning."

"You're so overbearing. Meanie. But fine. After all, I am your mother. When my child asks me to wait, I simply have to wait. Is that the treasure map? Let me see."

Catherine took up a position by the dining room table and let out a little cheer when she saw the pieces of paper Richard had arranged. She said that when she was hiding the marbles, she hadn't thought the paper she was wrapping them in was the map. She kept exclaiming "wonderful" in both English and French.

"Is this the villa's garden? So it's buried underground? Goodness."

"Maybe, maybe not. Do you remember any sort of cellar here?"

"Maybe the wine cellar? I think there's still one outside, but what about it?"

"There's something I'd like to check."

Richard already had his shoes on. He encouraged Catherine, who was wearing slippers, to put on more appropriate footwear before heading for the garden.

The garden really did have a peculiar power. As you moved into all that green, the air suddenly got thicker and felt different to breathe. And then there were the trees. The flood of sparkling green contrasting with the ashen trunks that all looked so sturdy. The only boring aspect of the whole area was the plain, rectangular pool.

The underground storage was a little shed made of stone in the corner of the yard. Inside, wine was chilling in a space dug about a meter and a half into the ground, reinforced with stone walls, just like Catherine had suggested. It was nice and cool to the touch, even though it wasn't a refrigerator. The technique must have been passed down through the ages.

Catherine grimaced, complaining of how it smelled of mildew. Beside her, Richard knelt on the floor and searched every corner of the small storage area. He seemed interested in the area where the wine crates were stored, and I hurried to help him when he went to lift one of the wooden boxes.

He was looking for something. But the spot marked on the treasure map was much farther away. And then...

The moment we lifted the box, the air began to move. Unbelievably musty air that smelled nothing like the air currently in the shed wafted up at us. Why? It didn't look like there were any holes in the wall.

Richard stared at the wall for a few seconds, before suddenly thrusting his hand between the gap in two stones and pulling it back out. The wall crumbled like it was nothing. What on earth was this man doing? I was about to stop him when I saw something that shocked me.

There was another wall behind it. At the foot of this other wall was a hole, big enough for a child to pass through.

"...I knew it."

"Goodness, what an awful hole. Is it broken? Is this why there are so many bugs in the villa? Oh my, maybe I should call a repairman."

It didn't look like damage to me. It was a round hole, but the opening was reinforced, and it was made of the same white stone that the old parts of Aix were built out of. It really didn't look like it was the result of wear and tear. Could this unimpressive storage space also be...

"Catherine, this is a secret escape route. The cellar is just camouflage. It's very likely that whoever owned this villa a hundred or two hundred years ago created it as an emergency exit just in case."

"Oh my! How romantic."

"So the map—"

"Don't spoil it. This path leads to the treasure, right? How exciting! But my word, it really is musty. Give me a moment, I'll get a handkerchief."

Catherine traipsed off back to the villa. Richard didn't wait for her to return. He held his cell phone in the hole and used the light to look around. It seemed to open up further beyond the entrance, so the light wasn't spreading very well.

"Was this mentioned in that letter, too?"

"Something to this effect at least. 'There's a secret place' it said. But if my suspicions are correct..."

"Do you need a shovel or something?"

"I think a bath towel would be more useful."

Got it. I grabbed a towel from the bathroom and came back. Catherine was still selecting handkerchiefs. Richard wrapped the towel around his arm, shoved it into the hole, and mercilessly destroyed the second wall. Was this really a good idea? We weren't going to get buried alive, right?

Despite my concerns, the wall collapsed with ease, increasing our field of view. It was a hollow space about a meter and a half tall. The entrance was designed to be small, so it wouldn't stand out so much, but it looked like you'd be able to walk hunched over once you were inside.

But...

About two meters in, the path just dead-ended at a fake-looking grey wall. It looked almost like some kind of bank vault. It was completely flat and seemed a lot newer than the surrounding walls. What was it?

"I thought so. It's the pool."

"Huh?"

"This villa didn't have a pool when I was a child. If I had to guess, whoever owned it after Marie-Claude may have added it, bringing in a premade pool shell and embedding it here."

A chill ran down my spine. Had the passage been unknowingly crushed? Did that mean...

"Do you think the treasure was destroyed? Goodness...how awful."

Catherine, rejoining us, listlessly stepped down the stairs. She handed me a handkerchief. It was blue with a yellow flower pattern, and it smelled like nice perfume. She gave Richard a white gauze one.

"Calm down." Richard very matter-of-factly explained that no contractor in their right mind would just drop a pool on top of an underground void. He had a point. There was a good chance that it had already caved in or otherwise been destroyed. Besides, it didn't make sense for a secret passage to not have an exit, and the spot marked on the treasure map was much closer to the edge of the yard than the pool. So...

"Let's search for the passage's exit. If we enter from there and head back in this direction, there's a good chance we'll find the treasure."

"...Richard, when did you get so smart?"

"Good question." Richard was playing dumb, a serious look on his face. I found it hard to believe anyone could even ask that question. I mean, this was Richard we were talking about. The peridot incident that happened when he was nine, alone, already made it obvious he was a very clever boy. And yet Catherine was genuinely astonished by her son's smarts. Was this just how parents were?

Deciding not to let it bother me, I raised my hand.

"How are we going to find the exit? Even if the cellar and the pool are connected in roughly a straight line, we can't be sure that it's straight all the way to the exit."

"Precisely. And that's where the map comes in."

Richard pulled up an image on his phone, which he'd been using as a flashlight until now. I couldn't be more thankful for the convenience of modern technology. It was an overhead shot of all thirty-two pieces of paper forming one whole map. In addition to the location of the treasure, there was a faint line marked on the map. Was that the secret passage across the yard?

The reduced scale was enough to give us a sense of the passage's rough direction and location. But we couldn't forget that we were in Provence, a land rich in nature. It was pretty much all grassland between the garden and the passage's exit. Could we make it through that?

Catherine looked a little exhausted as she stretched when she came out of the cellar.

"Sounds like quite the picnic excursion. What shall we pack for lunch?"

"Catherine, I'd like you to stand by back in the villa."

"Oh, but why?"

Richard gently pacified Catherine, telling her that we were expecting a visitor this afternoon. That was right—Pierre should be coming to deliver that letter. Someone had to stay behind in the villa. It had to be either the beautiful mother or son, and an investigation wouldn't get very far without its detective. That meant Catherine had to stay back.

"It's a very important role. It's the hostess's job to receive guests. Could you please wait for us?"

"Leave it to me! Hospitality is my specialty. And if he's an old acquaintance of my mother's, I'll give him the warmest of welcomes. I can't wait. I'm so sorry I can't go with you."

Richard nodded, telling her not to worry about it, and escorted her back to the villa. I waited until she was relaxing on the couch, enjoying her sparkling water, before I whispered to Richard.

"...Hey, are you sure about this?"

"Of course. This task isn't so difficult that Catherine can't handle it. I don't think we'll see a repeat of yesterday's disgraceful behavior."

"That's not what I meant."

His face really was red. It didn't look like sunburn, either. Was he a little feverish today or something?

I apologized and then grabbed his hand. Just as I thought, it was warm. I'd been a little surprised to see him take down the wall with that towel, but I guess he got a bit more daring when he wasn't feeling well? The impulses that usually kept his sense of reason in check must overflow, making him even more aggressive than he got when eating large quantities of sweets or giving me a one-on-one English lecture.

Richard stared blankly at me for a moment, but when he noticed the worried look on my face after I let go of his hand, he burst out laughing.

"Ridiculous. While I may be suffering from some lack of sleep from staying in a new place, there is nothing else wrong with me. Let's hurry up and get this done. Once this is over, you can go back to Sri Lanka, too."

"It's not like we have to rush. Let's have a nice vacation. Also, couldn't I go alone? Just to scout things out."

"I'm not trying to rush, but I'm not interested in wasting time, either. The weather forecast predicts rain this evening. We should head out once we have what we need. Preparation is key. Don't forget your backup charger."

"...Well, I suppose it's better than taking a walk in the rain."

"Exactly."

I guess this was inevitable. I wasn't trying to be Don Quixote's loyal attendant, but where Richard went, so did I. I couldn't stand the thought of him being alone on the off chance something happened.

Richard took an image of a map of the area surrounding the villa, which I assumed he'd gotten from the library, and overlaid it with the puzzle-piece treasure map in a graphics editing program to figure out the scale of things. I was concerned that the shape of the villa seemed a little off, but it was good enough to get a general distance and direction to head in. We'd be able to make it work.

With hats on our heads, sunglasses on our faces, handkerchiefs around our necks, and gloves and drinks in our backpacks,

Richard and I set out on our treasure hunting picnic. It was only a kilometer or two at most, but it was all off-road. Between the villa on the hill and the surrounding farmlands was a gently sloping expanse of wild grasslands. "Untrodden ground" seemed like the perfect way to describe this space, full of sturdy grasses and red flowers. We probably could have used some jungle adventure gear for this. I had to take care not to miss my footing.

Richard led the way, and we pushed on without talking much.

"Are you enjoying Provence?"

"Of course. You know, I've been wondering what those red flowers are called this whole time. The ones blooming here and there."

"*Coquelicot*. You probably know them as the common red poppy. They're a very French flower."

Richard would normally have called me pathetic and teased me for my lack of knowledge, but there wasn't even a hint of that in his voice. He really wasn't himself. And like, what was the code Octavia concealed in all that poetry, anyway? The fact that it was hidden made me all the more curious about it. But there was no point getting down about it. I should focus on the treasure.

"So that old man I talked to yesterday. He said that in the past, this villa was probably owned by some rich person who had to drop everything and run when the revolution came, so it wouldn't be weird if they left something behind. I wonder if there's anything to that?"

"If they really were famous aristocrats or wealthy merchants, their relatives would have come to claim the hidden treasure after the Restoration. The area surrounding the villa is a bit remote, but it's not entirely uninhabited. It is entirely possible that someone's gotten in there already. Don't get your hopes up too high."

"Well, sure. But what if it's like a big ruby or sapphire or something?"

Richard only responded to about a third of my questions. Even if it was just because he was concentrating on navigating the terrain, I was still worried. The man I knew was rarely reluctant to speak to me.

I kept asking him if he was sure we shouldn't turn back, but he ignored me every time. We kept on walking until we were drenched in sweat. We were going the right direction, probably walking directly over the secret passage. The exit should have been in sight soon. Even if the whole area was a wild field now.

"Hey, are you sure we—"

Before I could finish asking if he was sure we shouldn't head back, Richard stopped in his tracks.

There was something in the middle of the field. It looked like a hole. Maybe it was a dried up well? It looked old, and there was no bucket. It unsurprisingly didn't seem to be in use, either.

Did we strike pay dirt already?

I cautiously peered into the ring of stones. I could see the bottom, but it was very deep. And covered in spiderwebs. It was probably about two meters down.

I had expected more of a steep slope like an air raid shelter at worst, not a dead drop. How were we supposed to get down there?

"...We're going to need a rope or something. I don't think scaling that without any equipment is a good idea."

"I agree, but I believe 'scale' is not the appropriate word when going down..."

"I know, I know."

We had found it. The scenery wasn't all that unique, so just for my peace of mind, I took some photos of the area to hopefully make it easier to find it again.

I told Richard we should head back to the villa for now, and he plopped down on the ground. He said he was taking a break. His voice was hoarse. *Told you so.*

"Wait there. Or hold on, maybe you should head back? I'll figure something out."

"...This is pathetic."

"Remember me back in London. I collapsed from a cold, remember? Now we're even."

Just as I grabbed Richard's hand to help him up, the ground shook. Huh?

I felt a jolt, like someone was pulling me backward with all their might. A few seconds later, I think I lost consciousness.

I still had a "huh?" on my lips when, before I knew it, I was lying down. My sense of balance was all off. I should have been standing, but I was looking up at the sky. And it was so high and far away. And everything smelled like mildew.

Had I fallen into a hole? I decided to check my head and back first. I didn't seem to be injured. No blood, either.

"What? How?"

"...The ground around the exit must have been weakened. With the weight of two adult men suddenly placed on it, it's not terribly surprising that it collapsed."

"Oh no, you fell in, too?"

I looked to the side and saw Richard beside me. He was on the ground just like me, and didn't look injured, either. There was a massive hole above us, and the mouth of what had looked like a well a short distance ahead. I guess we had walked over a weak part of the ceiling and fallen down one floor. *Oh, come on.*

The stones lining the passage were slightly damp, and my back was cold from laying on them. The way the musty smell inevitably filled my nose when I breathed was intolerable. The ceiling was a little more than two meters above us, so I was sure that we should be able to figure something out.

"One of us could give the other a boost, so at least someone could get out of here. Come on, stand on my shoulders and go get some help."

"I might be willing to go for that plan if it were the other way around. You should be the one to get help."

"But my French is terrible, remember? Realistically, the person who would have an easier time getting help should be the one to go."

"I'm tired, so let me rest a while."

What the hell is this guy saying? Why does he wanna rest somewhere that could easily become our final resting place? I touched Richard's hand. It was even warmer than before. Not forcing him to stay behind in the villa was becoming one of the greatest regrets of my life.

While I was freaking out, Richard pulled out his phone. Once he confirmed that it had a working battery, he immediately began dialing. It was a very simple number. Emergency services. Richard was so calm and levelheaded even in times like this.

Richard spoke to the person on the other end in fluent but listless French. He was probably explaining that we were walking in the yard and suddenly fell into a hole, however hard to believe that might be. He gave his name as Richard de Vulpian, a name he rarely used, before hanging up and tossing his phone to me for some reason.

"I'm sleepy. You handle the rest."

I decided to interpret that "sleepy" as "exhausted." I remembered reading some internal affairs document about how in Japan, it took on average nine minutes from initial contact for emergency services to arrive. I wondered what that time lapse was in France.

"We should contact Catherine—"

"Emergency services will let her know when they arrive. I'm more afraid of calling her and having her end up down here with us."

I knew what he was getting at. I didn't want to think of how upset she'd be if she knew about our current predicament, but it didn't seem like letting emergency services show up out of the blue and tell her that her son contacted them because he'd fallen into a hole would have a much better outcome. I tried to suggest at least sending her a text, but Richard didn't even nod.

Who should you call in a situation like this anyway? I didn't have an answer. So I made a call on my phone, too, and politely handed Richard's back to him. Whether it would take ten minutes, thirty minutes, or even longer, our only real option was to sit here and stare at the sky.

Or not.

Richard lazily opened his mouth at almost the exact same moment it hit me. He shifted sluggishly, as if the dampness was bothering him, and leaned against the neat masonry. His throat was red. If people could die from worry, my life would be in serious danger.

"...Pathetic. Is this really any time for you to be observing me? If we ever want to explore this place, this might be our last chance. Aren't you worried that the people prioritizing safety may hinder our attempts to find the treasure later? If this entrance is filled in, finding the treasure will be impossible."

"I don't think this is the time for that. Are you sure we shouldn't be shouting for help? I guess no one would hear us out here. I wonder if there's some way we can get out. O-oh no, I'm starting to panic. I need to calm down."

"...I understand what Catherine was saying."

Huh?

Richard stared at me from where he sat against the wall. He fidgeted and let out a chuckle.

"The incident where she said I treated you like an underling and ran off bowling. When she came home, she did actually amend her comment. I 'treat you like a child' she said."

"Is this really what you want to be talking about now?"

"And do what instead? Panic with you? Settle down."

I kind of understood what she meant by that. She was talking about how he was overprotective and fussed over me too much, right? But that was just because Richard was an absurdly incredible person. He'd do the same for just about anyone.

"But Catherine is too focused on me; her observation of you has been quite lacking. Her observation doesn't just apply to me."

Richard looked at me, his face feverish. He didn't look like he was about to collapse at any moment, but walking would probably be a struggle for him. I pulled a drink from the backpack that I'd crushed beneath me in the fall and offered it to him. Richard thanked me and reached for it but didn't actually grab on to it.

"Why is it that you treat me like a child, too? You're welcome to dismiss this as silly nonsense, but sometimes when I look at you, I feel as though I have been nothing but a bad influence on you. You have learned just how to please me ages ago, but it is not as if looking at my smile is your only skill. Do you know that? You're quite unusual for a Japanese person—you've become proficient in English and other foreign languages, you are very skilled socially, you have keen powers of observation, you're deeply considerate of others, and more than anything you are still young. Why are you so attached to me? The world is a vast place and—"

"While I do love listening to you talk, I hope you can excuse me for a moment. I'm going to head off to find the treasure."

"...Is that so?"

"If this is something you really want to talk about, I promise I'll listen to every word of it later. But right now, I want you to get some rest."

THE CASE FILES OF JEWELER RICHARD

I told him to shout or call me if anything happened, and Richard replied with a cheerful "Will do!" in the same intonation that Catherine usually used. Man, was there some rule that said people had to start muttering nonsense when they weren't feeling well or something? I decided to take everything he'd just said with a grain of salt.

I used the flashlight mode on my phone to light my way and started down the tunnel. The path had a gentle upward incline with the walls, floor, and ceiling made up of surprisingly large stones. After a few meters, I couldn't see anything that I wasn't pointing my light at. All I could see was where I was walking. It really felt like a real treasure hunt.

"Hey, maybe I should sing. It might cheer you up, and you'll know if anything happens to me, too," I shouted. It echoed down the passage.

"Be my guest," I heard a quiet voice reply. At least, I was pretty sure I heard it.

I had to decide what to sing now. What would be a good choice? I kind of remembered the French song Catherine was always playing in the car. I could try just making up the lyrics for the parts I could remember. I did have the chorus down since, it was just *paroles, paroles* over and over. I wondered if it was really all in French and looked up the lyrics, but the pronunciation seemed a little off.

I remembered checking the map when we were walking above ground. We passed the point that I'm pretty sure was directly over the treasure about five minutes or so before we arrived at the well.

The paved path underground was night and day compared to walking through that wild field, so I figured I'd probably be there in about three minutes. Just enough time to sing the first part of the song.

When I thought I might have walked a little too far, I turned around and slowly backtracked, carefully shining my light on the walls, floor, and ceiling. Surely, I'd find the treasure if I kept doing this?

Still...I know Marie-Claude sent a letter about how she regretted losing her opportunity to collect the treasure, but why did she hide it somewhere so hard to reach in the first place? It would have been easier to access before the pool was put in, but still, I wished she'd considered how much trouble it would be for the next people who went looking for it.

The sturdily built stone path didn't change, no matter how far I went. I was glad that it was just one straight path. It'd be easy to get lost in here if there were branches.

Was there even really a treasure? And what kind of treasure was it? Was it in a bag? Or a box? Or buried in the ground? I didn't think so. These rocks didn't look like they could be moved very easily. And was it even here in the first place?

The place felt all the more oppressive in the faint darkness. Richard had told me not to get my hopes up too much. Even if it was underground, the place wasn't immune to the elements. An animal could have picked it up and run off with it, for all we knew. I felt bad for Richard and Catherine, but honestly, I was starting to think I was going to have to tell them, "There wasn't anything th—"

"Huh?"

I abruptly stopped singing the probably 80-percent-made-up song.

It looks like I wasn't going to have to say that after all.

There was a hollow by my feet on the right-hand wall. If this were Japan, it'd be the kind of space you'd expect to find a *dousojin*, but instead of a little stone statue, there was something else. A box. It was about thirty centimeters square, and I could vaguely make out the name of an alcohol and a year on it. 1969. If nothing else that confirmed that it couldn't have been left there earlier than that. Pierre said he'd gotten that letter about twenty years ago, so maybe this was it.

I gingerly picked it up. It wasn't piled high with so much dust that I'd be worried about what would happen if I blew it off, so I was pretty sure I could carry it back as is. It sounded like something was shifting around inside. It was a light rustling sound. Maybe it had been packed with old newspapers for cushioning or something. The lid was nailed in place, so it would take some effort to open. The whole thing felt almost too on the nose.

A smile naturally formed on my face. I found it. I'd been lowering my expectations, thinking it might not even exist, but here it was. How could I even express the joy I was feeling?

While I remained moved to silence, I suddenly heard a piercing voice from the other end of the passage. "Seigi! Did something happen? Answer me!"

Crap. I stopped singing, so he must've gotten worried. I had to say something. Something.

"I found it! And I'm fine! I found a box!"

I told him I'd be right there and to wait, but the sound of hurried footsteps covered up my voice. At first, I thought it was emergency services, but I was wrong. It was only one person.

I hurriedly ran back along the corridor. Was it Richard? I prayed that it wasn't. I didn't want to make him run in that condition.

Just as the area began to get a little brighter, someone appeared before me. Thankfully, it wasn't Richard.

Pink sneakers and a jacket with phoenix embroidery. I could clearly make out the shape of his shoes from a few meters away because of the reflective material. He was holding a massive flashlight at about waist height.

"...What are you doing? Or are you always like this?"

It was Vince.

He looked annoyed as he stared at me. Half-annoyed, half-outright angry, but not surprised in the least. While I was waffling about whether or not to contact Catherine, I remembered something. That a certain someone was definitely watching me, even if I didn't know how.

"If you keep getting mixed up in these grand adventures, sooner or later you're not going to come back."

"You got here faster than I expected. So you really were stalking me after all."

"I'm going to beat you up and bury you here."

He violently grabbed my arms and pulled them behind my back like a prison guard manhandling a prisoner. *I thought the hotel you were staying in wasn't in Aix?* I'd figured he was either using a listening device or watching me, but considering how fast he'd gotten here, it had to be the latter. Which worked out for me.

"What about Richard?"

"Already rescued. You really are an idiot. Didn't you even consider using a line or something before you came down here? Or do you just have dungeon explorer blood running through your veins? Do you see a dark underground passage and feel the urge to dive right in, regardless of your current level? Do you have a death wish?"

"We fell in by accident. But I'm glad to hear he's safe."

"Stop talking and listen up, chixian!"

What the hell was "chixian"? I didn't have an opportunity to ask. Vince grabbed me by the collar and forced my eyes downward.

"Don't get any more involved with him than you already are. He has too much baggage for you to carry. You're going to kill yourself trying."

"...Is that how you really feel, Vince?"

At first, I'd thought he was worried about Richard. I thought he was just another person, like me, who had been utterly charmed by him. But now I was sure I hadn't known the half of it.

"Thank you very much. Now I know what I have to do."

"Did I just feed your contrarian fire? Have you resolved to dedicate your entire life to *him*?"

"I want to talk to you more. I want to know what you're think-ing and why you're so concerned about me. Please, I want to know."

For all his talk about Richard this and Richard that, all his concern was focused on me. Was it just because he was helping Octavia with her revenge plot and couldn't stand to see an in-nocent person being dragged into it? Or did he have some other reason? There had to be a reason he was helping me, despite the hostility. It didn't make any sense. I wanted to have it explained in terms that even I could understand.

Even in the dim light, the apathetic look on Vince's face was obvious. He didn't say another word for the rest of the trip. The light was getting closer. Sitting in the well entrance was, if my eyes weren't playing tricks on me, the very same stepladder I'd used during the painting incident yesterday. When it was fully extended, it seemed like it could reach about two meters.

When I looked up out of the hole, I saw Richard and the two people who were painting with me yesterday. I guess he borrowed some hands in addition to the stepladder.

"You sure have been busy, Vince..."

"Don't get the wrong idea. *Madame* is the one who brought them along."

"Catherine did?"

"When I arrived at the villa in response to your call and ex-plained the situation, she hopped into her car like the wind and went to drag those two over to help, like some kind of demon. I only spoke to her briefly when I delivered the solitaire board, but she really is a woman of many faces. Actresses certainly are terrifying."

Despite his grumbling, Vince led me to the stepladder and pushed me up. The fresh air tasted delicious. I let out a sigh and something leapt at me.

Bright blue eyes and golden hair. Porcelain skin and glossy lips.

It was Catherine. Tears had gathered between her golden eyelashes. I had no way to resist her intense hug in the position I was in.

"Seigi! Thank goodness! I was so anxious about what could have happened to you when he showed up. I called emergency services and they told me they had already gotten a report, too. Why didn't you contact me? All I could imagine were such awful things. I'm so glad you're all right. I've been trying to figure out what to say to your mother this whole time. Thank you, Vincent. God bless you."

"Save it for someone else. God's done more than enough for me as it is. I'll let you handle the rest."

Vince tried to get out of there, leaving the two bewildered house flippers, Catherine, me, and Richard behind.

But someone called his name. Richard.

They probably hadn't seen each other since the cruise. There was no particular emotion on Vince's face as he looked at his rather ill-looking former boss.

"Is this what the beautiful Richard has been reduced to? You should be standing there like a statue carved from ice with your pretty little nose turned up. If you let your precious guard dog see you like this, he'll start howling. Hurry up and finish that energy drink and get better. And eat a balanced diet. Too much sugar is bad for you."

For a second, I felt like I was witnessing a strange illusion. For some reason I couldn't quite understand, the man in the pink sneakers who was lecturing Richard looked just like a man I knew very well: the twentysomething Asian man who looked back at me in the mirror every morning. Would that man become just like him in five years or so?

I was going to stop him but found myself staying silent. Vince smiled over his shoulder and walked off.

By the time emergency services finally arrived, he was nowhere to be seen in that grassy plain in Provence.

"Now, let's open it! Our troubled little prince is resting. He always falls right asleep when he has a fever. But sleep will make him better. He really hasn't changed at all since he was three years old."

Catherine and I stood, motionless, in front of the dirty box that sat in the middle of the dining room table. Richard had gone to bed on the second floor after we explained what had happened to the first responders, and they arranged to have the local government send someone out soon to inspect the area because it could pose a hazard. I went to bring him a cold compress, but he had reverted to blanket monster form, so I couldn't even see his face. I started pacing near the door because I couldn't tell if he was sleeping soundly or if he'd passed out, but I couldn't bring myself to lift the blanket.

That was when Catherine slipped right past me and checked for herself. She gently lifted one corner of the blanket, careful to not even stir the air. She turned to me and smiled—she looked exactly like a certain someone when he was feeling well—and said he was sleeping. What a relief. We should just let him sleep, then.

I was still worried, though. I started thinking about whether I should prepare a light meal for when he would wake up, or maybe go to the pharmacy to get energy drinks and some aspirin, and that got me thinking about other things we might need and how I should make a list.

While I fretted, Catherine had already found a hammer and was ready to go to town on the wooden box. I guess she couldn't relax until she saw what was inside. I could sympathize, even if it was a little extreme. I did want to see the box's contents, too, but even ignoring the fact that the person who did most of the work wasn't here, was it really okay for us to open it? And if there was some glittering gemstone or something like that inside, would I be able to ascertain its value? I, who still felt presumptuous calling myself a jeweler's apprentice and only started studying in Sri Lanka six months ago?

At least it was old enough that we wouldn't have to worry about it exploding. We should just open it. Yeah.

I politely took the hammer from Catherine and hid it some-where inconspicuous. I spread some scrap cloth on the table, set the box on top, and started prying the rusty nails out with a crowbar. I couldn't stop thinking about how it made that rustling sound every time I moved it.

Once I pulled the fourth nail out, the lid suddenly opened.

The box was stuffed full of leaves. I guess they were serving a similar purpose to old newspapers.

"Goodness...are those plane tree leaves? Or maybe these are a different kind of leaf. What wonderful cushioning they provide."

The leaves were basically mummified, with only a faint trace of yellow remaining. And in the middle of it all was nestled a single little box.

A jewelry box.

I exchanged a glance with Catherine, took off my gloves, and picked up the little box with my bare hands. The little gilded enamel box, which seemed made to sit in a woman's lap, was inlaid here with glittering pieces of mother of pearl. Lidded decorative boxes like this were called caskets, if I recall correctly. I had no idea when Marie-Claude had discovered it and hidden it again, but I was impressed by how beautiful it still was.

Catherine looked up at me when I handed her the box.

"Are you sure you don't mind if I open it? You're the one who found it."

"Sure, but this is something your mother wanted to retrieve but couldn't, right? Please, go ahead. I don't think it's dangerous."

"...Goodness, what if it turns out to be a jack-in-the-box or something and a doll leaps out at me?"

"Does that sound like something your mother would do?"

"Good question. If I'm being honest, I never knew her very well. I know she was a very talented model, but the industry isn't very kind to women with children. She doted on me like a doll when I was young, but she found fault with the way I spent money until the day she died. I was too scared to even call her 'mother.' I actually felt a sense of relief at the funeral."

She smiled as she spoke, but her cheeks were tense. I stood by, ready to catch her if she fainted as she opened the lid. She quietly said *merci* to me, readied herself, and flipped the lid open.

Inside the jewelry box, sitting on the dusty blue velvet was a single bracelet inlaid with cabochon stones. It was an extremely simple piece.

"Oh my...I know this bracelet."

"You do?"

"Of course. It was my mother's favorite piece of jewelry. It looks exactly the same, too. It's amazing. I wonder when the last time I saw it was. She wore it often, yes, especially when we stayed here. It was something she treasured because a dear friend had given it to her or something."

"...Do you mind if I pick it up?"

"Go right ahead," Catherine reassured.

I picked the bracelet up out of her hands as gently as possible. There were twenty stones, with golden metal links between them. The metal, the weight, and the texture of the stones all felt pleasant to the touch.

The rounded stones were probably things like quartz, agate, coral, and lapis lazuli. They were all in fairly good condition. A few scratches here and there, but that was to be expected with daily wear. The faceted stones had a remarkable sparkle to them. They seemed to be made to resemble diamonds, but I had little doubt that they were all fake.

Even if the quartz and agate were real, the coral, lapis, and diamond weren't. And the links were probably just plated. The bracelet was far too light. The design of linked round stones was cute, and would certainly look attractive on the arm of a beautiful woman, but—not to disparage it or anything—it was a piece of costume jewelry that you might be able to find at a random street stall just about anywhere in the world. The only value it likely had was of the sentimental variety.

So why did Marie-Claude go out of her way to hide this in that underground passage? And make a treasure map? Was she scammed into buying it for a high price in the past or something? That was hard to believe. Would someone who appeared in magazines that people in the countryside didn't even know the name of and regularly wore such high-priced clothes make a mistake like that?

"...You two sound like you're having fun."

Catherine and I both looked up at the same time.

Richard came down the stairs much like Catherine had that morning, dragging the hem of his nightgown behind him. It was hard to see him in such a wretched state...though how was it that, no matter what state this man was in, he possessed all the magnetism of the golden sun? Even sick, he was too beautiful by far.

He raked his fingers through his sleep tousled hair as his mother held out the bracelet toward him.

"Look! It's a memento of your grandma's! I can't believe it. I thought everything had been auctioned off."

Auctioned off?

I looked confused, and a misty-eyed Catherine explained it to me. As I'd heard before, her family, the de Vulpians, had very few assets to their name despite being nobility. Marie-Claude couldn't escape that fate, either. When she died in Paris, everything in her apartment was auctioned off. The villa had been mortgaged, too. Catherine tried her best to hold on to it at the time, but after the divorce, she was forced to give it up.

"If this bracelet had been in the Paris apartment or this villa, it would have been sold off. Mother must have anticipated that. Thank you, *maman*, I love you. I'm sure you're watching over me from heaven even now."

So that's what was going on. But she must've had a reason for going to such trouble to hide something with no real value?

Richard fished around in the pockets of his nightgown and pulled something out to hand to Catherine.

It was three sheets of paper folded in half. Oh, the letter from inside the solitaire board. He hadn't let Catherine read it, saying it would be better if she did so later.

Catherine snatched it from her hands and began reading the first page aloud.

"'*My dear countess, I would love to return what I borrowed from you, but my body is failing me. I curse my lot in life to be unable to repay your kindness. Enclosed is a map. Give it to the appropriate person at the appropriate time so they may come retrieve it...*' Goodness..."

Huh? She wanted to return something? And have someone retrieve it?

I was struggling to take in everything when I heard the cheer-ful sound of a car horn from in front of the house.

"Is anyone there? I came by earlier, but no one was home. I thought I'd try again."

I rushed out of the house. Just outside the gate was the little truck with the rental bike on the back. When the driver side door popped open, an old man in overalls hopped out. It was Pierre.

He cheerfully waved to me when he saw me. "Hello, my friend from the other side of the world. Seigi, right? I brought the letter."

"Thank you so much! You have perfect timing."

"Mind if I come in? Are you home alone?"

"Um, well."

"We just found the treasure."

As I stumbled over my words, Richard came up from behind me and spoke for me.

Richard, Pierre, and I took up seats around the large dining room table. We should probably have used the salon for this, but it was still pretty dirty and there were cleaning supplies piled up in one corner.

Catherine was still standing, having set the box on the table. She held the letters in her hand, and her posture was imposing.

She now had four letters.

The first three had been hidden in the solitaire board—exchanges between the countess and Marie-Claude, written in

English. The fourth letter, which Pierre had brought, was from Marie-Claude near the end of her life. It was written in French.

Catherine began to read them aloud. Starting with the first three.

"My dear countess, I would love to return what I borrowed from you, but my body is failing me. I curse my lot in life to be unable to repay your kindness. Enclosed is a map. Give it to the appropriate person at the appropriate time so they may come retrieve it. This is my dying wish. I hope you remain well. —Marie-Claude."

"My beloved Marie-Claude, that was a gift from me to you. Do you still have it? Do with it whatever you like. It does not belong to me anymore. It pains me not to be able to see my old friend. I pray for your recovery. —Leandra."

"Dear Leandra, it seems the end is near for me. Please look after my daughter. She has the kindness of a saint, at times, and the skill needed to brave the wilderness all on her own. I am very grateful for the jeweled gift of kindness you have given me. I hope that, if at all possible, my body can be buried in the summer garden. —Marie-Claude."

I guess she had written that one right before the end. Now for the fourth. Pierre's eyes were already red when Catherine began to read the letter he brought. He crumpled his cap in his hands. Catherine, in contrast, had completely maintained her composure. It was almost as if she were just an actress playing the role of "the woman who reads letters"—someone with no connection to the people in those letters.

"My dearest Pierre, are you well? Just thinking about your bread gives me strength, but it seems the end is near for me. It vexes me that I can no longer enjoy the weather in Provence, but such is life. I discovered something very valuable in that villa but was ultimately unable to give it to the person to whom it should belong. Perhaps someone will find it, someday, but it still pains me so. Thank you for all the wonderful memories. *Adieu*. —Marie-Claude."

After she finished reading, Catherine carefully folded the letter back up and returned it to Pierre. Pierre wiped his tears away with a handkerchief and thanked her. He mumbled as he gently caressed the dining table.

"Marie-Claude, they found it. I hope you can rest in peace now. So, what was this treasure?"

I shot Catherine a look. She showed Pierre the bracelet and his expression soured a bit. Did he remember it, too? The two of them began reminiscing about Marie-Claude in rapid-fire French. I couldn't participate with my elementary-level grasp of the language. If only I could ask Professor Richard's advice...

Actually, where *was* Richard? I didn't see him. He'd been in the chair next to me a moment ago. Where had he gone? Had he collapsed on the floor?

I looked around the dining room and found him, looking unkempt and hunched over the old wooden box, fishing around in the leaves. Did he think there was still something else in there?

"Richard, calm down. Let's do that outside. That's going to make a mess in here."

"I never met her myself, but I've heard that Marie-Claude was a clever woman. There's a good chance that she set a trap with a dummy treasure so that anyone looking to cause mischief would happily take the fake and leave."

"A trap?"

"This box is lined. And these leaves aren't real, they're made out of thin cloth. Did you notice that? A pile of leaves left in a place like that, even in a box, would have been devoured by insects by now. There would be nothing left."

You know, now that he mentioned it...

So was there some significance behind this big pile of artificial leaves?

The two French people finally started to pay attention to what Richard was up to. It almost looked like a workshop floor covered in sawdust. *At least help them clean it up...*

Richard continued to fish around in the box, then suddenly stopped. A bewildered expression crossed his face for just a moment, before he went completely emotionless again.

What? The other two shouldn't have been able to see his face, so why?

Richard started moving again before he said anything. He slowly turned to face me, seeming almost hesitant. He was holding something.

"Behold—I've found something beautiful."

It was...a leaf.

A golden leaf.

A leaf made of metal seemingly molded off a laurel leaf. The same kind I had added two of to the bouillabaisse as an herb: a bay leaf. It wasn't just a flat piece of metal either. It had all of the delicate curves of a real leaf along with every little vein. And it wasn't tarnished in the slightest. It looked almost like...no, not *almost* like. It *was* genuine, extremely high-purity gold.

I panicked. That had a much higher price tag than that piece of costume jewelry. It was tiny, only about two thumbs long, but definitely worth at least a hundred thousand yen. But I didn't know if Catherine knew that.

"Goodness, that was in there too? What a pretty leaf. What is that, gold? Look, Pierre."

"*Mon dieu*, perhaps this is what Marie-Claude was actually talking about."

"Perhaps," Richard added softly. But his expression didn't clear up. Was he really okay? If he was still suffering the effects of pushing himself too hard, he should probably go back to bed. I could bring him anything he needed.

I gazed at his beautiful face, thinking those thoughts. Richard smiled faintly, though he still looked listless. He had to know how much of a sucker I was for that face. He was probably trying to tell me I was being too much of a worrywart, but it was only natural that I'd be worried. Especially after all that stuff he said down in that hole, about how I was basically handicapping myself by being near him. It hadn't even come from Vince this time.

Catherine and Pierre were holding the piece of golden craftsmanship up to the light and remarking on how beautiful it was. For a second, I thought she might be talking about giving it to Pierre. He was someone Marie-Claude seemed to feel a deep sense of gratitude for. If this was all about holding on to memories, giving it to someone with a connection to her might be the best way to accomplish that.

But then she suddenly looked at me, smiled resolutely, and walked toward me.

"Seigi, hold out your hand."

"...Huh?"

"Like this?" I said, extending it as if to shake her hand. She turned my hand so my palm faced the ceiling and set the golden leaf on top of it. "I want you to have it. You came all this way and you mean so much to both me and my Richard. Unless I shouldn't, Richard?"

Why wasn't she asking *me* how I felt about it? Richard seemed astonished, too.

"...I see you still have a habit of giving people expensive things on a whim."

"But of course. Isn't that a good thing? You see, truly wonderful things shouldn't stay in one person's possession forever. What's wrong with giving them to someone you care about, while you still can? Seigi, as long as you're okay with it, I'd like you to have this. The bracelet is more than enough for me."

I hadn't expected this development. "But, um..."

I kept fumbling my words, and Richard wouldn't look at me.

Help, please! There was no way I could accept something like this. This was on a totally different level from being treated to dinner.

I tried my absolute best to appeal to common sense, suggesting there was a good chance this leaf might have been an important possession of her mother's, just like the bracelet, and she should take some more time deciding what to do with it, but Catherine stubbornly refused to budge. Last time, the gift had been a white sapphire. It really would be okay if the apple fell a little further from the tree when it came to this particular trait...

"...Do you mind if I say I'm only accepting it for now?"

"You really don't know when to give up, huh? I want you to have it. Is that so wrong?"

Catherine wrapped both of her hands around mine and gently leaned toward me. I casually took a step back, and she took a step and a half forward. Fine. I guess I had to give an answer immediately.

"O-okay. I gratefully accept. But if something happens—"

"Thank you, Seigi. You've made me very happy. Hold on to the memories we made this summer," she said, taking that last half step toward me and giving me a gentle kiss on the cheek. The feeling of her lips lingered on my skin. I felt myself trembling a bit. Was this a normal thing for French people to do? I was losing track of how many times I'd had this thought, but our cultures really were different.

"Now! We're having a party tonight. Pierre, you should invite your family. And anyone in the neighborhood who's free. I hope you won't mind, Richard. You seem to be feeling better now.

I actually found something wonderful upstairs. It starts with a V and ends with an N. Can you guess what it is?"

Richard waved his hand, as if to say he wasn't going to bother answering.

"That settles it!" Catherine sang, her voice going up half an octave.

A party. That's right, my half-finished preparations from yesterday were still sitting in the fridge. But what was this thing that started with a V and ended with an N?

"We'll have a garden party out in the yard at seven. And we'll open plenty of wine. I'm sure it will be great fun."

"Then we'll make it a farewell party. Seigi and I will have to excuse ourselves tomorrow."

"Goodness, that's so sudden." Catherine squirmed, but she didn't seem all that upset. I guess she'd just accepted that the two intrepid adventurers would be leaving once the treasure was found.

I said I'd help clean in an attempt to keep Richard from worrying, but Catherine told me she was going to hire people to take care of all that. Pierre said he couldn't stay long because he had to prepare for work tomorrow, but he would be dropping by at least. And with that, the party arrangements were settled. Was it really this easy for people who regularly held garden parties to just throw together an event?

"I can't wait," Catherine said, showering about 80 percent of Pierre's cheeks with kisses before he left. Of course this time he left the bike behind. The green leaves of the two trees growing next to the gate rustled as he drove away.

Was it really all right for me to accept the golden leaf?

I returned to the entry hall and gave Richard a mildly pleading look.

"Hey, Richard, so about this."

"If it's really going to bother you, I can hang on to it for you. I'm sure you're going to be helping Catherine prepare for her little 'party,' and it would be unwise to walk around with something like that while you're otherwise occupied."

He read me like a book. I *had* been thinking about helping with the cooking, at least. I took him up on the offer and held out the golden leaf to him, pinching it by the stem. Richard teasingly held out both hands and bowed slightly as he accepted the leaf. The beautiful man declared that he would be going back to bed and retreated upstairs.

I hoped he'd get some decent rest. I'd have to make him something to eat and bring it up later.

"Now, Seigi, we have much to do!"

"We sure do. I guess I'll get going on that lamb roast today then..."

"And I have to prepare the dragonfly. We need to set up the tables in the yard and put out the tablecloths, and—oh, yes, I found some fairy lights in storage earlier. Perfect for an evening party! You'll help me, won't you?"

"Sure..."

This was a battle against the clock. There were a ton of little things that needed to be done. And still, my heart felt lighter.

Catherine was wearing the bracelet made of fake stones on her gorgeous wrist. Every so often, she stroked it tenderly.

It was 7 p.m., and the party had finally begun. Five tables had been set up in the garden, strings of orange fairy lights hung between the trees, and Catherine had her dragonfly wings on. As for me—Richard had texted me, telling me not to do anything that might make people mistake people for waitstaff, so I'd donned a very formal outfit. But when Pierre showed up in his little truck with his sons carrying sandwiches and wine, all in a jovial mood, I decided not to sweat the small stuff.

The sandwiches were packed full of truffles. I asked Pierre if he was sure he wanted to give us something like that, and he responded with a very serious look on his face, "Do you think you can cut a truffle, bury it in the ground, and grow more truffles?" I figured that if showing too much restraint would be considered odd behavior, I should just gratefully accept it.

It was delicious. It filled my stomach and wiped away my exhaustion. Tomorrow was going to be a big travel day, too.

Pierre chatted with his sons and other elderly folks who seemed to remember Marie-Claude. The average age in the garden must've been over seventy. It was quite a sight to behold. Mind you, "average" was the key word here. Most of the elderly folks were over eighty, accompanied by their sons and daughters who were providing transportation. We didn't have enough chairs for everyone, so a number of people sat around the edge of the pool, enjoying their wine. I found myself marveling at the wonderful sight as I served my lamb roast. The red wine was a hit, so I was glad I'd taken Catherine's suggestion to buy as many extra bottles as my wallet allowed at the supermarket.

It was a little chilly, but it reminded me a bit of a summer festival at a shrine in Japan. Everyone was enjoying themselves, eating, and reminiscing about the past.

Marie-Claude had died in Paris. She must have had friends there. I didn't know if she got her wish to be buried in the summer garden, but to me, this felt like the greatest tribute we could possibly offer to a woman who had died several decades prior. Japanese and French sensibilities might be pretty different, but if I were in her place, a ceremony like this would make me very happy. What greater honor could there be than being the impetus to bring so many people joy for a little while?

I was fixing the fairy lights I'd frantically set up as the sun was setting, admiring the view of the party, when someone suddenly grabbed me by the shoulders and dragged me to the middle of the garden. It was Catherine. Richard was standing there like he had been waiting. He was wearing a black shirt—not a typical color for him—and carrying some kind of case. He had the aura of a musician. I'd music coming from the second floor while we were preparing for the party, so I had a pretty good idea of what was going on.

Catherine clinked the champagne glass she was holding with a spoon, attracting everyone's attention with the sharp, bell-like sound. She called everyone over in French. All right, I was going to have to put my listening skills to the test.

"This is my son, Richard, and next to him is his dear friend Seigi. They've come to visit for summer vacation. I'm honored to have the opportunity to introduce them to you all."

The party erupted in applause. I lowered my head and started thanking everyone, but Richard told me to stop and I hurriedly straightened back up. What was going to happen next?

Catherine and Richard exchanged a look, and Richard nodded.

"Richard, are you feeling better already? Can I count on you?"

"I'm keeping my promise. But only for one song."

"That's more than enough," Catherine said with a smile. This time she took me to the edge of the pool and sat me right in the center. The two older women beside me seemed to be enjoying themselves, which made me glad.

The spot gave me a good view of the middle of the garden. Catherine smiled at me. Richard, standing a little behind her, pulled the item that started with a "v" and ended with an "n" from the case.

It was a violin.

The mother and son synchronized their breathing and began their duet.

Richard provided the music while Catherine danced.

The gentle stream of violin music sounded vaguely familiar to me. It was one of the pieces that the college orchestral music club had performed when I helped attract customers to their butler café. It must've been a very famous piece. But the sound felt so much nicer to my ears than it had back then. This man really could do anything.

Catherine danced on tiptoe like a ballerina, still wearing her pumps, all across the garden. I would have thought the wings on her back would've gotten in the way, but they didn't hamper her at all. She moved almost as if she had been born with fairy wings. I guess this was the "dragonfly" she was so proud of. I'd been surprised the props were in the villa, but on closer inspection, it was cellophane coming off the ends of those wires. They didn't *look* homemade, but she'd certainly found those tools quickly when we were opening the box, so maybe Catherine had put all her effort into making them?

I decided it was probably better not to ask. The answer didn't really matter, after all. She would have told me about it herself if she had wanted me to know.

I *was* curious about the name of the song though. I politely asked one of Pierre's sons—one of the people there who could speak English—what it was when he walked by. He stroked his face with his hand and replied, *"Beau Romarin,"* before correcting himself to *"Schön Rosmarin."*

"That's the name of the song?" I asked, looking a little confused, and he corrected himself a third time. "Beautiful Rosemary." I had no idea what language was being translated to what anymore, but I was sure I could run a search for any of those names and find the song for sale online somewhere. I was definitely going to buy it, so I could listen to it when I was alone and remember this evening.

Catherine had become the queen of the dragonflies there in the damp evening air of the summer garden.

She got up on tiptoe and paused, striking a pose, shuffled her feet again, returned to the tips of her toes, and once again paused, raising her arms above her head. The way her wings' movement was delayed just a beat before stopping made her look like a beautiful living statue. When I'd first heard the story that just seeing her perform like this made a man want to marry her, I had a hard time believing it, but she certainly had enough magic to make that seem possible. More than enough, really.

She maintained the same smile she always used on me throughout the whole violin piece.

With the amber-colored violin pressed against his cheek, Richard moved the bow gracefully with his right hand, pressing on the strings with his left, adding a friendly flourish to the end of the song. While the mostly elderly crowd clapped for Catherine, my applause was for Richard. Richard responded to the applause by taking a bow. Even if you couldn't hear the voices going, "That's her grandson? He looks just like her," and so on, you could generally guess what people were saying. Richard ignored them and disappeared, peering into his phone again.

After the party was over and Pierre's grandkid, who was a staunch teetotaler, had finished taking all the old folks home, Catherine finally removed her wings. She looked very pleased with herself. The sink was piled high with plates and cutlery, leaving me struggling to accept that it was okay not to clean up.

"Good work tonight, Seigi. I haven't had such a delightful party in ages. You should get some good rest tonight."

"I hope you do, too, *madame*. You amazed me with how incredible you were. I didn't know you were a dancer."

"Oh, you flatter me. When I was a child, I dreamed of becoming the étoile of the opera house. That's the ballerina who dances front and center. But I wasn't ever all that good, so I shifted to acting. And it was a good choice—I love the sound of my own voice, and dancers don't talk. Oh, the solitaire board. I'll have to fix it."

"I'll do it."

"No, no. Cleanup can wait. You need to sleep. You have to catch the train at 10 a.m. tomorrow, don't you?"

She was right. We would head to Marseilles by car and catch the TGV to Paris from there. But I was going to spend a night in Paris to catch an early flight the next morning, so there was no need to rush. But Catherine ignored me when I explained and gently patted me on the shoulder.

I walked upstairs as quietly as possible and opened the door to the guest bedroom. It was really too little too late, but we had gotten another bedroom into shape today. Finally, our own rooms. But I had to collect my things first.

"...Are you up? I just came to grab my stuff."

"Go right ahead," a voice beckoned, and I stepped into the dimly lit room. Richard was still awake. He was sitting in bed looking at something in the meager lamplight. The glimmer that was as piercing as the midday sun made it obvious that it was gold.

Richard held up the leaf and called me over.

"Do you have a moment?"

"Only if your fever is down, you're not hurting anywhere, and you're healthy enough to have a concrete idea of what you want to eat tomorrow."

"Tomorrow, I'd like to eat a rustic tarte tatin. And canelé with extra honey would be nice, too. But if sweets are out, then I'd like duck confit over thinly sliced pain de campagne with a warm herbal tea."

Okay, a Richard who could talk about food with such a lively look on his face was a healthy Richard. I sat down on the other bed facing him, and Richard gave me the golden leaf again. He really could have just held on to it...

There was something about the leaf's perfect imperfection, which made it look more real than the real thing, that made me feel uncomfortable just holding it.

"I did a little research while I was resting and I'm fairly certain now."

"Certain of what?"

"Just to be safe, I have to ask, are you familiar with Napoleon?"

Of course I knew who Napoleon was. I was the same Seigi Nakata who knew enough French history to know who Count Mirabeau was now. He was a charismatic leader who came to power after the French Revolution, the star of the First French Empire, Emperor Napoleon. His wife, Josephine, was famed for her love of jewelry, and her influence laid the foundation for today's high end jewelry designers. I should mention that

I got most of this from the internet. I was curious about this Saint-Juste guy after the chat I had with Pierre at the arcade, so I looked him up. He was also involved in the French Revolution and was known to be a cruel yet very handsome man. Thank you, internet.

I replied that he was the Emperor of France, and Richard gave a nod that was about as good as a passing grade. He showed me an image on his phone. It was a painting. The same one I'd seen a massive print of in Charles de Gaulle.

It was an image of a coronation.

Napoleon was placing the empress's crown on his wife, Josephine. And Josephine was on her knees as she received the cro—wait a second.

"Notice anything?"

Richard slid his fingers over the screen, enlarging part of the image. He had zoomed in on not Josephine's head but Napoleon's. I guess he was already Emperor at this point, because he was wearing a crown. But it wasn't the kind of crown a little kid might draw. It had much more delicate workmanship—

That was right. In ancient Greece and Rome, the customary sign of political power was—

—wearing a crown of laurel.

And his was made of exquisite golden leaves.

"Huh?"

"The tale is rather old. After Napoleon's fall from power, his laurel crown was melted down. The gold itself would become the foundation of a new power's authority, but it's said that before the coronation, Napoleon had four golden leaves removed, claiming that the crown was too heavy."

"Wh-what happened to them?"

Richard silently opened something else on his phone. This time it was a famous English news site. The title was, "Golden Leaf from Napoleon's Coronation Crown Won at Auction." But the biggest text on the page wasn't the title. It was the amount of the winning bid.

A single leaf had gone for 625,000 euros.

It was clearly not the value of the gold itself, but the value of something worn by someone whose name is known the world over. That, and the historical significance of a piece made by a jewelry workshop that still existed to this day. That much, I could understand. I could make a decent guess at how much that was in yen by adding a couple of zeros to the end, but I really didn't want to do that. I mean, it would be a completely insane number. Way too scary to think about.

Especially with the thing right in front of my eyes.

"Ohhhhhh..."

"The four leaves, including the one that just sold at auction, are said to be managed by the workshop that created the original crown. But not only does the crown itself no longer exist, no one knows if those four are the only remaining leaves. At the current exchange rate, the final auction price is somewhere in the ballpark of eighty million yen, I believe."

"Ahhhhh..."

Was it? Was it really that? Really? He'd just said he was certain.

This was clearly—no, *absolutely*—not something that anyone would be giving me on a whim.

"What should we do? Actually, no, how did it even end up here in the first place?"

"The 'treasure' that Catherine's mother, Marie-Claude, wanted to return to the countess was likely not the bracelet but this leaf."

I finally came to my senses as his calm voice explained the situation. This was no time to be sitting around making weird noises. We still had a riddle to solve.

Where did the leaf come from, how did it end up in this villa, and how did it end up hidden in that secret underground passage? Was it originally a treasure that belonged to the Claremonts, Richard's father's family?

My curiosity was piqued. The beautiful man began by saying this would be a rather long explanation.

"I should start by explaining the connection between the de Vulpians and the Claremonts. While my parents, Catherine and Ashcroft, met by happenstance, it appears that Catherine was invited to the party where they met because of Marie-Claude's connection to Leah. The Claremont family regularly holds charity events, but they're typically limited to members of the family and close friends. The party Catherine was invited to was thrown for the family's very closest friends. Her putting her hidden talent on display was initially met with disapproval, except from the youngest son, who had a fondness for insects. He was quite taken with her. Perhaps, in a sense, Leah did fulfill the request Marie-Claude made in her final letter."

"Do you think they got married because Leah had pushed for it?"

"As far as that goes..." Richard trailed off and shrugged. His gesture seemed to be communicating less that he didn't know and more that he didn't really think so. He probably felt pretty confident that he knew his parents' personalities, and his face suggested they weren't the kind of people to be so easily influenced.

Got it. Let's continue.

Richard's paternal grandmother, Leah, had come to England from Sri Lanka during the war as a bride who wasn't particularly welcomed by anyone. She was a white woman born in the colony and raised in a church of some sort with her parents. Despite initial objections that she was unsuitable as a marriage partner, with no other heirs present and the threat of the line ending and their assets being seized, she was eventually welcomed by the family.

What awaited her and her husband, the new earl, was an endless parade of never-ending social obligations.

"So long as one belongs to human society, no one can exist completely free from social obligation. They quickly grew tired of life in England and, I'm told, withdrew to live a quiet life together birdwatching. However, that only lasted so long. The eighth Earl of Claremont had always rebelled against his father, and lacked his political talents to boot. What the Claremont family did have at its disposal, however, was money. As long as there is money, people will come. Their wealth attracted people like ants to sugar, and they had to deal with those people in the right way. Leah seemed prepared for this."

She was born and raised in Ratnapura, after all, and she had an eye for gemstones. While her accent might have been different from the people surrounding her, she could tell the origin and value of their precious gems—and whether or not they were real, too. This occasionally led her to solve a few mysteries surrounding those very stones.

The knowledge she acquired was her weapon to survive the British high society, where she had no support.

Her nickname, Leah, was sealed away, and she became Countess Leandra.

"...She sounds kinda like you."

"What makes you say that?"

"I mean you use your knowledge of facts and culture to beautifully explain the mysteries concealed in gemstones."

Wasn't that the perfect description of Richard when he was in Étranger in Ginza?

Richard sulked for a moment before going, "Well, you're welcome to your opinion," and pouring himself a cup of water from the glass pitcher to moisten his lips. I guess he was ready to continue.

And so Leah had grown famous as a "jewelry detective" of sorts. She wasn't just secretly tasked with appraising the value of quality stones, she was the backbone of her husband's fortune. Occasionally she'd buy stones of unknown provenance for bargain prices, and other times she would replace fake stones that would be a great embarrassment if discovered with similar real ones for the price of a favor. All in secret of course. In order to protect their assets, the British nobility passed on all of their family property only to the eldest son, so many families who were wealthy in the past remained wealthy today. Those people's dirty laundry was like top secret MI6 documents in terms of confidentiality.

But all people eventually died.

Leah's husband suffered from dementia, and she left this world a little before he did. It was a sad story. If only she had lived a little longer, maybe she could have laughed off that nightmarish inheritance debacle and ended it before it started.

As Richard continued speaking in the dim light, he wasn't just beautiful—he had a strange intensity to him, too. Like a painting that a painter had poured their soul into coming to life.

"I wouldn't describe Leah as a uniquely prolific letter writer, but she did keep in contact with people. It's only natural that those records would serve to keep her and her husband safe. Although, of course, any records pertaining to her secret dealings were stored securely in a safe."

In the course of cleaning due to certain recent circumstances, those very records were discovered in a secret room in the country villa where the couple had hidden themselves away. The servants who had known her habits were certain that they had to be somewhere in the house. They were so extensive that even reading through them was quite the task. So the Claremont family had someone they could trust take over reading their contents. Henry, maybe? Probably not. He had mostly recovered, but based on what Jeffrey had said, he likely wasn't well enough to work outside of his own domain.

Richard explained that those records contained evidence of underhanded dealings. Not just on the part of the people they were trading with but the family as well.

"You mean like selling off fake stones claiming they were real?"

"Or, for example, a transaction both parties agreed to, but any record of which could cause one of the parties significant harm."

Kind of like what the seventh earl had done, when he got their help to purchase a white sapphire in place of a diamond for the inheritance scheme.

And those records remained like a restless spirit even after the countess had passed.

I felt like I could kind of understand. Richard looked me in the eye and continued.

"I believe you have some sense of this from what that walking credit card told you, but Godfrey, the ninth Earl of Claremont, Jeffrey and Henry's father and the man who raised me, is terminal and currently receiving palliative care at home."

Ugh, not another character to add to the cast. Not that I could say that out loud—this was someone Richard was close to, after all. This was the first time I'd heard the name of the current earl, but in short, there was going to be a new earl soon. There were a lot of things set in stone about succession in the British nobility, so even if there was a confirmed heir, the title holder could not pass it during his lifetime. I'm sure Henry was getting impatient.

"Leandra was his mother. Having been made aware of the very human frauds she committed, Godfrey seems to be trying to set things right before he passes. I think it's safe to assume he's doing it for his son's future. Of course, he isn't in any condition to do any of this himself, so the servants of the Claremont family's butler's office are working together to make it happen. I should note, that a butler is not the same as a footman. You could think of him as a servant who is permitted to proactively make efforts to assist his employer and offer counsel, even if it may not be the most pleasant of sorts."

"So am I understanding this correctly? The servants of the butler's office read through the records of Leah's dealings, and are currently cleaning up after them to avoid putting the earl's descendants in a disadvantageous position?"

"Bravo. You're surprisingly sharp for someone who's just come from a party."

"Most of the alcohol was gone before I got to it. Everyone had a lot of fun."

Richard was only half listening to me as he got up and fished around in his bag. He pulled out a supple leather case that looked like it could be for a wristwatch and took something sparkling wrapped in cloth out from it.

It was a pendant, no the chain was too short for that, with a pink sapphire. I'd never seen a piece of jewelry quite like it before, but I wondered if it might be some kind of headpiece.

"It's a headpiece Leah lent to the late founder of Gargantua."

"Gargantua? That Gargantua?"

Richard nodded. The pink stone glimmered in the low light. It looked like padparadscha, but something about its sparkle seemed off. I didn't think my eyes were playing tricks on me.

"And that's a fake, too, isn't it?"

Richard nodded. I guess it was self-explanatory.

"The founder wanted this piece as a font of inspiration, and Leah lent it for a fee of three thousand pounds. But it was only worth a handful of pounds at most. It wouldn't be strange to consider that fraud."

"O-oh no."

"If someone who didn't know anything about the situation saw those papers, there's a good chance that's how they would interpret it. The secrets contained within those documents could also present a tax issue, and during the course of a succession, the government might send someone to go through all those troublesome documents. And if it's judged to be tax evasion, we could be hit with a very hefty fine."

Lord Godfrey was on his deathbed, and soon Henry's succession party would begin. Even if cleanup was underway, there wasn't much time left. Richard continued. It was roundabout, but I could tell that we were slowly approaching the heart of the matter. Just a little further. Just a little further and it felt like it would all open up.

He returned the fake pink sapphire to its case and drank some water before speaking again. If only I could make him tea like usual.

"I was sent on the Gargantua cruise under the pretense of a request from Lord Godfrey, via the butler's office. 'Circumstances demand that we request the return of a particular headpiece. We require cooperation, to that end. The specifics of the request will be confirmed with you on-site. Do whatever it takes to acquire the item.'"

So basically, Richard was issued a completely absurd order to just give the person in question whatever they wanted? And considering how indebted he probably felt to the man who essentially raised him, he couldn't easily refuse. I was still amazed that a member of Richard's own family could ask him to do such a thing when just the thought of it made *me* seethe with rage, but I guess that's just how it was.

Richard was a capable man. Surely, he could have gotten out of it if he'd wanted to. He would have known who was actually issuing him the order in question, even if the request came through what was essentially their secretary's office and only claimed to be from someone he felt deeply indebted to. Richard wasn't the kind to sell himself short, and I'd never want him to be.

And yet, Richard did not run away. I knew that, because I'd been on that ship. And I hadn't been invited by the butler's office or whatever but by Octavia, who had bought out Jeffrey's so-called "shadow handler." She harbored some sort of personal grudge against Richard and was executing an incomprehensible revenge plan. But was she the only one who would benefit from it?

I decided to try to think about it with the information Richard had just explained. In concrete terms, who was actually benefiting from all this? Wasn't it the butler's office, or whatever it was, with their goal of settling the family's past misdeeds in a positive way?

My eyes glimmered with excitement as I looked at Richard's beautiful face, and he flashed me a scolding smile.

"It's funny, isn't it? How is it that a young girl with more money than she could ever possibly need, and a group of servants trying to permanently bury the failings of the family they serve before an impending succession, have such similar goals?"

"...So what about the current situation? Are they trying to get the leaf back?"

"That's probably part of it," Richard said, swiftly doing something on his phone. This time, he showed me an email from Henry. It looked like Richard had tasked him with researching something for him. The email was written in concise bullet points, easy enough for me to understand.

Leandra's diary. October 1979. Marie-Claude de Vulpian. Model. Met visiting injured soldiers at a veteran's hospital. Bought a bracelet. 8,000 pounds. Entry ends with a triangle mark.

"Is this..."

"A record of Marie-Claude buying a bracelet from Leandra for a price of 8,000 pounds. But no such bracelet exists, nor does a record of a deposit of 8,000 pounds in my grandmother's secret ledgers."

Well, yeah. Was Marie-Claude ever that wealthy? I guess she could have had some incredible patron in the 70s or something, but I didn't really think that was the case.

"It appears to be one of Leah's little tricks. The triangle mark is proof of that. She would note fake transactions with that symbol. She had many upper-class 'friends,' so rumors of her jewel sales spread like wildfire. I'm sure you can imagine what solace gossip of the sort that brought people before the age of the internet."

"So, it was all to start a rumor that even though Marie-Claude, a model, didn't look particularly wealthy, she was actually super rich?"

"*Très bien*. Exactly."

"Could you say that one more time?"

Richard looked at me confused, but repeated his *très bien* for me, albeit with a little less enthusiasm. He was so cool. Especially the way he said *"très."* I loved the way Richard pronounced French. Wait, no, this was no time to be impressed by Richard. We needed to continue the conversation.

"Was there some point to spreading a rumor like that, though?"

"Of course there was. Even if she couldn't be overt about it, even the rumor of a purchase that large brought with it a certain amount of prestige. She would have already had Catherine at that point and seized at any opportunity to get in with a wealthier crowd. And we have enough records to prove that Leah wasn't particularly stingy when it came to helping women like her."

Well, that made that transaction make sense, but we still hadn't gotten to the main point. What of the golden leaf?

"Here's another of her records."

He showed me another email. *August 1983. Marie-Claude de Vulpian. "A memento."* This line ended with an X.

"Transactions with this mark seem to indicate people Leah transferred Claremont family property to on her own discretion.

We don't have the letters, but it's likely that Marie-Claude had already fallen ill by this point. We can assume that the transaction coincided with her no longer being able to work, so it might be best to think of it as a form of financial assistance."

"Couldn't she just send money normally? Wait. I think I asked something like that before."

"If you mean with respect to what happened about two and a half years ago, then yes I believe you did."

I think the question I'd asked back then was about the earl in England sending money to his son in Sri Lanka and why he had done it the way he did. I still remembered the answer: The only way to provide a substantial sum of financial assistance to a personal friend without attracting the ire of others was to secretly send a small item.

Like a gemstone for example. Or, perhaps, a leaf made of gold.

Who could blame them for taking such a troublesome route? Both Leah and Marie-Claude must've been desperate.

Earlier, Richard said that most of Napoleon's crown had been melted down. Part of the reason it was so popular to have gold jewelry remade was because melting it down and reusing the gold wasn't very difficult. It was hard to imagine being able to easily turn something with this much historical value into cash, though, so was Leah telling her to melt it down and use the gold?

I asked as much, and the beautiful man snorted.

"That's a very creative idea, but I think something else was going on. A method that wouldn't require completely destroying a priceless historical artifact."

"...Like what?"

"Like claiming that it had been discovered in the secret passageway of a villa that once belonged to an old noble family. You could simply plant the leaf on your own property and 'discover' it later, claiming you had no idea that such a treasure existed on the property—it's certainly not something that belongs there, after all. That way, no one could question the owner once it was made public."

Oh.

So basically, if you did what we'd tried to do on this vacation—or rather, what we actually did end up doing—the item would likely be considered a "found object" of sorts and not be taxed like a gift or inheritance. That was clever. And France was the perfect place for such a scheme. With all the chaos of the revolution, it really wouldn't be that odd for something to be discovered in this way. Even the people who lived in the area suggested as much.

But then why?

"...Why didn't Marie-Claude actually do it?"

"We don't have any records regarding that, but perhaps she simply got a bit sentimental about it? Or maybe she was so shocked at its value she was hesitant to sell it."

Either seemed reasonable. Regardless of how much Leah cared for Marie-Claude, it was an outrageous amount of money.

"This is just speculation. I don't think I need to tell you that the glamorous era Marie-Claude lived in was very difficult for a woman with a child to survive in. Much more so than it is now. The way she lived, even under those circumstances, is quite remarkable and magnificent. Even after she quit working as a model, she must've had a talent for self-restraint unlike the rest of the de Vulpian family, given that she managed to hold on to the villa. If I were in her position, having some 'insurance,' so to speak, might give me peace of mind."

You never knew when life was going to deal you a raw hand. You might be getting by for the time being, but know that hard times could be just around the corner. If you knew you had a treasure worth a great fortune, not unlike the magic hammer of Japanese folklore, available to you in a time of need...then, if nothing else, you could be safe in the knowledge that you'd never have to make a painful decision because you didn't have the money.

Marie-Claude must have felt that way. She'd held on to that powerful piece of insurance until the end of her life.

She must've had a good head on her shoulders. Something beyond your control can happen to anyone, at any time, and the desire to get rich quick exists within us all. It must have been very tempting to use her option of last resort...but maybe I had it backward. No matter how hard things got, she never ever reached for the ace she had up her sleeve.

I tried thinking about the tanzanite cuff links my stepfather, Mr. Nakata, had given me. One of the unique features of gem-stones is that they can be turned into cash in emergencies. But stones also carry memories. And the more valuable the item, the more sentimental value it might hold. I'd much rather never be in the sort of position where I needed to do such a thing, but if I were, *could* I do it? Could I part with them? That memento, that powerful proof of how much he cared about me?

Nothing is out of the question when you're poor. My grandma was proof of that. But, thankfully, I wasn't in that kind of situation. *Let's shelve that hypothetical for now.*

"...What if Marie-Claude had sent the treasure map that was hidden in those tiny pieces to Leah 'just in case'? She did say it was so someone could come retrieve it."

"That does seem very likely."

I guess it was just as the letter said. It had been given in secrecy to the Claremonts, too. It would have been real bad if the postal service had accidentally exposed its contents or the letter had met a watery grave in a transit accident or something. I was just glad it had been found.

"...She didn't have to return it. Couldn't she have found a way to give it to Catherine?"

"You mean give it to the daughter with the talent to brave the wilderness, knowing she'd likely give it away to someone else? Had I been Marie-Claude, I certainly wouldn't have done that. Catherine is the kind of person where the bigger the prize, the less she wants to keep it," Richard said as he showed me his phone again. "And this is the last part."

This time it was neither a painting nor a record. It was a photo. A professional one. It looked like an old color photo that was clearly from a women's fashion magazine. The kind of publication that both now and in the past featured attractive women wearing expensive clothing standing in fashionable places.

It was of a blonde woman with a pixie cut, looking standoffish. It looked like it had been taken in the fall. She was wearing loose pants and a tight high-neck sweater with a cap like a coal miner might wear on her head and a cigarette in her mouth. The backdrop looked like a park in Paris. Slender golden leaves fell from the sky above the model's head, like confetti during the finale of a play. She looked far less like Richard and Catherine than I'd expected. But she was definitely beautiful. In her strong-willed brow and her pale-colored eyes, I could see hints of the most beautiful person I knew of in the world. But it was in their words that the real resemblance lay.

There was an interview next to the photo. She must have been pretty famous. I didn't claim to know much about the industry, but models didn't usually talk, right?

The article, titled, "The Marie-Claude Way," was written in English. And there, in large letters, was what appeared to be a favorite saying of hers:

Love is the jewelry of life. You may be able to live without it, but having it is oh so wonderful.

France was said to be the country of love. How much resolve did it take for someone from such a country to say she could live without it? I couldn't know. But the fact that this was in Richard's inbox suggested that it was a magazine clipping Leah had kept. There was a year printed in the margin. 1969. Long before Leah and Marie-Claude's first "transaction" had taken place.

I felt something fall into place in my heart. I had thought it odd that Leah had gone to such dangerous lengths for someone who wasn't even family, but it wasn't odd at all.

She was a fan.

As someone struggling in difficult circumstances, I imagine those words provided great comfort.

I wondered if Marie-Claude, who had opened the first of those letters with the very formal "my dear countess," knew that. But really, what did it matter? Even if she didn't know that Leah had been a fan of hers, they both had warm feelings for each other. She may have shown it in a bit of a dangerous way, but I think that was another expression of "the jewelry of life."

I understood the strange connection Richard's two grand-mothers had had with each other. I decided to backtrack a bit.

I needed to know more about Octavia and the butler's office.

I probably had a bit of an intense look in my eye, because Richard set his phone down on the bed and looked at me.

"Richard, was the invitation to the villa—"

"All I could get from Catherine was that it was a joint project between her and Octavia. She doesn't appear to know anything beyond that. But the letters that came out of the solitaire board are something that only a certain group of people connected to the Claremont family are permitted to see. They're not something a young girl holed up in Switzerland could get her hands on alone. Which means there must have been some intention in releasing that information."

"So does that mean what you've been thinking is—"

Richard nodded. At this point we were basically just check-ing his work.

"This came up when we were discussing legal options as well.

There would be no point in just going after Octavia. Moreover, for Henry and Jeffrey it could end up being a roundabout attack on their own people."

Was the Claremont butler's office using Octavia or was she using them? Well, they were probably using each other.

I wished I could just tell them to stop. I was pretty sure there was no point in saying that sort of thing to someone letting their emotions drive them, but I wished I could at least say it to the butler's office. I'd like to tell Lord Godfrey on his deathbed to fire the lot of them for playing the part of loyal and innocent servants while dragging a seventeen-year-old girl into their attempts to settle old financial issues and commit borderline-illegal acts.

But it was Lord Godfrey's love for his children that was allowing them to act in the first place. And if he'd been discharged from the hospital to receive palliative care at home, that meant he had no chance of recovery. How much power did he really have? And who would let him do this?

Either path before us seemed rough.

"So who do you think plotted this treasure hunting excursion?"

"I think it was likely a joint effort just like the Gargantua cruise. The code Octavia sent was definitely targeted at me, but the treasure hunt itself was likely the butler's office's scheme. It's only logical that upon discovering that a leaf from Napoleon's coronation crown was missing from the Claremont family's hidden assets and that it may likely be in the French countryside they would want to retrieve it."

But they must have had the treasure map from the documents Leah left behind. Why did they have to go out of their way to send me and Richard for it? Couldn't they have dispatched one of their lowest-ranking servants, like an assistant to a butler in training or something, to retrieve it under the guise of someone coming out to do some civil engineering work? Wouldn't that have settled it? That's what would have made sense to me.

"And the rest of it was Octavia's orders?"

"I believe so. Additionally, there must be a reason for having sent me specifically. While it's hard to say that I have been living my life as such, I am technically someone within the earl's sphere. I'm grateful that they have enough faith in me to believe I wouldn't do anything to harm the family."

I felt half regretful and half grateful that he wasn't looking right at me when he said that. There was an unspoken anger in his voice as if to say, "Have you people forgotten what you've put me through?" At times like this, Richard's raw emotions showed on his face.

Richard leaned forward and hung his legs off the side of the bed to face me.

"As I mentioned back in Kandy, it seems I will be causing trouble for you for a while longer."

"I like the way your face looks now a lot more than it did when you said that to me before. Well, I guess I like both, but the way you look now is..."

"How do I look now?"

"Like a warrior."

After a moment, Richard smiled gently. The first adjective that came to mind was "ferocious" but that didn't really sound like praise. I was thinking like, lion, you know? The creature that both had a connection to his name and was the symbol of kings.

"If there's anything I can help you with, I will. And I'll do my own research into some things that have been on my mind. You can count on me."

"Understood. But promise me you won't forget one thing."

This must be why he'd sat up fully.

"Your job is to refine your eye as a jeweler's apprentice. And to prepare to return home in a year and a half and retake the civil service exam. Those two things. I feel like I am doing a terrible disservice to Mr. Nakata by wasting your time making you worry about me like this."

"Huh? Did you see my stepfather again? Have you been seeing him often?"

"He visits the shop in Ginza from time to time. He often says he wishes he could have visited when you were still working there. As for any other purchases...it seems his wife has stopped him on that front."

It felt a little weird to hear Hiromi called "his wife," but it made me happy to hear Richard talk about them. We texted and spoke over the phone regularly, but I hadn't seen them. My memories of Mr. Nakata telling me I was going away to hone my skills, and me replying with a cheerful "sure am!" were still pretty fresh. I wanted to be strong and not give him the impression that I might be feeling homesick.

"...Are you finding yourself longing for Japan yet?"

Richard's question was gentle. What he was really asking was whether I felt like I'd be comfortable walking in Tokyo's crowds again yet. Of course I thought I'd be okay, but thoughts and reality aren't always the same. But I had something I wanted to do more than anything now.

While in Sri Lanka, I'd been largely cut off from my friends and family in Japan. It felt like the very air I breathed was sending me the same message, over and over: You don't really need to be here. You weren't born here, you don't have any professional obligations that you absolutely have to accomplish, you don't need to be here at all.

It was the first time I had ever felt that way. Maybe it was just that, as someone who was born in Japan and went to school in Japan and had worked steadily at a part-time job to save up money, it was such an unfamiliar experience it felt almost like being launched out into space. Setting aside for a moment all the help I'd gotten from different people, I kept asking myself why I was even there, but the conclusion I came to for the time being was that it'd be no different were I in Japan instead.

I wasn't a farmer under a feudal lord, so I guess it's kind of weird to get hung up on the notion of the place you're *supposed* to be. Obviously, there was no place anyone was *supposed* to be. To look at it from another angle, I guess I was just surprised at how much I'd unconsciously internalized the idea that living and working in Japan was what I *should* be doing. Maybe it was just an issue of mindset.

You can go anywhere if you put your mind to it—like how Haruyoshi Shimomura dropped out of college and dove headfirst into learning the guitar. I'd learned from all sorts of people that there were a lot of paths you could explore in life, even if they came with their own risks. I just hadn't seen any of those paths for myself until now.

I couldn't help but wonder if this was how people felt when they thought about changing careers. I'd had two irons in the fire while I was living in Sri Lanka. During the day, I improved my eye for gems and learned to haggle over the price of loose stones, while at night, I studied for the civil service exam. The effort I put into one or the other of those two things would prove to be very pointless in the future...but funnily, I still enjoyed both and found they served me well in my daily life.

Whatever path I ended up on in the future, I didn't want to feel like I'd wasted any of the time I'd spent doing what I was doing now.

"Not really, honestly. At this point I feel like I want to continue living like this for a little while longer, at least. I'm living in Sri Lanka now, but I've been to Florida and now France—I've been traveling all over the place lately. I'm starting to worry that the neighborhood kids are going to forget who I am."

"You really do make friends no matter where you are."

"I have you to thank for that."

Étranger.

A stranger.

Someone who isn't *supposed* to be there.

Whenever I began to feel like that, and wonder what I should do, I had Richard shining in my mind like the north star. I couldn't imagine not needing that. Now that I'd begun to walk a path with no rails, that overwhelming beauty had saved me more times than I could count.

Could I ever be like that, too?

"You booked us on the ten o'clock train tomorrow, right? What time should we leave?"

"Eight at the latest. We still have to pick up the tickets. I'll—"

"No, I'll drive to the station. You should sleep. I'm more of a morning person, after all."

"......"

Richard mumbled something about being a disgrace, but thankfully, seemed to agree with me. I was slowly gaining a few responsibilities.

And I felt a little lighter, too.

I felt so much better knowing what I was up against. Octavia might continue causing us trouble in the future, but if you knew where the enemy troops were located, you could come up with a strategy to face them. And just like Jeffrey said, we might get an opportunity to see Henry show off, too. I wanted to be able to rely on them.

I entrusted the golden leaf that was presumably worth something in the ballpark of eighty million yen to Richard, picked up my things, and left the room. Having a room all to myself was nice but a little chilly. I could faintly see the outline of the window frame through the curtains, just like in the room Richard was sleeping in.

Tomorrow, I decided, I would wake early and clean the house. I quietly did my usual exercise routine, curled up in my blanket, and closed my eyes.

"Wake up, Seigi. Wake up. Let's play solitaire."
"...Solitaire...?"

Did I forget to lock my door? I guess I hadn't even thought about it. Catherine was standing there in the pale blue early morning light, peering at my face from right beside my pillow. What on earth?

I hurried out of bed as if tempted by a fairy in a dream and went downstairs. I looked at the grandfather clock when I entered the dining room. It was five thirty in the morning. That wasn't more than just a little early—I'd thought Catherine wasn't a morning person?

She wore a pale green stole over her white dress and she had sandals on. She had an otherworldly aura about her that made me want to ask what world she had come from. I was overwhelmed.

At her behest, I came out into the garden. The vestiges of last night's party were still where they had been, but one thing had changed. One table had been set up in the center of the garden, with two chairs facing each other on either side.

And atop the table was the game board full of marbles.

"We never got a chance to play. Do you know the rules?"
"I don't, sorry..."
"We start by taking the center stone."

Catherine cheerfully took her seat and removed the transparent quartz marble from the middle spot on the board. There was a channel running along the edge of the board, surrounding all the divots that seemed perfect for holding eggs. I guess that channel was where you put the stones you removed. The quartz marble rolled around the path.

"You can play it by yourself, but you can also play it with others. You jump one marble over the other, and then you can remove the marble that was jumped. You can only jump one marble at a time. And we take alternating turns moving the marbles."

Catherine moved the rose quartz marble from two spaces away into the center slot and dropped the black and white jasper marble it had jumped into the channel. Now there were fewer marbles. Thirty-one left. So that was how the game worked.

"The game ends when there's only one stone left. If you have two or three left and no other moves, then you've lost. In the multiplayer version, you lose when you can no longer make a move. Understand?"

"I think so."

Catherine encouraged me to take my turn, with the cool, damp garden as our backdrop. I picked up a chilly marble, jumped another, and just as I was about to pick up the marble I had jumped, her slender hand stopped me.

"Seigi, what kind of stone is that?"

"This? I think it's probably amazonite."

"It's from the Amazon? Goodness, that place is full of all sorts of dreadful memories. It's home to so many rare butterflies."

"I think this one's a kind of stone called microcline...but it comes from all sorts of places around the world. Including Russia and Libya. There are even records of its use dating back to ancient Egypt, so it's a stone that has had a long relationship with humanity."

"My!"

After that, every time a stone was removed, she'd ask me what it was. About 80 percent of them were kinds of chalcedony, like quartz and agate, but there were a few stones in the mix that felt almost like trick questions. I did find it a bit odd that despite being dragged out of bed in the wee hours of the morning, I was enjoying talking about stones.

Labradorite displays an iridescent optical effect called labradorescence.

The pale blue stone, celestine, which bears the Japanese name tenseiseki—*heavenly blue stone. One of my favorites.*

A purple imitation of sugilite. The stone was named for Dr. Sugi, a Japanese petrologist. It's also called royal azel for its noble color.

Catherine listened intently to all of my comments. Little by little, stones disappeared from the game board. Thoughtful choices were paramount. But just as I was thinking that—

"You..."

Catherine began to speak as she was selecting a marble. She'd been such an eerily good listener so far, I didn't think she felt like talking.

"You think my son is beautiful, don't you?"

There was a loud *clink*. The channel around the board was packed with stones, and it was getting hard to find an open spot. Little sparks were starting to fly in my head.

"W-well, um, yes. I do. Yes."

I pointlessly repeated my answer, started to panic and got flustered. Where was this coming from, all of a sudden? It was my turn. I was starting to get the hang of the game

Catherine paid no mind to what I was doing but continued talking. "You really think he's beautiful, huh?"

I dropped a bloodstone marble into the channel. With its black ground and flecks of red, the stone's eerie appearance is said to have made it valued as a sorcerer's amulet. But she didn't ask me to explain what it was. I replied, "Yes," again, and she looked at me rather than the solitaire board.

"Do you actually understand what that means?"

"...What *beautiful* means?"

"No. What telling him that means."

She went on to explain what the word "beautiful" meant. There are two main types, she said. The first was the sort of beauty that elicited interest and affection, that gives art its value, like the delightful sweetness of a dessert. "You understand, right?" she said.

I was pretty sure I did. I felt like innumerable spirits of the departed were concealed behind her sweet smile.

The other was the kind of beauty born out of concern for someone you care about—a beauty that came from the depths of your heart and had nothing to do with objective standards of attractiveness. It was the word you said when you wipe away your baby's tears, or to your loved one when they'd dressed up just for you.

"Which kind of 'beauty' is the one you feel, I wonder? Neither, perhaps?"

It was like the peak of a mountain at daybreak. Or the ocean at sunset. Like the sparkle of shattered glass or a slick graph illustrating the spread of manufactured goods.

That's kind of how I would explain Richard's beauty. He was really cool, and I respected him as a person, but I didn't think that was the type of beauty I was initially taken with. If you put a magnet into a sandbox, you'd undoubtedly find some iron sand sticking to it. That was the closest I could get to finding a word for it. I knew I should hold it in, but he accepted it, and allowed it, so I just kept doing it until now.

No matter how hard I thought, I couldn't tell you which kind it was. I started to say that he was just humoring me, and I was actually being very rude to him, but Catherine cut me off.

"Non," she said with fire in her eyes. "That's not it at all. None of that matters. You really don't get it. You've plunged countless knives into that poor boy's chest. Think about it for a moment. Imagine if the person who always told you that you were beautiful, so beautiful, as if the fact they found you beautiful was just a given, one day just stopped. Like they had suddenly turned to stone. Have you ever thought about that? Have you? You haven't, have you? I'm glad."

"That's where I am," she mumbled softly to herself as she discarded another marble into the channel.

I knew it was my turn, but I couldn't make my hand move.

"Words are living things. You're not throwing words at an unspeaking statue in a museum. That boy is kinder than anyone, and he knows that you don't understand what you're doing, but he still forgives you. Why does my precious baby have to do that? If I were him, I would distance myself from you. But he likes being with you. I'm sure he loves delighting other people by giving them what I could never give him. That's why he's stayed by your side for so many years. It's not fair. What are you doing? Hurry up and make your move, or I'll never get my turn."

I jumped a carnelian marble with a blackish-green diopside one. Catherine began speaking again.

"Would you promise me something, Seigi?"

"...Depends on what you're asking."

"Oh, but of course. I knew you'd say that. He's such a nice boy, he'll never ask much of you. But I'm not nice at all, so I have no issue making demands of you." She continued. "Promise me that tomorrow, and the day after that, a year from now, ten years from now, forever and ever, you'll still be able to call Richard 'beautiful.' For all eternity, as long as you're part of his life, be it morning or night, in good times or ill. Just the way you do now, from the heart, without any pretense. I want you to take responsibility for what you've started. It's only logical. Think about it—really think about it. If you don't think you can do it, pack your bags and leave this instant. Disappear from his life. You won't bring either of you happiness if you can't do that."

"W-what if he comes after me?"

"Then run. And keep on running, to the Amazon or the Sahara, it doesn't matter. But if you don't leave, then be prepared."

In the past, when they adorned heroes' heads with crowns of laurel, they used to listen to the words of oracles and priestesses. If that practice were revived today, maybe this is what it might look like. Her blue eyes looked at me over the game board. It felt like, were it not for the table, she'd turn into a dragon and gobble me up headfirst.

"Tell my boy he's beautiful forever. Even when he's angry or crying, even when he shows you a side of him you'll never see again, even if he pledges his eternal love to someone who isn't you. Promise me that. And never break that promise."

I needed to think clearly.

When would I call Richard beautiful?

Or maybe I should think about it from the other angle: When *couldn't* I call him beautiful?

I had numerous embarrassing memories of saying it when I shouldn't have. But those struggles had become a distant memory ever since he gave me permission. It just seemed obvious that if I thought he was beautiful today, I'd still think so tomorrow. But I didn't have a concrete image of what exactly that was. But I think the feeling I got whenever I was near him, that the world was a truly incredible place, was the kind of "beauty" I was thinking of. The same feeling you get when you spontaneously encounter music or art or gems.

Could I even imagine a situation where I wouldn't be able to say that to him?

I thought and I thought.

And eventually came to a conclusion.

I mustered up the courage to smile at the woman radiating a flame-like aura.

"I gave it some serious thought, and I don't think it sounds all that difficult. I promise I will. I'll call him beautiful forever. As long as he doesn't threaten to kill me if I don't stop, that is."

"I wish you'd say you'd do it even if he did threaten to kill you. You might be better off dead. Don't you agree?"

"I, uh, I'm not so sure about that one."

"Heh heh heh."

Catherine giggled mischievously. She spun around and rocked from side to side a bit before selecting a marble and dropping it into the channel. I followed suit and picked up a stone.

And then there was only one marble remaining, this one made of clear quartz.

"Well, I think that's a win. Congratulations, Seigi. That was your first time, wasn't it? Did you find it difficult?"

"Not at all, thanks to your explanation. It was fun getting the hang of it."

Although...I didn't know if this applied when you played it by yourself, but in a multiplayer game, especially with two players, the real key to the game wasn't so much how you move the marbles. If you wanted to win, you had to figure out what your opponent was thinking, what they wanted to do, and then match their pace. If you wanted to corner your opponent, you read their cues and outsmarted them. The nature of the game would be completely different if both players were working together with the same strategy versus if they're each trying to make their opponent self-destruct, right?

Catherine made some tricky moves from time to time, but the more I thought about it while I chatted about gemstone trivia, I realized she was only picking the stones that would show me the way forward. Her tone and her expressions were a bit scary at times, but she wasn't actually trying to beat me. Of that I was certain.

It was a little scary, but in the end, I think she decided to make it a game that was easy on a first-timer.

When Catherine spun around and took her eyes off me for a moment, she put her predatory aura away, somewhere out of sight. A friendly, smiling mother stood before me instead. But there was still something mildly unsettling about the atmosphere.

As we celebrated the game and put all the marbles back in their spots, I found myself closing my eyes.

Day was breaking.

The dark green garden had regained its vibrant summer hue. The light was golden, like wheat. It ran straight across the dewy lawn. Morning was coming from beyond the mountains. The air was getting gradually warmer, warming even my lungs. Inexhaustible light showered every living thing in this land, as if to bless it.

"It's so pretty here," I whispered and Catherine smiled. She picked up the game board to return it to the dining room.

"Well, fun's over. Seigi, let's prepare some sandwiches. I want to make you two lunches to take with you. Would you mind giving me some advice?"

"Of course. Um...I'm sorry for making you worry."

I'd wound up apologizing again. But Catherine held back a chuckle. "It's fine," she said, face serene. She still had a hint of that dragon in her voice. "You really are good at games, Seigi. You passed with flying colors."

"Passed?"

"Indeed," she said, pressing her body against me, making a show of the skin from her neck to her collarbones. She really was soft. I gently pushed her away, and she giggled, amused.

"It's funny. You spent the whole time with me here in this villa until we found the treasure. I was so sure you'd leave before then."

"...What's that supposed to mean?"

She smiled and explained.

"If you had even once told me I was beautiful while you were staying here, that would have been it. You would have been out. Richard and I look very much alike, after all, I even tried to do my makeup more naturally, like that college friend of yours you mentioned. But two people in one house can't both be 'beautiful.' It's unacceptable. And I want nothing to do with a man like that."

She went on to explain that she'd planned to ship me right back off to Sri Lanka or Japan, claiming I was having stomach troubles.

"I'm so glad. Maybe you do understand a little more than I'm giving you credit for. That's much better than the alternative. Now, what shall we put in these sandwiches? What do you like, Seigi?"

As she smiled and rolled up her sleeves, she looked almost like an angel from another world to me. She was terrifying. A being that, despite its lovely form, could not be reasoned with normally. I let out a deep breath, wondering if this was what it meant to be in "awe" of someone—but a little later, that turned to fear.

In the car all the way to the station, Catherine boasted about her sandwiches all the while Richard dodged her comments in the passenger seat like a martial arts master. The car stereo was off-limits and the car's owner didn't attempt to turn it on. I didn't say a word as I drove. I just focused on obeying the traffic signs. The route hadn't changed at all from three days ago when I arrived— fields of sunflower and lavender. Ears of barley. Grapes and olives. And every so often I'd catch a glimpse of children wearing hats and adults watching over them.

Richard suddenly interrupted Catherine as she was extolling the health benefits of fresh watercress. I wondered what he was going to say.

"Where is Marie-Claude's body now?"

"In a cemetery in Paris. Same place she's always been."

That's right, Marie-Claude had written in one of those letters that she wanted to be buried in the summer garden. I wondered if Catherine was thinking about whether she could do something about that in the future. She was wearing a William Morris print jacket with a red scarf wrapped around her head. She put her chin in her hands in the back seat of the car as she spoke.

"But you know, I don't think I'll be able to do anything there. I'm going to have to let the villa go again after all."

I was startled by that. What? But didn't Octavia just give her several tens of thousands of euros? I briefly glanced at Richard in the passenger seat. He didn't look terribly surprised. But he did look like he had a headache.

"...You loaned them money again, didn't you?"

"I didn't loan them anything. I gave it to them. It's not like they would ever have paid it back, anyway. If I wanted to buy the villa back, I could have spent all the money on that. But I was happy enough to have the opportunity to entertain the two of you this summer, so I just talked to the current owner about renting it for a little while."

"People behave differently depending on whether you call it a loan or a gift. Like that self-proclaimed 'movie director' or similarly self-proclaimed 'musician.'"

"Oh, stop it, would you? If that were true, all actors would be just 'self-proclaimed' when they didn't have a gig. They're always struggling so much, it would be wrong for me to use all that money for myself. I'm living in A'dam right now, anyway. There's no way I'd be able to maintain a house in Provence."

"A'dam? You're living in Amsterdam? What happened to southern France?"

"I moved. It's a nice place. With wonderful people. But it's going to start getting much colder soon, so perhaps I should find another new city to live in. And find a new love."

This time, her son sighed. I sure couldn't tell how serious she was being, especially after the side of her she'd let me see that morning.

She giggled, and sang, "Richard, Seigi, thank you. My last memory of that villa will be of spending a beautiful summer with the two of you. Maybe it came with a little too much suspense, but you're both safe and sound and you found the treasure, so it was the most wonderful summer. I thank you from the very bottom of my heart."

"Please look after your health, at least. I'm not interested in carting your dead body back from an unfamiliar place."

"What a disturbing thing to say! I've never been one to indulge so much that it puts my health at risk."

"And don't overdo it with the marijuana. I can smell it on you."

"Oh, goodness, not in front of Seigi. I thought my perfume would cover up the smell."

"The smell is not the issue."

I kept on driving. Eventually, we arrived at the station, which vaguely reminded me of a car repair shop. Tears abruptly filled Catherine's eyes. To me she said, "Thank you, *adieu, adieu!*" and to Richard, *"à bientôt!"* Easy enough French for a beginner to understand. It was basically the difference between, "goodbye basically forever" and "see you again soon."

"I want to see you again. Hopefully after a shorter gap than this time. You hear me? I may not be the kind of woman who will greet you with a freshly baked pie every time we see each other, but I await the day that you'll call me 'Mother' again."

Richard and I went "huh?" at almost exactly the same time. It was such a decidedly Japanese-sounding "huh" that Catherine was a little confused. She kept looking at the both of us wondering what it was.

I snuck a look at Richard's expression. I'd have to let him handle this one.

The beautiful Richard looked like he had a terrible migraine again as he turned to Catherine and said, "With all due respect, were you not the one who told me, 'Don't call me *Maman*'?"

"Who? Me?"

I'd heard that, too. And my boss wasn't one to lie about things like this.

Silence hung between us. Catherine opened her eyes wide and blinked several times so dramatically that I could have sworn I could hear it. The world was a big place, but I thought there might be only two people in it who could create such a spectacular atmosphere just by blinking at each other.

"No...I wouldn't do that... At least I don't think I would. But when was that?"

Richard hesitantly described exactly when and what had happened. It was right after she left England. She was single again and didn't want to be addressed like a married woman. Catherine was flustered, and then she looked up at the sky and sighed.

"...Goodness. I was so certain that you had decided to stop calling me *Maman* because you were angry with me. But I guess I asked you to do that. Ahh, the Lord certainly likes to play fair. I created my own punishment."

"There's nothing funny about it. It wasn't the least bit fair to me."

"I guess that's true. At least for me, what you've just told me has more than made up for all the pain I've been through. I'm so sorry, Richard. I can't believe I..."

Catherine was about to pull away, but Richard stopped her with a hug. It was a sight to behold—Richard, hugging someone. The beautiful man began to speak softly as he held her. In French, with that familiar songlike rhythm.

"I know you feel responsible for my being born with the burden of this face. I wasn't as mature as I am now, back then, and I did feel a degree of certain resentment. But weren't you always fond of saying, 'Your appearance is insignificant in comparison to your thoughts and your actions'? I don't resent or hate you, *Maman*. It has just added some more spice to my life."

Richard released Catherine after he finished speaking, but this time Catherine hugged him. He held him tight as she bawled her eyes out. The amount of attention they had attracted was incredible. Richard was trapped in the dramatic hug until Catherine finished crying. I wasn't about to run off on my own, so I ended up just circling mother and son like a guard dog with nothing to do.

Catherine wiped away her tears as we walked through the crowded station and let out a little lament to herself, "I should have called Marie-Claude *Maman* more often."

I had heard her, but I had no idea what to say.

We picked up our tickets and hurried to board the TGV. Richard's face finally relaxed once we were on board. He massaged his brow. Good job. Seriously. I couldn't really think of anything else to say.

There was no one else sitting next to us in our booth-style seats designed for four people, so the two of us sat across from each other with two whole seats to ourselves. Hm. You know, I think I deserve a "good job," too.

"Man, this sure ended up being an eventful trip, huh?"

"So it seems. What were you doing with her this morning?"

I asked Richard if he'd seen us, and Richard played dumb, saying he'd just caught a glimpse through the window. I guess he didn't hear our conversation. I wasn't sure I should just be upfront and tell him it was no big deal, I just swore to his mother that I'd call him beautiful for all eternity? I think he'd just get the wrong idea. I mean, to me it was just like saying "good morning" to someone when they wake up. Maybe he'd let me get away with not giving him the rundown.

"I-It's a secret? ...You're not gonna let that slide, are you?"

"Absolutely not."

"Thought so."

"To cut a long story short, she gave me a lecture about the importance of decorum even among friends," I said honestly. And, I mean, I didn't think that's a wholly inaccurate way to describe it. Richard looked a little taken aback to hear me say that, but after a few moments he let out a bitter chuckle.

Catherine really did seem to be Richard's Achilles heel, but if Octavia was trying to sow chaos like she had on the cruise, I think she'd missed the mark this time. I think they were struggling with the same kind of discord most parents and children the world over deal with—when you're too close, it's easy to talk right past each other. But it wasn't a hostile relationship, by any means.

The train was just passing Avignon, and Richard was eating his egg and watercress sandwich while drinking fresh lemonade. The man who liked to claim that tea dies the moment it touches a plastic bottle had given up on the milk tea and enthusiastically joined Catherine in making lemonade. Apparently, his trick was to reduce the sugar a bit and add a dash of mint syrup.

"That reminds me," I broke the silence. "Octavia's code...you said it was for you."

Surely, I wouldn't be punished for asking what it was. If it contained something extremely personal, I'd rather he didn't tell me. But if it was just something rude that I had the right to be mad about, too, I wanted him to talk to me about it so he didn't have to deal with it alone. Maybe it wasn't the right call. I didn't know. That's why I decided to ask.

Once Richard had finished his sandwich, he gazed out the window and said softly, "It was."

To my Japanese sensibilities, this long-distance train seemed to be moving about as fast as a local express train. I guess the country was just that big, but I did wish it would get us to Paris just a little faster.

"...It was a poem."

"A poem?"

"It was a poem that had been part of our correspondence in the past. It wasn't anything bad."

He pulled out his phone again to show me something. He explained how he deciphered the anagram and wrote the English poem on a paper napkin in front of me. It was two lines.

About jewelry.

The first read, *"If only you were a jeweled bangle, I could wrap you about my wrist and keep you with me always, but alas, you are a person of flesh and blood, so it cannot be so."* The second read, *"If I am to suffer so, I would rather become just such a bangle, that I might rest upon your arm."*

It appeared to be an exchange between two people—love poetry, and surprisingly direct, at that.

"I'm feeling a little culture shock here. Those kinds of overt expressions are too much for a shy Japanese boy like me."

"What on earth are you saying? The authors of those poems are from your country."

"What?"

And then Richard wrote a long string of complicated Japanese characters next to the English poems.

Otomo no Sakanoue no Oiratsume.

Otomo no Yakamochi.

My mouth hung agape, and Richard looked at me with a half smile.

"They're from the Man'yoshu. It's the oldest known collection of Japanese poetry, compiled some time in the eighth century."

"...Huh."

"In the English-speaking world it's better known as the Anthology of Ten Thousand Leaves or the Myriad Leaves. It's a piece of literature that has long since been translated into English. I can't imagine even a Japanese person who knows a few Yeats or Keats poems is all that unusual. I cannot deny that I am a bit more of a fanatic than most, but it's no different."

Professor Richard went on to explain that these were love poems exchanged between two people before they were eventually married. I didn't know which of us was the Japanese culture expert here anymore. I was about to give him my usual awkward smile and promise that I'd study more when I realized—

Richard was looking out the window again.

I wondered why. Did he just not want to look at my dumb face? No, it seemed more like he didn't want to look at anything at all.

My boss's weary face was reflected in the train window over the scenery streaming by, almost like some kind of ghost.

That was right, though... He'd studied Japan at a famous British university. I shouldn't have been surprised that he was versed in the classics. And as I recall, the person he met there...

...was the same woman Octavia had been "rooting for."

There was only one person that I could imagine Octavia's note bringing to Richard's mind. I'd never met her before, but she was the woman who still quietly occupied the prime spot in his heart.

I guess Octavia really had set up a secret message just for Richard. But to what end? Was she just trying to tell him that she felt betrayed by how the relationship she'd been championing had ended? Did she want to make him remember it, to make him feel as bad as she did?

I felt like that couldn't be all there was to it. If all she wanted to do was make him feel bad, surely there were better ways to do that than this love poem, like something he'd written to Deborah when they were both still in Octavia's life or a message Deborah had sent Richard. Admittedly, I had no idea how much of any of that Octavia would have access to. But there had to be any number of more effective options than poems from the Man'yoshu.

I had a vague sense that she was motivated by more than malice. But maybe that was just wishful thinking. There's a limit to how much you can understand of what's in another person's heart from the outside, and not just because she was a seventeen-year-old European girl and I a Japanese man in my twenties.

I was sure Octavia had something going beyond what she relayed to me in that video message. She hasn't shown it to me yet, but there was something.

As a certain somebody who had a tendency to insinuate things and then run off flashed through my mind, I felt myself getting just a little irritated. Vince. I'd already sent him a message thanking him for saving us, but I hadn't gotten any reply. Not that I expected one. I'd brought the shirt I'd borrowed from him with me, still wrapped in the dry cleaner's bag, on the off chance that I ran into him, but I never got the opportunity to return it and ended up having to take it back with me again. I wanted to make sure that didn't happen next time.

As the TGV entered a tunnel, the hazy reflection in the glass became almost clear as a mirror, and Richard pulled himself together and looked at me. Crap. I guess my face was reflected in the glass, too, and Richard could tell I was looking at him. He was smiling.

"That reminds me. You really surprised me back there in the tunnel."

"You mean how I left you to go find the treasure? I was worried about what might happen if the entrance was destroyed after we were rescued."

Richard shook his head, "That's not what I mean." He mouthed something as he hummed.

Amore, amore? No. It was *Paroles, paroles.* Oh.

"You mean that French song? I just kind of ended up learning it because Catherine always played it in the car. Was she always fond of that song?"

I was thankful no one else was sitting in the booth with us, because that meant I could sing a little bit of it quietly without bothering anyone. I sang just a little bit of it, still mostly making up the lyrics, and for some reason, Richard stared at me like he'd just swallowed a handful of rocks.

"What?"

"She was listening to that? In the car? Inconceivable. She always hated the radio and TV."

That didn't sound right. When she picked me up from the station and when we went to the supermarket together, she always had music by the singer Dalida playing. I smiled and suggested that maybe her tastes had changed since he'd last seen her, but Richard's expression was stiff. And then for some reason he started messing with his phone. What? Please, talk to me a little more?

You're just making me anxious. At which point, Richard showed his phone to me. It was a bunch of text.

Lyrics?

"You might want to reconsider whether to add that one to your repertoire once you've read this," Richard said, showing me a page with both the French lyrics and a Japanese translation. Apparently, the song had been a hit in Japan, too, with a Japanese language cover released under the title *"Amai Sasayaki"* or "Sweet Whispers." It turned out the French version itself was a cover of an Italian song, and the slightly odd pronunciation I had noticed was likely a result of the fact that Dalida was a native Italian speaker.

The song was about a man lavishing a woman with praise, and the woman singing boldly, "your tender, candy-coated words, land in my mouth but never in my heart." It felt like the sort of thing that would be painful to listen to for a certain subset of people, but maybe you could interpret it like some kind of anti-catcalling anthem, too.

I don't know how many times Catherine had made me listen to it. She probably did so knowing I couldn't understand the words. Well, I guess it wouldn't have made any difference if I had understood it. She would have just smiled at me, and I wouldn't have been able to say a word.

I thought back to what she told me in the garden that morning. Continually calling someone beautiful is like repeatedly plunging knives into their chest.

Maybe she had reasons for cooperating with Octavia other than finding the treasure her mother left behind. There would have been no reason to invite me along if that was all there was to it.

The pressure of her, "What are you doing to my precious baby boy" made me sigh. *I'm sorry. I'm so sorry. I'm exceedingly sorry.* I thought beautiful things were beautiful, but I couldn't exactly blame his family for not wanting to hear that. I needed to really reflect on my behavior. I should stick to saying it in places where I was less likely to cause offense. Or was that not good enough? This was hard.

"...I guess I'll hold off for now."

"Smart."

And then Richard began to giggle, for some reason. The way he couldn't hold back his laughter even though it wasn't the most appropriate time for it told me that he really had been holding it in. What was so funny though? I was pretty shocked, to be honest.

"Catherine was complaining before—'I got myself all dolled up and Seigi won't even call me pretty. I'm devastated!' She was obviously joking, but I am curious as to why you didn't."

I could sense Catherine's kindness in his question. She hadn't needed to say anything like that to him. If she wanted to get rid of me, she would have probably told Richard about how "he mistook me for you when we first met," and made him feel uncomfortable. Richard was a master at seeing through lies. He could almost certainly tell how much of that was true and how much was nonsense.

I decided to tell him about what had happened at Gare de Lyon Station before it became a problem. He cut me off while I was explaining how sorry I was for the mistake, and the conversation veered off on a tangent about how he kind of expected her to pull something like that, since she'd tried a similar stunt on some of his friends in college before. What on earth? Well, it sounded like he forgave me at least. I was thankful for that.

I quietly felt more encouraged and decided to answer the question Richard had posed.

"...My sensibilities might be a bit odd or even old fashioned, but—"

"Spare me the preamble."

"Got it."

I thought back to junior high, when I was over at a friend's house after school to play video games. I'm pretty sure his surname was Kuroda. His mom was always home, and our group of four was always hanging over at their house, and she'd always serve us tea and snacks with a smile. Thinking back on it now, having four boys running around your house must've been really annoying, but she never complained. And she never treated me any differently from the others, even though I never had any games to lend my friends.

But that's what your friends' moms are like, right?

How would it have changed things between us if back then I'd told Kuroda, "Your mom is so nice, and she's so pretty"? Kuroda was an impressive guy who was good at both fighting games and science experiments, but I think that would have made things really weird between us. I mean, we were in junior high, so maybe we could've just laughed it off and that would have been the end of it, but now that I was mostly grown up, saying something like that about someone's mom would feel a little wrong to me. Don't get me wrong—I don't mean this in terms of manners but rather in terms of what it could do to your friendship. If I had a male friend who started talking about how pretty my mom was, I'd feel creeped out and ask him what the hell he was talking about. And I didn't want to make Richard feel that way.

I more or less explained the feelings I'd been wrestling with, and Richard, who was no longer smiling, accepted my explanation with an "Is that so?"

"You were struggling, so that's why...I decided not to say anything. I do...think so, though. I mean, of course I do. When someone who sparkles like a yellow diamond shows up right in front of you, it'd be stranger not to feel anything, right? But I—"

I didn't know what to say exactly. I knew what I was feeling, but I didn't know how to express it. The door to our car opened, and the conductor came through. If I waffled for too long, he'd get in the way of me ever saying it.

"...I don't want to lose you."

Richard silently took our tickets out of his wallet to show the conductor. After a moment, the conductor seemed to tell Richard there was an issue. Richard was startled and looked at what he'd handed him only to realize it was a store loyalty card or something like that. The beautiful man apologized in his elegant tone and produced the correct tickets this time. The conductor tipped his hat and moved on to the next section of seats.

Richard remained silent for a while after the conductor left. Was he okay?

"Richard?"

"When, exactly, did I become your property?"

"Sorry! I didn't mean it like that! I was trying to say that I didn't want to lose your trust. Agh, soon I'm only going to be able to speak broken Japanese and broken English..."

"Where's this coming from all of a sudden? I thought your carelessness was one of your prime selling points?"

"Ugh, thanks for kicking me while I'm down. But, hm, I guess you're right."

"You needn't abandon the merits of throwing yourself head-long into things without a shred of fear. You just have to be aware that it could put you at a disadvantage at times and be ready to fight back, right?"

Richard smiled. He looked a little frustrated, as if to say, "That's what you always do anyway, right?" But in a gentle way. I appreciated it, but I didn't want to rely on his kindness like that forever.

"Well...even if I'm fighting back, I don't want to abandon my manners. I'm trying to be better about that every day."

"Do keep up the good work."

We were almost like a teacher and his pupil sitting across from each other in a tea room as we put our hands in our laps and bowed to one another. Even though we were on the TGV. We glanced up, exchanged a look like, "What are we even doing?" and both laughed a little. I asked what he'd be doing until his flight after we arrived in Paris and had lunch, and Richard put on an eye mask and declared he was going to sleep. I hoped faintly that he would dream of sweets and jewels, rather than anything to do with secret codes or love poems from the Man'yoshu.

Once the man in the eye mask's breathing began to slow, I pulled out my phone. I looked up the contact "Hiromi." It was a seven-hour difference between here and Tokyo. It shouldn't be too late over there yet. Or at least I hoped it wasn't.

I thought about what I could learn from the long-standing discord between Richard and Catherine, and the regrets both Catherine and Marie-Claude had. And after throwing all my high school era embarrassment to the wind, I sent her a text.

"How are you? I've been doing well. I'm heading back to Sri Lanka from France soon."

"I know I've been calling you Hiromi for like, ever, basically, but would you mind if I started calling you Mom instead?"

A second after I hit send, I already wanted to claw my hair out. "Do you mind if I start calling you Mom?" Was there a more cowardly way to phrase that?

I let the movement of the train rock me back and forth as I argued with myself. Hiromi was the one who had permitted me to call her "Hiromi." I didn't call her that because of an unreasonable request like the one Catherine had made. So why was I phrasing it like it was on her? And why did I *text* her about it? Shouldn't I have just started calling her "Mom" without making a thing out of it next time I came home?

I started typing another message—"I'm sorry for how I've behaved toward you until now. I'm sorry. I'm trying to be more

THE CASE FILES OF JEWELER RICHARD

mature from now on—" when a reply arrived. Thank you, inter-net. There really aren't any borders in the world anymore.

It was from Hiromi.

"Did you eat something weird?"

"I don't know if I could get used to it at this point. Just keep call-ing me Hiromi."

"They both mean the same thing anyhow, right?"

And then she reported that she and my stepfather were enjoy-ing some sushi together.

I felt my heart tingle. Whether it was joy or sadness, I couldn't really tell. Probably some combination of both.

It's not easy to set things that have built up over time on a different course overnight. It was kind of like sedimentary rock, built up of layers upon layers of leaves and dirt and shells and carcasses that have turned into stone—a completely different creation process from rock that gushes up from inside the earth. But it's still rock, and it's just as hard and massive as rock that comes from magma, and they're all part of the Earth.

Sometimes, you just have to accept what already exists. From now, I'd probably feel like my immature self was punishing me whenever I called her "Hiromi." But if, sooner or later, I decided to start just casually changing that...then maybe one out of every ten times, I'd try—

—calling her "Mom."

Epilogue

THE CASE FILES
OF
JEWELER
RICHARD

AUGUST 21ST

Iggy here. It sure has been a while, hasn't it? I just got back from Europe.

I'm sorry to everyone who's been following this blog to hear about gemstones in Sri Lanka. I wrote about going to buy stones in Ratnapura and having to haggle with the traders there in a previous post, so I'd encourage you to go back and read that if you'd like.

This was my first time in continental Europe, and everything practically sparkled.

It's a big tourist spot, so maybe uploading a few photos will be okay?

Here's the Eiffel Tower, the Louvre Palace, the Museum of Decorative Arts. Art Nouveau and Art Deco-styled furniture was on display as if people were still living there, and I learned a lot about the evolution of fashion and jewelry trends. The desserts were great, too, but if I started uploading pictures of those, I would never stop.

It's given me a lot to think about.

Like how there's not really any particular reason I *have* to be here. But I am here. Stuff like that. To be a little dramatic, I sometimes kind of feel like I've been thrown out into space without a lifeline, but that's gotten better now.

I'm feeling even more motivated to give it my all while I'm here. That said, I never thought I'd feel so happy to head out on my three-wheeler with the green reusable shopping bag from the supermarket with me.

I have a new family member to introduce to you all.

This is my dog, J! He's a slim mutt with short fur and big, triangular ears. I guess he looks a little foxlike, maybe? He's a boy. I don't know exactly how old he is, but I think he's under a year. He does have a real name, but I don't know who could be reading this blog, so I hope you'll forgive me for using a letter.

To be completely honest, if my friend who helped me name J ever sees this blog, I'll be so embarrassed. I'm sure you can guess it's the "Hawk Eye" I mentioned earlier. I'd really like to surprise him with how much better my English has gotten, if I can. I want him to think my sudden improvement is so incredible.

It sure does sound a bit childish when I write it out like that. I'm so embarrassing.

J makes such a happy face when you scratch behind his ears, I can't stop petting him with a big smile on my face. When I first met him, I was feeling down and he was keeping me company. But he didn't seem to have an owner, and he's been looking kind of thin lately, so I made up my mind to take him in.

I hope we continue to get along well.

But boy is he cute. So cute!

You wanna know a secret? Owning a dog has always been a dream of mine, and now it's come true.

When I start thinking about my future, and having to see things through to the end, I get a little anxious. But despite that, I'm happy right now. I want to find a local vet as soon as I can and take J in to get checked out and get his shots.

Another peaceful day in Sri Lanka.

I thought I was petting Jiro and calling him cute, but then, all of a sudden, I woke up in bed with Jiro nowhere to be seen. I guess I'd been dreaming—probably because I was writing a blog post right before bed.

I first started thinking about getting a dog when I was in Paris. Richard wasn't opposed to it, and he asked me if I had any ideas for a name. I nearly told him that I hadn't thought about it at all and asked him if he could come up with one for me, but I stopped myself.

What kind of dog owner would I be if I couldn't even name my own dog?

I decided that this was a serious matter that I had to settle on my own, so I just told Richard I'd surprise him and we said our goodbyes. I spent my time until I had to go to the airport the next day going to all sorts of bakeries, since I was encouraged to take advantage of being in the heart of French candy-making to learn some things. Come to think of it, that was probably the most touristy day of my whole trip.

Now, I didn't name my dog Jiro because Richard's childhood dog was named Taro. I mean, okay, that was part of it, but while I was in France, I'd also learned that the name "Giraud," a common French name, was pronounced the same way, which I found a little surprising. And if you go more Italian with it, it becomes "Giro" which can mean "to wander" and if that doesn't sound like a certain somebody who flies all over the world on the regular, I don't know what does. Well, I guess I've done a bit of that myself recently.

Anyway, his name is Jiro, and he's very cute. I worried about him a lot, because I didn't have a collar for him yet and he still needed his shots, but I had a feeling we were gonna get along swimmingly. At least, I hoped so.

Jiro was barking in the yard. I still had a few things to take care of before I could let a dog in the house, and I wanted to formally get Saul's permission, too. He never really said anything other than "go ahead and do it," no matter what I asked to do, but having a pet introduces some sanitation questions, so I figured it'd be best to get it out of the way before it got messy.

Still, he really was barking a lot...

It was still only six in the morning. Didn't he get enough attention yesterday? When he was still a stray, he was so deferential and standoffish, but I guess he was up and making demands the second his stomach began to rumble, now. What a calculating little guy. I'd have to give him some ear scritches.

I couldn't get back to sleep.

As I tossed and turned a few times in bed, it hit me that maybe that wasn't Jiro barking. It was so sudden I struggled to believe it. It was hard to imagine, but were those gunshots I just heard?

I leapt to my feet and ran downstairs. I forgot to grab my phone off the charger, so I ran back to my room in a panic. I opened the news app while I walked back toward the stairs, and this time, I heard it for sure. I couldn't tell if it was close or far away. But it sounded like some kind of explosion.

What on earth was going on?

I came down into the living/dining room and turned on the TV to a public station. The news was always reported in such fast-paced Sinhala that there was still a lot that I couldn't understand, but you could switch to the English broadcast. They always aired important news that way, so I put it on in English to ensure I wouldn't miss anything important.

I didn't need to this time. The image on the screen was of something burning. It looked like a shop—just one specific shop, not a whole area or anything. I wasn't familiar with the street, but the subtitle read "Kandy." That was here. The place I'd been living for the past six months, which was famously a peaceful city full of Buddhist temples, elephants, and Victoria Reservoir.

Why was this happening here? Did it have something to do with those gunshots? And what were those explosions?

I finally looked at my news app.

My eyes landed on a simple phrase.

Martial law.

I remembered something kind of silly. This phrase, if I recall correctly, was placed in the "good to remember if you can" section of the fairly small set of vocabulary flashcards I used when studying for my high school exams. National martial law. Now I understood what it meant. It was when the government gave the power of the state to the military during situations like a foreign invasion or civil unrest. It was a declaration of a national emergency.

Jiro actually started howling outside. He might be in danger, so I opened the porch door and called him in before locking the door again. If Saul got mad at me, I would just have to apologize. I could hear the sound of explosions, but I didn't see any fire. The newscasters cried out on the TV screen, just like Jiro.

Riot in Kandy.

Multiple people were dead. They didn't have an exact count yet, but it was at least two so far.

The shop that was on fire was the result of arson.

And the cause was religious conflict.

Jiro buried his nose against me as I hugged him, focusing all my listening skills to pick up what I could from the Sinhala. I switched over to the English broadcast when it repeated. I hadn't misunderstood any of it. And there was no new information.

No one knew what would happen next.

The news switched to footage of men in military garb walking the streets. They were carrying guns with them. The word "curfew" appeared on screen in red letters. They were just declaring that now? Did the arson and the deaths all happen while I was sleeping? Was this really happening? Really? In the risk assessment the Ministry of Foreign Affairs put out about other countries, Sri Lanka was always level one. Wasn't that supposed to be the safest?

Of course, I had learned before coming here that this country was embroiled in civil war until the twenty-first century. My friends had been worried about this sort of thing when I told them I was going to Sri Lanka, and I'd heard that some areas still weren't very safe. But I'd also heard that it was mostly religious conflict and that I'd be fine as long as I didn't poke my nose into dangerous areas. Saul wasn't quite as confident about it, but he'd said I would probably be fine. But most importantly, the Kandy I'd known so far was a very peaceful city. Wasn't it?

I needed to pull myself together. I needed to prioritize telling everyone that I was safe first and foremost. News traveled around the world in mere seconds. It probably wouldn't be long before my phone was exploding with people asking if I was okay, and I wanted to preempt that and reassure the people I loved, at least.

But *was* I really safe? The news wasn't really telling me anything, so I couldn't say with confidence that I was.

Jiro must've been able to smell my anxiety, because he tucked his tail between his legs and started whining. Well, I wasn't going to achieve anything going in circles like this. And it certainly didn't help that both of us were hungry. First, we eat. Then we deal with whatever comes our way, and then we start contacting people. That was the plan.

"Jiro, let's have breakfast together. It'll cheer you up."

He didn't reply, but to be honest, I was kind of glad to have company that couldn't talk. I heard an explosion in the distance, and the ground shook. *Please, give me a break...*

I decided to drink something. I knew just what to make: royal milk tea. I could search until the ends of the earth and not find another drink that calmed my heart quite as much.

At which point.

Just as the water started to boil, my phone buzzed. I wondered who it could be. Richard maybe? Or Mr. Nakata? Or Hiromi?

But the sender wasn't one of the people I'd imagined. It was Vince. Was he trying to find out if I was safe? That seemed unlikely.

"Let's talk," read the subject line.

As gunshots rang out in the distance, I opened his email.